Issue 12
December 2018 - January 2019

Lezli Robyn & Tina Smith, Editors
Shahid Mahmud, Publisher

Published by Arc Manor/Heart's Nest Press
P.O. Box 10339
Rockville, MD 20849-0339

Heart's Kiss is published in February, April, June, August, October and December.

www.HeartsKiss.com

Pleaee refer to our website for information on how to submit material for *Heart's Kiss* magazine.

Available by subscription (www.HeartsKiss.com) or through your favorite online store (Amazon.com, BN.com, etc.).

ISBN: 978-1-61242-442-2

Contents

OPENING EDITORIAL

by Lezli Robyn

We hope you are all warmed up for our next issue of *Heart's Kiss*. Leading into our holiday offering, the last issue in our first year as editors of this magazine—Wow, what a year!—Tina and I discussed our wish to represent different types of festive occasions, because not everyone celebrates the end of an often hectic but successful year the same way with their family. While some people enjoy a beautiful white Christmas akin to the ones you witness in your favorite Hallmark movies, others celebrate a Christmas Day in singlet tops and shorts on the other side of the world, sweating off a year's worth of food indulgences while they roast way too many meats in the outside weber (cooker) in 109 degree heat. Others do not celebrate Christmas at all.

So for Issue 12, we're delighted that Debra Jess decided to write us a story, "Shaped by You", that focuses on finding love during a Jewish holiday season. Tina Gower also delights us with her pagan and paranormal offering, "The Lipski Partner Axiom"—jackals and gremlins and angels, oh my!—where her romantic leads celebrate Yule, finding love during their attempts to foil a crime.

The author we're featuring this issue is the amazing Susan Donovan, whose novella was so flawless Tina and I were hard pressed to find anything to edit, except to say it was amazing, and invoked all the right feels. It depicts a British immigrant's jour-

ney through loneliness and unintentional fumbles in the lead up to Christmas, as she falls in love with a man in uniform and discovers the family she was missing. We also interviewed Susan about her writing process and how her life as influenced her writing. It's an equally fascinating read.

For something different, Gracie Wilson's story, "Song of the Brave", takes place on New Year's Eve, a holiday where people celebrate the year just gone, and the promise of the year to come—and to more importantly gather the courage to kiss the one they love when the clock strikes twelve. Or if you are wanting a good swoon, bestseller Anthea Lawson will take you back in time to deliver us love in Victorian times.

Once you are done with the fiction, this issue's non-fiction section includes more recommended reads by C.S. DeAvilla, a discussion on different holiday traditions and tropes in Julie Pitzel's regular "You Read *That?*" column and the recipe for a Chocolate Ganache Cake by our personal temptress, Andrea Abedi, that will make you fall in love with her.

And last, but definitely not least, we have an exciting update written by Christine Feehan, the queen of paranormal fiction, telling us about an exciting development in her Carpathian Series. You will not want to miss out on that. (How many of you are now flipping to the back of the issue to read it? Wait—I've got more to tell you!)

Maybe you will heat up some eggnog, skewer marshmallows on a hardy stick or fire pocker, and plant yourself in the front of the fire in your warmest sweater and eighties-inspired legwarmers to read the holiday issue of *Heart's Kiss* on your e-reader. Or, perhaps you slip on your bathers (Aussie for swimsuit), grab some fish and chips, and head to your local beach to devour the print copy of the magazine as you recline in your beach-chair, beer in hand.

However you are spending your end-of-year holidays, we hope the contents of this issue warm you up in all the right ways. I could just wish you all a Happy Holidays, but that seems to be cheating, somehow. So I wish you all a loving Christmas, Hannukah, Kwanzaa or New Year's—or Christmahannukwanzear for short. We hope your holidays are filled with family and amazing food, and most importantly, love.

Publisher's Weekly calls Susan Donovan's novels "the perfect blend of romance and women's fiction." Susan is the New York Times *and* USA Today *bestselling author of twenty-eight novels and novellas, including the Bayberry Island Series, The San Francisco Dog Walker series, and the Bigler, North Carolina series. Her novels have won awards and accolades for their humor, characterization, and sexual tension—"brain candy for smart women," as she calls it—and have been translated into dozens of languages. Susan is a former newspaper journalist with degrees from Northwestern University's Medill School of Journalism. She lives in New Mexico with her family and assorted dogs.*

HEART'S KISS INTERVIEWS SUSAN DONOVAN

by Lezli Robyn

It was my pleasure to call Susan, at her New Mexico home, for a fascinating interview about the romance field. She was just as warm, delightful and funny as her books are and very insightful on what it takes to be a romance writer. Meeting her at the RWA conference in Denver this year was a highlight for both Tina and I and I cannot wait for you to read the novella she wrote for us in this issue.

Lezli Robyn: Hello, this is Lezli—how are you?

Susan Donovan: Hello, Lezli. I'm good! How are you?

LR: Wonderful, now that we have connected. As I warn everyone, you'll have to get used to an Aussie accent. *laughs*

SD: *laughs* I think I can handle it. It's lovely.

LR: Thank you. I often forget I have it, until people ask, "What did you say?" and I realize I must sound completely different.

SD: Well, I just got back from a week in west Texas, so let me just say that your Australian accent is—shall I say it again?—*lovely.*

LR: *laughs* I'm glad we could find time to talk today!

SD: Yes! I will admit, I'm a little worn out—I've had a busy few months. My daughter graduated from college, I had a play that was put on in New York, I have been travelling a lot, and I had to teach last week. And I have also been on deadline, with not only my writing projects, but the full-time job I have. *laughs*

LR: So, not much to do, then?

SD: No. *chuckles* Slightly insane, the last few months.

LR: I sympathize, as an assistant publisher working on many books, an editor of a magazine, and then trying to also find time to pen my own words.

SD: Wow, you are plugged in.

LR: Okay, we always ask one question of all of our authors, and we've had the best reaction. If you could pick one female heroine out of one of your novels, and a male hero out of another of your novels, that you would think could make a great couple, who would you pick?

SD: Ohmigosh!

LR: I know. *laughs* The mind boggles.

SD: I need to think about that. That is very difficult to answer. I'll get back to you.

LR: Got it. I will ask you again later on in the interview.

I read on your website that you started writing when you were looking after your kids. But before that you already had an amazing career. What made you switch from a business career to one of the arts?

SD: Well, I think that I have always had dual goals—for my career. I always wanted to write fiction. I always wanted to be a novelist. But I also had a practical side, and so I studied journalism in my university and I focused on working in hardcore news. And—I loved it. It taught me a lot of respect for deadlines and accuracy.

LR: And research.

SD: Yes. And talking to people. I've certainly used my interviewing skills from journalism in fiction writing, when I prepare for novels.

But I have always wanted to be a novelist. When I was really young, I figured that by the time I turned forty I would have my first novel written. Then one day I woke up and I realized I was thirty-nine.

LR: So you started writing.

SD: Yes. I gave myself one year to sell a novel.

You know, I feel fortunate, in my life, to have had a variety of careers. But my heart has always been in fiction.

LR: Beautiful. Did you always think of writing with the intention of doing romance?

SD: Yes. I did. But…I will confess…I had never read a romance novel, when I decided I wanted to write them. *sounds sheepish*

LR: *laughs* Oh, that is a pearler. [Aussie slang, roughly translating to "That is priceless."]

SD: I had never read a single romance in my life. I gave myself a year and I decided to do some research. I had decided to discover what were the best opportunities for me at that time. What were the chances of getting published in all the different genres? And then I had to decide…what would I *want* to write?

What I discovered, when I was looking at horror, mystery, police procedural, suspense, fantasy and sci-fi, was that romance was *everything*. If you wrote anything, set anywhere, at any time, in any circumstance, as long as there was a committed relationship at the core of the story, it was romance. And that really appealed to me.

LR: Oh, fascinating.

SD: Yes. And especially when I started, there was very little focus on branding, and having every book feel be familiar to the reader. So I was attracted to the concept that I could write all kinds of books.

But, I did fall into a comfortable place for me, which was writing a contemporary romance with comedy elements, suspense elements and also emotional impact. That is what my brand became.

And I was very fortunate in the beginning to read other authors first, while I was deciding, and I realized I could just be myself.

LR: That is an important realization.

SD: Yes. I gave myself permission to write the way I wanted to write.

LR: And you could see examples of other authors' novel branding. And you realized through reading those examples what *was* and was *not* your voice.

SD: Yes. And I also realized the restrictions that I assumed existed—because I had not read romance *laughs*—just didn't exist. There was the same kind of irreverent humor I have in some of the authors I read, and I was relieved. I could just be myself. And once I settled into that idea, I started selling books, and I never stopped.

LR: I do have to ask the question, since you referenced it earlier. Was there a guideline that said it was possible to do everything in one year? Because when I read that I was amazed.

SD: Well, in one year I wrote three novels.

LR: Oh, that is impressive. I know there are amazing writers like you that can sell really quick. But what I meant was that you said that from start-to-finish you wanted to sell your first book within a year.

SD: Right. I gave myself a year. When I got the call from St. Martin's Press, it was about two weeks after the deadline I gave myself had passed—but I forgave myself.

LR: I would too. *laughs*

SD: But, you see, the thing with me was that I had little kids and I worked part time and I was also married. My husband said, "We can only afford for you not to be working for one year." So, that was my guideline.

And so, basically, I was a woman possessed. I was on a mission; I could not stop writing. I always liken it to someone popping the cork on a wine bottle. I had permission to write and then it just all came out.

I got a lot of work done in that year. And I got an agent. I got an editor, and then a publisher. And I had my first contract signed by July of 2001.

LR: It probably took longer for your first book to come out after you sold it, then it took for you to write and sell it.

SD: Oh, yes, absolutely. That is the very slow pace of New York publishing.

LR: If you read your first book now, do you think you have changed your writing process, from start to finish? Or do you think your brand has changed over the years?

SD: We're talking about nearly eighteen years. Nobody is the same after eighteen years. Especially with all the major life catastrophes I have lived through since then. Life changes you—and that's not a bad thing.

But I do think that there are elements to my writing that are still the same. My dialogue, the rhythm to my dialogue, my sense of humor, my ability to see things a little skewed, my fondness for quirky characters—those elements stay the same, even if the plots, settings and characters change between each book.

LR: I would agree with this based on your fiction I have read. You have a clear "feel" to your books.

SD: Mmm-hmmm. I also think my writing has deepened a lot, and I think it has also mellowed a little. I'm not pushing too hard for the slapstick or the physical comedy. Every once in the awhile it's there, but it's taken a back seat to sly sense of humor and a psychological humor between characters.

All my books have always been character driven, and that has never changed.

LR: That is my focus as a writer, too. That is what has always appealed to me as a writer and reader.

Do you have a book that created the most impact on you as a writer? Whether it was the writing of it, or how successful it was when it sold?

SD: I would say it would have to be *The Girl Most Likely To...*, which came out in—I believe—2009. It was my first *New York Times* bestseller. It was also the first book I wrote in entirety after I walked out on my marriage. So it was a) very difficult to write a romantic comedy when that was happening, and b) I had so many things pulling me in other directions in my life, including needing to get another job during the transition time, that it took me longer to write.

I also felt that I crossed some sort of milestone with that book, in that the subject matter was a little bit more intense. And the characters were extremely hurt. They were damaged.

LR: They were coming from a place of hurt, like you were.

SD: Yes, exactly. But, I also managed to get some comedy in there. There was a happy ending, but it was a very emotional book to complete. That was a very big change for me.

Also, I have to say in 2012-2016 my Bayberry Island Series was a little different too, because that was the first fiction I wrote after my illness. It was very interesting, because I was scared. I was scared because I was told I might have profound brain damage from my illness. And so I had to prove to myself that I could still think and write and create a story.

LR: The creative mechanics of putting a book together.

SD: Yes. But I had come across this great idea and it was fun. It helped bring me back to life. Seriously, I mean that. It helped reacquaint myself with...myself. *laughs*

LR: That is amazing. I'm so glad you are still here.

What is your preference regarding standalones versus series?

SD: Ah, well, the publisher has a preference. The publisher prefers a series. It hooks a reader and they will come back and read you next book, and your next, if you do it right.

As an author. I do not know. I've gotten a lot of joy out of writing a series, because these people become like family to me. You live with them for four or five years. You have to put in a lot of work up front, and do a lot of planning, but then that place and those people become very comfortable and familiar. You can return to them again and again, and you also can see character arcs that extend all the way across the entire series.

LR: I find that as a reader I love that too; I'm very family oriented. I love seeing the characters that were secondary characters in the last book, maybe damaged or alone, then you get to see them get their partners in "their" book, and then you get to see them living their happily-ever-afters as secondary characters in future books.

SD: Another thing that is fun about a series, especially Bayberry Island, is I had an opportunity to develop a theme across all the books. I didn't have to wrap things up or explain everything by the end of the series, although each book had their own ending. This series had an element of magical realism to it, and it allowed the reader to make the decision—whether they believed the mermaid had some magical power, or whether they believed the magical power was generated by the humans involved. I could string it along…

LR: …and make it more magical. You're building upon your previous creations.

SD: Yes. Yes, absolutely.

On the other hand, I love that thrill of starting over. New place, new people. New problem. New sense of humor. New Stakes. *Everything.* And since my books are character driven, I find delight in coming up with two new characters, and then I can create a whole new world on top of that—it's a lot of fun.

LR: Do you think the industry has changed since you started?

SD: Ha!

LR: I heard that! *laughs*

SD: The answer would be—as soon as I stop snorting with laughter—yes. *laughs*

LR: The biggest change would be ebooks.

SD: Yes, because the influx of ebooks means a lot more writers, which makes it a lot harder to make a living.

I took a hiatus from the romance community, after my illness. It took me many years to get back to a place where I was even comfortable to go to public events. Now I've got mobility back and I feel less self-conscious and I have more energy. It just took me forever to get bounce back; it really did.

When that happened, I fell out of sync with my readers. Books that were supposed to be turned in as part of a series, didn't get written until four years later. But there was nothing that could be done. I had to find a way to survive and get my life back.

When I came back to the field, so much had changed. You have to keep the books coming.

LR: That must have been hard.

SD: Yes, but I am back and I have reestablished connections with other romance authors. I have gotten back into meetings, and I am enjoying it. I even just recently had a book come out: *Breathless*. It got a starred review from *Publishers' Weekly*, which is not all that common for romance. It's the sequel in the Courtesan Series, written with Celeste Bradley.

LR: Congratulations. That is amazing!

SD: Thank you! It took me a long time, but I'm back in the swing. I am still writing romance, but I am also looking at other avenues for income as an author—like everyone else is. I have a writer that I work with, who is TV screenwriter—experienced—and we are writing romance stories for Hallmark and other networks. We're pitching to different people and I'm really enjoying that. I'm learning about teleplays, and I'm learning about story structure in other formats other than novels. I'm learning a lot.

LR: It definitely pays to be a multi-medium writer.

Have you put some thought into the "Which two characters from different books would you put together?" question I asked you earlier?

SD: Ahhh—okay. So…

LR: *laughs*

SD: First of all, I am going to tell you why it is so hard to answer that. *laughs* And I'm sure other authors have made this excuse: When you create characters in a romance novel, you make them for each other. For example, in all of my books, my job as a romance author is to make the reader believe that their love matters more than anything else in the world and that they are meant for each other. There is a sense of destiny, A sense of puzzle pieces fitting together without any gaps.

Because I start there—designing the hero and the heroine to be with each other, and then creating the book around them—I don't know if I can take a character from one book and another book and put them easily together.

Let me tell you this, though. I know I have characters I could put together where the sparks would fly. *laughs*

LR: But they might not be a perfect fit.

SD: Right. Definitely the sparks would fly. I could put a bunch of characters together from separate book and it could be hot hot hot! And funny—and even steamy. But I don't know if I can convince a reader that they had a long term committed promise of happiness. I just don't know.

LR: Well, that is fair enough. And that is a definite answer. *laughs*

SD: Ha! Glad I could oblige!

LR: I wanted to ask you about the retreat you offer…. Where do you live?

SD: I live in Placitas, New Mexico. It's in between Santa Fe and Albuquerque. It's close enough to both so that I can ride in for anything I might want to go to: concerts, plays, really good restaurants. But it is also far enough out that it is peaceful and quiet.

I have no neighbors. I have a straight view of the mountains; no buildings in the way. I'm very very lucky. I love it.

LR: It looks very beautiful from the photos.

SD: Yes. Thank you.

I offer retreats for writers. There are many different ways they can take advantage of what I'm offering. They can come here and stay, opting to not get any coaching or editing suggestions. If they just want to hide, they can finish their manuscript in peace.

LR: That sounds like heaven.

SD: Many of us writers, in the years, have gone to a hotel to isolate ourselves in order to make a deadline.

LR: Yes, I've done that myself. *laughs*

SD: You can do that here. And it's beautiful and quiet and peaceful and comfortable. I've designed the guest house to accommodate a writer. That is what it was specifically built for.

You can also come and get a full week of author coaching from me, in addition to the time and space to write. I have had all type of clients: I've had literary, romance, mystery, sci-fi, YA, or steampunk writers. Everybody comes with something different they need. One person might need to plot an entire book—from ground zero. Another person might need to know how to link together twenty-five short stories they have written in the same universe and create a single novel. Some people need to simply be edited; they need someone to look at their manuscript and tell them what is not working. So many of us can work out that *something* is not working, but not exactly *what* it is.

LR: Sometimes you are too close to the project.

SD: Yes. I will take the manuscript. I will dissect it. I will tell them: "Your conflict is weak." "Your motivation is not there." "Your character is inconsistent."

I will tailor my coaching to what is needed.

LR: The options are amazing. I thought the minimal price jump between the second tier level and the third tier level does not give you enough money considering the hours of coaching you offer has doubled. It's a great deal for authors.

SD: I know. I'm trying to make it affordable for writers. There are so many retreats where you go with fourteen other writers, and there is one author coaching them all. Most of the coaching time is shared and you only get one hour of private coaching during the entire trip—or one private meal—and it's five thousand dollars! It's crazy.

LR: Exactly.

SD: It can be as little or as much as you want to pay. I have had clients come here and they've taken advantage of every option available. They have a private chef. A massage therapist each day.

LR: So the authors make use of their visit as a personal retreat as well as a writing coaching session.

SD: Definitely. It can be very rewarding. Most will leave feeling more confident and rested, with a completed manuscript or much needed direction on *how* to complete their manuscript.

LR: That sounds amazing.

Thank you very much for doing this interview! And for writing a wonderful novella for our holiday issue

SD: Oh, absolutely! Take care of yourself.

A PARTRIDGE IN THE AU PAIR'S TREE

by Susan Donovan

CHAPTER ONE

Noelle Clarke tucked her chin into her pea coat and waved goodbye to the occupants of the Range Rover. "Safe travels! Have a smashing time!"

The passenger window lowered, revealing a perfectly coiffed blond head, an unnaturally smooth forehead, and a pair of dubious blue eyes, all of which belonged to Noelle's employer, Pru DiPaolo. "Take the Lexus if you have to run an errand, Noelle. It has four-wheel drive and the tank is full."

"Tell her not to drive the Tesla."

Pru rolled her eyes and snapped at her husband. "Did you not hear what I just said, Steve? I told her to take the Lexus."

"Fine."

Pru turned her attention to Noelle again as the car backed out to the private cul-de-sac. "Make sure Siggy gets his antacid medicine at least a half hour before he has breakfast. He'll throw up if you cut it too close."

This is breaking news? "Of course, Mrs. DiPaolo."

"Oh, and he'll need his heartworm medication soon."

"Absolutely. It's on the calendar."

The car was at the end of the drive now and Pru began to shout. "You're sure you understand the new security system?"

"Everything will be fine. Don't worry. Have a lovely holiday."

Pru's brows arched with doubt—well, as much as the Botox would allow—then she eyed Noelle up and down, passing judgment on her appearance, no doubt, subtracting points for the worn trainers, lack of makeup, and messy ponytail. "Call if there's an issue." The window rolled up, and seconds later, the luxury SUV turned down the street and out of sight.

Only then did Noelle release the breath she'd been holding. She raised her eyes to the gunmetal-gray sky as a smile slipped over her face. "Happy bloody American Christmas to me."

Taking care not to slip on the rutted ice, Noelle trudged up the drive. She made her way through the cavernous garage of the DiPaolo's suburban Chicago manse and entered the mud room. Noelle walked right past the boot bench and storage cubbies. She ignored the closet for the rubbers, footballs, hockey skates, and ballet shoes. She paid no mind to the butler's pantry, where she would find the chunky peanut butter preferred by Grayson and the frosted biscuits Phoebe ate by the boxful. With a defiant sniff, Noelle walked right past the dry-erase board featuring the family's planning calendar of sporting events, dance recitals, and social events.

For the next fortnight, she was officially, gloriously—blessedly—off the clock.

Noelle tossed her coat on a kitchen island stool—didn't even hang it up—and kicked off her snow boots. She made a beeline for the wine cabinet, snagging the 2000 Chateau Gruaud-Larose St. Julien that she'd long had her eye upon, then grabbed a corkscrew and goblet. As she crossed the marble mosaic of the foyer to the grand staircase, she wondered, *Is it pathetic that all I wish to do is hide in my room, my only company a bottle of wine and a flat-screen TV?*

"Bloody hell not. Quite right, Siggy?" The dog galumphed up the grand staircase by her side. "And anyone who disapproves can just bugger off." She made her way down the long hallway until she reached her suite. "Ha! That's another bonus—I can curse like a dockworker all day and night if I wish, eh Sig?"

She placed the wine on the bed stand. "Yes, world. It's me—Noelle, the naughty nanny!" With a laugh, she flopped down on top of her duvet and fluffed the matching European pillow shams for the perfect telly-watching angle.

Pru didn't like that word "nanny", of course. She preferred the term au pair, claiming it had a whiff of exclusivity to it. Noelle couldn't disagree, since nothing said "elite" like hiring an utter stranger to take care of one's children.

She poured herself a bit of the ruby-red Bordeaux and began clicking away on the remote control. She waited. And waited. How odd…

Here she was, all alone. No one hounded her, and nothing absolutely had to be done. The house was quiet as a cloister. So why couldn't she relax, dammit? Maybe it would take a few days to wind down.

Serving as sherpa for the overscheduled and underdisciplined DiPaolo offspring had been exhausting, to say the least. The months had whipped along in a blur of organized sports, after-school activities, science fair projects, and temper tantrums. Time off had been rare, and Noelle often found herself too depleted to enjoy what little freedom she'd earned. She was the DiPaolo's first nanny, and Grayson and Phoebe were Noelle's first attempt at nannying. The learning curve had been steep for everyone involved.

She sipped and channel surfed, settling on an episode of Public Television's *Sherlock* that she'd seen at least six times.

Noelle raised her glass to Benedict Cumberbatch, the most pleasing incarnation of the Scotland Yard freelancer the world had ever known. He'd been her man-port in the storm these last months. The sound of his velvety British voice had transitioned her from unpleasant reality to pleasant dreams on many a night. So who cared if she'd practically memorized the dialogue from this episode?

"Here's to us, Benny, you sex muffin." Noelle toasted his high-definition image. "Alone at last, luv."

"Brruuhhf! Gack! Gwuuhk!"

Perhaps she'd been too quick to celebrate. The source of the dreadful sound stood hunched over in the doorway. Siegfried, the DiPaolo's daft Goldendoodle, was presently hacking up a plastic object, likely another low-hanging bauble from the Christmas tree. She closed her eyes, remembering the conversation she'd had with her employer a week ago.

"Are you sure you don't want to join us? It's not too late to change your mind." Pru DiPaolo had tilted her head and frowned—as much as the Botox would permit. "The chalet is a short snowmobile ride to the lifts. You'd love Aspen. The scenery is stunning, and the vibe is very chic. There's a large contingent of tourists from across the pond, as you Brits like to say."

No, we Brits do not like to say that. Noelle was from the working-class Wembley neighborhood of London, and not once in her twenty-six years had she heard that expression, and even if she had, she was not stupid enough to take the bait. Noelle knew her employer was serving up another big porky with the promise of all that stunning chic-ness. If Noelle agreed to go along on this family holiday, she wouldn't see the inside of a snowmobile or ski lift unless she was wrangling the children. The trip would be nothing but a repeat of the summer's South Carolina beach holiday, only colder.

"I do appreciate your offer, Mrs. DiPaolo, but I'm quite sure I'd like to stay." Noelle had smiled politely "I can look after Siggy, the dear boy, so he won't have to go to the kennel. And besides, I don't know how to ski."

Pru had narrowed her gaze—as much as the Botox would permit. "But what will you do all by yourself for two weeks?"

Noelle had somehow managed not to laugh as images of napping, sleeping, and more napping formed in her mind. "Oh, just read a bit and catch up on e-mails to friends," she'd said. "Maybe I'll take the train down to Chicago for the day."

"That's your prerogative, I suppose, since you've already fulfilled your vacation responsibilities for the year." Pru had pursed her plumped lips. "I thought it only polite to ask, since…well, it's not like you'll ever be able to afford this kind of trip on your own."

"Ha!" Noelle took a swig of wine and refocused on her two-dimensional hot date. "Bloody well right it's my prerogative, eh Benny?"

"Gack!"

"Bollocks!" Noelle set her wineglass on the bedside table, ran to the en suite bathroom to fetch supplies, and cleaned up what appeared to be the partially-digested head of Father Christmas himself.

"Let's go, Sig. Come on boy. Outside!" She reached the top of the stairs and looked over her shoulder at the guilty party. Siegfried was endearingly cute, which was fortunate, because his brain was the size of a dried currant. There he was, leaning against the wall in all his yellow fluffiness, his big chocolate eyes ready for some type of vomit-related reprimand. She tried to sound more enthusiastic. "Come on, boy! Chivvy along, dearest. Let's get you outside."

Nothing.

Noelle slapped the front of her thigh. "Siegfried! Come along you silly prat!"

That seemed to do the trick. The dog scurried along the hallway, slipped past her, and made his way down the stairway. She followed, disposing of Saint Nick's remains and washing up before she let the dog into the garden.

Noelle stood just outside the French doors, shivering in her stocking feet, noting that it was almost dark at 4:30 p.m. A wave of sadness settled over her, leaving a hard lump of regret in her chest. Could it be true? Yet another year had slipped by, and what did she have to show for it? Her academic dreams were still on hold. There was no one special in her life. Months had been spent in a job she didn't love, in a city she didn't know.

"All right. Come along, Sig. It's cold as brass monkey balls out here."

Change could be around the corner—at least in the academic department.

Noelle had a secret, one she'd not dared to share with another soul. She had submitted an early admission application to the University of Chicago's English Literature Ph.D. program. It was such a gamble—such a complete shot in the dark—that she'd decided not to tell a soul. Her parents would find out only if she got accepted.

Today was December 22, which meant the fateful letter was probably already on its way.

She peered into the fading light. "Siggy, you knob head! Where did you go?"

Noelle was a proud realist. She knew she didn't have supermodel looks or Nobel Prize-winning brains, but she wasn't an ass-ugly dullard, either. In fact, she'd been told on numerous occasions that she was fairly attractive and measurably clever. So the question remained: Why had nothing interesting happened to her since she'd come to the U.S.? Where was the excitement? Why did it seem as though she was doomed to endure a thoroughly boring life no matter where she lived?

Noelle leaned back against the French doors and remembered that fateful day last spring. She'd signed with the international nanny agency after the London-based recruiter promised her a future of cultural exchange, adventure, and an expansion of her horizons. It was all right there in the brochure! And since Noelle had been two years out of uni at the time—a Chaucer scholar working in a coffee shop—the sales pitch sounded rather brilliant.

Perhaps it was time to admit the truth. The last six months had been more frustration than culture, adventure, or expansion. The last six months had been a rip-roaring mistake.

The problem wasn't the children, really. Beneath all the layers of spoiled-rotten entitlement, Grayson and Phoebe DiPaolo were bright, playful, and occasionally sweet. But bloody hell! Working for Pru DiPaolo was simply…depressing.

The woman's entire existence revolved around appearances—her home, her children, her husband and, most importantly, herself. Pru's days were filled with shopping, grooming, redecorating, and keeping fit. Her evenings were for dinner parties, the theater, the symphony, and Steve's work-related social events. Pru wasn't an awful human being, but she was a shockingly shallow one, and she'd made it clear that Noelle had been hired to tend to the needs of the children so that she wouldn't have to.

She watched her breath hang in the still, cold air. A flittering of snowflakes tickled the tip of her nose. She saw Siegfried pass beneath the security lights, sniffing along the back privacy fence. "Sig! Come on, boy! Let's go back in, shall we?"

He stopped sniffing long enough to shoot her a blank, defiant stare. He didn't move.

"Siegfried, come!"

He lifted his leg and pissed in the snow.

"Bloody dumb dog."

That's when it hit her. Christmas was just days on, and for the first time in her life, Noelle would spend it away from London and the familiar chaos of her parents, grandparents, siblings, aunts and uncles, and nieces and nephews. Though she desperately needed a break from the DiPaolos, she suspected that at some point during the holiday, gut-level loneliness would find her. Unfortunately, she hadn't made a single friend since her arrival in the States—she hadn't had the time.

Oh, well. She'd simply have to bash on.

"What the—" Siegfried slammed into her shin on his way back inside the warm house. "Where are your manners, you fuzzy little twit?"

Noelle closed the door and rearmed the security system, doing her best to remember the operating instructions. Steve had given her a lesson yesterday and Pru had raced through a refresher just prior to the family's departure. Noelle hoped she remembered all the steps correctly.

She tapped the homeowner code on the keypad and hit the ENTER button. Noelle activated the interior and exterior motion sensors. She checked to make sure the window and door alarms were armed, then set the timer for the lights. No sooner had her finger left the touchpad when an ear-splitting alarm rattled the house.

"Bugger it!" She punched random buttons in a panic to shut the thing off. She got lucky and the God-awful racket eventually stopped—just as the phone rang.

Noelle answered with her customary politeness, but her voice trembled with adrenaline. "DiPaolo residence. This is Noelle Clarke speaking."

"This is Northshore Security Services responding to an alarm activation. Is there an emergency?"

"What? Oh heavens, no. Apologies. I hit the wrong button on the keypad when I let the dog inside. There's no problem whatsoever." Noelle saw that her hands were unsteady.

"All right." The woman sounded entirely bored, and Noelle had to wonder how many false alarms she had to deal with on a daily basis. "Miss Clarke, I see you are on our list of occupants of the home."

"Yes. I'm the nanny." Noelle rubbed her forehead. "It was an accident."

"You're listed here as the oh pear—is that how you pronounce it?"

Noelle rolled her eyes up to the custom-designed pot rack. It seemed she was the au pair across the board now—to Pru's tennis partners, the pool man, and even the security company.

"It's the same thing."

"I see, but because the homeowners reported they would be on vacation at this time, we're obligated to contact the local police. A patrol officer will verify that the premises are secure."

"Police? But there's really no cause to…" Out of the corner of her eye, Noelle saw Siegfried run into the kitchen from the great room, another ornament dangling from his bearded dog lips. He began to skitter around in circles on the hardwood floor, as if overwhelmed by the excitement of it all.

"An officer should be arriving soon. Why don't you stay on the phone with me until he arrives?"

"Sounds brilliant." Noelle put her hand over the receiver. "What the—drop the Magi, you bad dog!"

Ryder Partridge tussled with the boys for a few more minutes, then Glynnis walked with him to the front door.

"Need me to pick up anything after my shift, Glynn?"

She nodded. Her cheeks were paler than usual today, and the dark circles around her eyes more pronounced. Ryder leaned in to leave a gentle kiss on her forehead. Even three months later, the scars at her hairline remained an angry shade of pink. The day would come when the stitches would barely be noticeable, but that would take time. For all of them, getting through this would take a lot more time.

"A loaf of whole wheat would be great."

"You got it."

"But not the nuts-and-seeds hippy kind. Get the kid bread—you know, the stuff that looks like white bread but is whole grain in disguise."

"I'm all over it." Ryder rested a hand on the shoulder seam of her bathrobe. "You sure you're ok?"

"Of course. Go. I don't want you to be late."

Ryder looked past her to see the boys racing back and forth across the living room, their stomping causing the Christmas tree lights to sway. Cole, the wild-child oldest, was barefoot. Ethan, the middle kid, was in his Spiderman jammies, per usual. And the baby, Seth, was teetering around on his two stubby legs and yelling for his brothers to wait for him.

"Call me if they burn the place to the ground. Otherwise, I'll be home regular time."

He made it halfway down the front steps when he heard his name. He turned.

"I…I just want you to know…"

When Glynnis pulled the robe tighter, Ryder saw the raised welts on the backs of her hands. Defensive injuries. But he knew the most painful scars were the ones no one could see.

"…I love you—we love you—and we appreciate everything you do for us. I don't know what we'd do without you, Ry."

Damn. His heart just roller-coastered down to the pit of his stomach.

In truth, he'd often asked himself the same question, though he'd never tell Glynnis that. She would worry that he'd made some kind of sacrifice to be here, that it had cost him somehow. It hadn't. That wasn't the way these things worked. He was here because he wanted to be.

"I love you too, Glynn."

The afternoon passed slowly, and ninety-minutes into his shift, Ryder was almost relieved when dispatch sent him on a 10-33 run. Normally, it was a pain in the ass to respond to a residential security alarm at one of those sprawling mansions along the lakefront. They were pure busy work, nothing but paperwork-generating false alarms. But on this slow, gray Saturday afternoon before Christmas, he appreciated the distraction. It would keep his mind off everything else.

Besides, the call just might be the real deal. Twelve residential burglaries had been reported in Glencoe in the last week, and in each instance the family was on vacation. The house on Lakeside Circle fit the profile, except for one detail—the security company had mentioned that the nanny was at home.

Ryder continued along southbound Sheridan Road. He listened to the hiss of his car's radial tires on wet pavement and the rhythm of windshield wipers brushing away snow flurries. Once past the country club, Ryder approached a small cluster of exclusive residential streets, turning when he located Lakeside Circle. A dozen or so luxury homes lined the narrow road, each tastefully decorated for the season in swags of greenery, red velvet bows, and delicate white lights. The driveways here were lined with the best that German engineering had to offer—nothing but Mercedes, Audis and BMWs as far as the eye could see.

He smiled to himself, thinking how different his life had been this time last year. The South Patrol Division of the St. Louis Police Department had been a world of sex offenders, drug traffickers, and drive-by shootings. Glencoe was like another planet, home to Chicago's one-percenters—doctors, lawyers, judges, CEOs, and captains of industry and finance. Sure, there was the occasional domestic battery and drug-related call, but Ryder's customary evening shift was filled with fender benders, property crimes, shoplifting, and neighborhood tussles over dog poop or extra-enthusiastic hedge trimming.

A few months ago, if someone had told him he'd be leaving the hard-core city for a snooty suburb, he would have laughed his ass off.

Never say never.

Ryder parked the patrol car in front of the attached three-car garage and headed toward the front door. On his way he noticed that the sprawling brick estate was well lit and featured a prominent home security sign and a "NO SMOKING" placard near a neat row of boxwoods. He saw no footprints in the new snow and no indication that anyone had tampered with the doors or windows. As he rang the bell, Ryder put his money on the false alarm.

CHAPTER TWO

Noelle remained on the line with the security company as Siegfried ran in circles, chewing on his latest plastic victim. She worried the alarm had short-circuited the animal's brain. When another call came in, she put the security company on hold.

"Hello, Mrs. DiPaolo."

"Dear God, Noelle!" Pru shrieked into her mobile phone in an attempt to drown out the background noise of arguing children. "Is everything all right at the house? We've barely been gone an hour and we get a security notification. Do we have to turn around from O'Hare and cancel our trip?"

And the Academy Award for best melodrama goes to…

"Everything's fine, Pru. Truly. It was a false alarm—entirely my fault. There's absolutely nothing to worry about."

Noelle imagined that Pru had just scrunched up her nose in disdain—as much as the Botox would allow. With another round of assurances, Noelle wished her a good holiday and told her not to worry. Then, she returned to the conversation with the alarm company.

"The officer is arriving now, Miss Clarke."

"Police! Please open the door!"

"I'm bloody coming!" Noelle hung up the landline and ran through the marble-floored atrium, Siggy barking at her heels. Thinking that this wasn't ex-

actly the kind of excitement she'd been pining for, she flung open the front door.

Oh, my. Perhaps she'd been too quick to judge. Because, truly, the officer standing in the doorway was simply smashing.

"Miss Clarke?"

She nodded, her eyes straying from his light brown hair and hazel eyes to his firm chin, gorgeous mouth, and brass-plated badge. It read "Officer Ryder Partridge."

"Hullo." Noelle felt herself smile.

"Hi." The police officer smiled back, his friendly eyes shining in the porch light. He had a lovely face, she thought. Friendly. Sexy. In fact, Noelle decided that he was extraordinary in most every way. He possessed the kind of lips that could provide a girl all the adventure she'd ever need. Those were the kind of lips that could expand her horizons and possibly even provide a lifetime's worth of cross-cultural exchange.

Siegfried chose that moment to poke his head through Noelle's legs and retch at the policeman's feet. Her handsome visitor glanced down at the dog and chuckled.

"Sorry." Noelle was horrified. "He likes to eat ornaments off the Christmas tree—angels, snowmen, candy canes, you name it. Seems like he's moved on to the nativity scene."

The policeman glanced up again, his eyes glittering behind thick lashes. "Looks like we've got a wise man down."

She blinked in surprise at his comment, then giggled. How perfectly delightful! This officer of the law was devastatingly attractive, and droll, to boot! She knew she was in danger of behaving like a complete man-starved git in his company.

"May I come in?"

"Whaa…oh! Of course. Of course." Noelle stepped aside so the police officer could circumvent the remains of what looked to be Melchior of Persia. "Please do come in."

As he walked, she heard the erotic squeaking sound of all his leather accessories—a utility belt, a large gun holster, shoes…and he smelled heavenly. It was a mixture of the leather, starched cotton, and hot authority on a cold December day.

She watched the tall policeman come to a stop in the center of the vestibule, directly under the sprig of mistletoe Pru had hung from the chandelier. Noelle couldn't help herself—her gaze darted from the mistletoe to the man, the man to the mistletoe, and back again. He glanced overhead to see what had her behaving so strangely.

The corner of his mouth twitched.

Noelle wanted to die from embarrassment, but the officer was all business, acting as if nothing untoward had transpired. He touched the walkie-talkie mounted to his shoulder, and it squelched to life.

"Glencoe Public Safety Patrol Officer Ryder Partridge, badge number 29, location 714 Lakeside Circle, responding to a 10-33 and possible 62R. In contact with resident."

Noelle felt her mouth open in wonder. This was her first in-the-flesh experience with an American "cop." For the most part, London bobbies did not carry guns. They didn't seem to swagger like this, either. And she racked her brain but couldn't recall ever seeing one as appealing as this American specimen.

Officer Partridge finished his radio call and smiled down at her. "I'll sweep the interior if you don't mind, check the alarm system, and give the grounds a quick look. Then I'll be out of your hair."

Her hair. Her hair! Noelle began patting her head, only to remember she had it pulled up in a lopsided pony tail. She peeked down at herself and groaned at the worn V-neck jumper and ratty pair of jeans she wore. And she was in her stocking feet, no less! Her complete lack of grooming was appalling.

"So, would you mind showing me around?"

She smiled and straightened her shoulders. "Yes, of course. Please follow me."

For the next ten minutes or so, Noelle gave the delicious Officer Partridge a guided tour of the DiPaolo home as Siegfried tagged along and sniffed at the back of his legs. She began on the first floor with the study, dining room, kitchen, great room, living room, library, and on to the mud room, butler's pantry, garage, and sun-room. Then she showed him the basement's media room, fully stocked bar and kitchenette, game room, home gym, racquetball court, luxurious bath and steam shower, and artificial-turf putting green. At this point she noticed that the policeman's eyes had gone buggy. Noelle knew what he was thinking, because she'd been thinking the same thing for six months: Why on earth would four normal-sized human beings need this much room and this many possessions?

"Not too shabby," was all he said.

Noelle laughed at the observation. "I suppose it's no wonder why my employers desire an alarm system."

The officer shook his head, as if sorting something out for himself. "Getting stuff, storing stuff, protecting, insuring, and worrying about it…people can spend their whole lives on that hamster wheel. And in the end that's all they've got—stuff. Seems crazy."

Noelle had been leading the policeman from the gym when he said those words. She stopped near the foot of the basement stairs and slowly turned toward him. As remarkable as it seemed, Officer Partridge had just eloquently summed up what bothered Noelle most about working for the DiPaolos—their priorities were material things. The children were almost afterthoughts.

"Are you all right, Miss Clarke?" He scanned her face, concern in his expression.

Noelle stared at him. No, she most certainly was not oh-kay. She was surprised by this stranger. She'd been caught off-guard by his good looks, humor, and sensitivity, and how she now found herself quite possibly smitten. Which would make her a daft cow, since no rational woman moistened her knickers fifteen minutes after meeting someone—no matter how totty he happened to be.

She couldn't help it. She looked at his left hand. No wedding ring. How was that even possible? But, of course, lack of a ring meant nothing. This man could not possibly be single. A man like this was almost certainly in a relationship—he had "taken" written all over him in permanent marker. He probably had kids, a mortgage, university savings plans…

"Miss Clarke?"

"I'm absolutely fine. It's just…" Noelle was appalled by her clumsy attempt at social intercourse. She'd gotten rusty in her six months of au pair purgatory. "What you said was spot on, and quite lovely. Sad, as well."

The officer's striking hazel eyes locked onto hers, and their gazes stayed connected longer than might be considered polite. Noelle felt heat spreading across her cheeks, rushing down her chest and belly.

She swallowed hard and did her very best to maintain her composure.

"Right, then! On to the bedrooms?" She spun around and immediately cringed at her gaffe. The totty cop was probably laughing behind her back, and she wouldn't blame him. "This way please."

The climb from the basement to the second floor consisted of two flights of stairs and several awkward moments during which Noelle's bum hovered mere inches from the attractive police officer's face. Perhaps she should have let him walk ahead. In fact, she was beginning to feel a bit cheated by the arrangement.

"I'll wait here in the hallway." Noelle stood at the top of the staircase and pointed to her right, then left. "The master suite is down there, and you'll find four more bedrooms and bathrooms on this side."

Officer Partridge didn't budge. Instead he looked at her with blatant curiosity. "So, you're a nanny?"

"I am."

"From England?"

"Quite right. London."

"The family went on vacation without you?"

"Um, yes. They're in Aspen for a fortnight."

He frowned. "You mean you're here by yourself for two whole weeks?"

Noelle didn't know what to think of this line of questioning. Yes, he was a police officer and was probably only doing his job, but she'd just answered several pointed questions from a man she didn't know, and the last one had made her feel vaguely uncomfortable. With her mother's dire warnings about aggressive American men echoing in her mind, Noelle slipped her hands into the front pockets of her jeans, hesitating before she gave away any more information.

The policeman shook his head. "Forgive me, Miss Clarke." He closed his eyes for an instant, then gave her a sheepish smile. "That didn't come out right, did it?"

Noelle shrugged.

"I'll be right back, okay?"

She wrapped her arms around her middle and waited while he checked the second floor. Watching him disappear into her room, she suddenly worried about the state of her suite. Had she left knickers scattered about? Bras? Jimjams? Did she leave her

birth control dispenser on the bathroom vanity? And oh, dear God! The wine bottle!

The policeman exited her room with a big smile on his face.

He thinks I've been sitting around getting rat-arsed. He thinks I bodged the alarm in a drunken stupor!

"Anyway…" The officer hooked his thumbs in his utility belt, a pose she found unbelievably sexy. "I asked if you were here alone because there's been a cluster of residential burglaries in this neighborhood, and in each case the homeowners were on vacation. I want you to be sure to set the alarm properly and lock up. Just be cautious, Miss Clarke."

Noelle felt her mouth fall open in surprise. "There's a crime wave in Glencoe?"

It was obvious that Officer Partridge was trying not to laugh, which meant he either was amused by Noelle or found her ridiculous, or possibly both. But he nodded politely and gestured for her to lead the way back downstairs. Their fingers accidentally touched on the banister. His skin was hot and smooth.

Too hot. Too smooth. She felt her face flush.

"Sorry," he whispered. He was so close that she could feel the warmth of his breath on the nape of her neck.

"No worries."

What a lie. Things were quite worrisome, indeed, because Noelle's entire body tingled from his proximity. Her breath came too fast. Good heavens—she was acting like she hadn't seen a deliciously attractive man in months!

Six months, to be exact, if she did not count Benedict.

Downstairs once more, Officer Partridge helped her review the operating instructions for the security system. Standing so close to him made her lightheaded. When he reached around her shoulder to activate the system, her knees weakened.

Too soon, he was ready to leave. While they stood in the foyer, he scribbled something on a business card and handed it to Noelle. "I work most evenings from three to midnight. Call if you have concerns while the family is away."

Noelle took the card, surprised to see that he'd written his mobile number on the card. His personal mobile number! She looked up at him, careful not to gawk.

"It was a pleasure to meet you, Miss Clarke." The officer opened the front door and stepped over the masticated wise man remains. "I'll take another look outside before I leave. Have a safe and happy holiday."

"And you as well, Officer."

Noelle waited as long as she could—a whopping five seconds—before she decided to run from window to window to watch him make his rounds. The policeman moved elegantly as he bent low to peer at the basement windows, the seat of his trousers pulling tight across his spectacular bum. She saw the power in his broad shoulders as he checked the lock on the side gate. And she got a good look at the strong line of his jaw when he glanced up at the motion-activated exterior lights.

That's when he caught her spying on him. Officer Partridge waved and gave her a shy smile so disarming that Noelle clutched at her chest. Though thoroughly mortified, she waved back, then spun around and stared at Siegfried.

"Bloody hell!" she whispered to the dog. "Did you see the smile on that man?"

Ryder turned up the heat in his cruiser and took another sip of bad coffee, watching the customers go in and out of the convenience store. It was nearly nine thirty. He'd completed three reports, including the one for the hot English nanny, and was just beginning to think about grabbing something to eat when his cell phone rang. It was Glynnis.

He smiled as he answered. "Hey, good lookin.'"

The sound of her laugh warmed his heart. They'd always been close—she was just a year younger than Ryder and his only sibling—but college and work had kept them from being part of each other's lives. Before September 30th, anyway.

"I don't mean to interrupt. I know you're busy."

"Another night on the mean streets of Glencoe."

"It's ugly, I bet."

"The shit's goin' down—right here at the 7-Eleven on Green Bay Road."

"Looking for underage smokers?"

"Damn straight."

He heard her sigh. "I hate to ask, but could you grab a gallon of milk, as well? Two-percent."

"No problem. I'll put it in your fridge when my shift's over."

"Just don't leave it in your car overnight. You know how Spidey feels about frozen milk."

Indeed he did know. Ethan had a complete shit-fit last week when he went to pour milk on his Cheerios and got slush instead. The kid who dressed like a superhero had developed a supersized temper to match.

In the past three months, Ryder had become familiar with the eccentricities of his sister's world. He knew the only storybook that would get Cole to fall asleep. He knew Seth's must-have bath toy. And he knew to provide a back-up uniform when Spidey's primary suit was in the wash.

The way Ryder looked at it, if he was lucky enough to have kids of his own one day, he'd be way ahead of the game.

"Ten-four," Ryder said.

"You're the best. Catch you later."

Ryder clicked off his mobile and returned it to the pocket of his trousers. Usually, he didn't allow his thoughts to dwell on the details of that September night, but he must have let his guard down at some point. Maybe the sound of his sister's laugh left him hopeful. Maybe he was preoccupied by the pretty British nanny.

Whatever the reason, the memory had forced its way into his thoughts, all the ugly details already unfolding in his mind's eye.

The drive from St. Louis had been a ninety-mile-an-hour nightmare. His head swam. Sweat rolled down his spine. Rage cut his insides to shreds. Would Glynnis die before he reached her side? How much had the kids witnessed? How long would it take to get them out of child protective services, and when he did, how would he deal with the fallout? Ryder had no idea how he'd repair the collateral damage to the people he loved most in the world, how he'd explain the unexplainable to the boys.

But he knew exactly what to do about Jay. That man would rot in prison for what he'd done to Glynnis. Ryder would make sure of it.

He'd reached Evanston Hospital at about two A.M. Ryder stood beside the intensive-care bed, his thumb gently stroking the only spot on her forearm not bandaged or poked with needles and tubes. His pretty, dark-haired little sister was nothing but an unrecognizable mound of flesh. Swollen. Bloodied. Broken at the hands of the man who had vowed to love her.

At sunrise, Ryder was on the phone with his commanding officer. He put in for an emergency leave of absence. He moved into the second-floor unit of his sister's Asbury Avenue house so he could take care of her boys, and once Glynnis was discharged from the hospital, he drove her to daily physical therapy and doctor's appointments.

Within a month, a second-shift Glencoe Public Safety patrol job opened up. Ryder grabbed it, resigning from the St. Louis PD. It was the best choice he could make in an impossible situation.

Sometimes, he could barely digest all the changes the last few months had produced. He coped the only way he could—by taking it one day at a time, one hour at a time, one step at a time—exactly the way Glynnis coped with her physical recovery. He had the option to return to his career in St. Louis one day, but for now, his primary duty was to Glynnis and the boys.

Ryder was just about to head into the store when the police radio crackled to life. Dispatch was sending him to another activated security alarm. He recognized the address.

"I've already responded to that call. I was there a couple hours ago."

Ryder waited for dispatch to admit they'd made a mistake.

"Affirmative. This is the second report from that address today."

He pulled out of the 7-Eleven lot and made a U-turn, shaking his head. He'd seen the lovely Miss Clarke peeking at him from the kitchen window. Could she have finished off that bottle of Bordeaux and tripped the alarm on purpose? It wouldn't be the first time a woman had pulled that stunt, but the nanny was much better looking—and younger—than the last homeowner who desired a return visit from Glencoe's finest.

Ryder laughed at himself. Sure, it had been several months since his last date, but he hadn't come back to Chicago to improve his love life. His love life had been pretty damn healthy back in St. Louis, if he didn't count the fact that every woman he'd been interested in in the last three years had lied to him about something—money, exes, children, marital status, arrest records, library fines, you name it. And anyway, the hot English nanny looked about nineteen years old, and he had no business messing with that, no matter how adorable she was, how much he loved her accent, or how much he'd been thinking about that brief brush of his hand against hers.

He took Green Bay to Sheridan, thinking that he'd always been the guy who could look at a jumble of puzzle pieces and know exactly how they clicked together. It's what made him a good cop. But when it came to the laws of attraction—sexual chemistry—Ryder had always suspected there was more magic involved than logic. He'd seen it often enough. Two people who, on the surface, looked as if they should fit together perfectly often did not. And two people who couldn't be more different sometimes joined with such ease and grace that their happiness was contagious. If Ryder got lucky, he hoped to one day have that kind of happiness. There was still time. He was only thirty-one. He was in no rush.

He pulled up the drive of the house on Lakeside Circle, parking in the same spot. He reached the front porch and was surprised when the English cutie threw open the front door before he had the chance to knock. She held a cordless phone to her flushed cheek. Her dark blond curls were loose against her shoulders. Her green eyes pleaded with him for patience as she motioned him inside.

"What? A hundred dollars? But it was an accident! That's a bloody lot of money!"

Ryder squatted down to greet the big fuzzy dog while the nanny finished her call. Obviously, she was speaking to the security company, and he knew they weren't just blowing sunshine up her skirt. The majority of Glencoe's eight thousand residents had home security systems and responding to false alarms had become a huge waste of government resources and personnel. Like many cities and towns, Glencoe had an ordinance that fined homeowners for repeated offenses, and a hundred bucks was just the starting point.

"Yes, yes. Lovely. Good-bye to you, too." The nanny clicked off the phone and stared down at Ryder, who was still petting the dog. "Bugger it!"

He rose, doing his best not to let on how entertained he was by her use of exotic cuss words. For a moment, the nanny just stared at him. Then her chin began to tremble, and she bit down on her lower lip. Was she about to cry? Oh man—not that.

"I'm so very sorry." She shook her head, clearly angry at herself. "I feel like such a plank for doing this again, but I think I waited too long to punch in the code. Gadgets aren't exactly my strong suit. Do come in."

Ryder smiled politely and stepped into the large foyer, immediately getting a whiff of freshly made popcorn. His stomach rumbled. He followed her into the kitchen, taking full advantage of yet another opportunity to appreciate her British booty. She really was a nice little package of feminine curves, probably about five-five, no more than one-hundred-thirty pounds. He bet that beneath those jeans she had great legs. And a lot more of that creamy, soft skin.

It was a relief to see she hadn't set off the alarm on purpose. A woman with an ulterior motive would have at least brushed her hair and changed out of that old sweater and jeans. Maybe even put on some lip gloss. She'd done none of those things.

And was prettier for it.

The nanny spoke to him without turning around. "I suppose you'll need another look about the house?"

Ryder cleared his throat. "Yes. It's standard operating procedure, Miss Clarke."

"Have at it, then. You know your way around by now, so I'll wait here." She set the phone on the marble countertop, plopped down on a kitchen stool, and rested her elbows on the island. When she dropped her forehead into her hands, all those soft curls fell around her face, making it impossible for Ryder to see her expression. He was suddenly hit with such an intense feeling of sympathy that it took real effort not to run his fingers through the blond corkscrews or place a comforting hand on her shoulder.

Miss Clarke was just a kid a long way from home, all by herself at Christmas.

"I'll be back soon." He walked away before he did something he'd regret—like hug her. Or let her cry on his shoulder.

Nope. Nope. Nope.

It took about ten minutes to check all three floors plus the garage. During his second visit to Miss Clarke's room, he'd discovered that she enjoyed watching Sherlock reruns, preferred copious amounts of butter on her popcorn, and, yes, that she could finish off an entire bottle of wine all by her lonesome. When he returned to the kitchen, he found the nanny where he'd left her, her face still hidden in her hands. He sat on the kitchen stool next to hers and pulled up the citation template on his tablet.

"May I see your ID, Miss Clarke? Do you have a driver's license?"

"What? Why?" She raised her head, and Ryder saw she'd been crying. Her cheeks were blotchy, and her long eyelashes were clumped with tears.

"I need your ID for the paperwork, Miss Clarke. I'm issuing you a warning."

Noelle groaned, pushing herself up from the stool and heading to the mudroom near the garage. She came back with a small wallet. "Is this really necessary? And how much is this warning of yours going to cost? More than a hundred dollars?"

"There's no monetary fine. I just have to document that I was here."

Her brows rose in surprise as she handed him an Illinois license. "Really? But…that's so kind of you!"

Ryder smiled as he entered her information into the template, then stopped. The license indicated that Noelle Elisabette Clarke was twenty-six years old—days away from twenty-seven. Not a kid at all.

"Hey, it's Christmas, right?" He finished the report and was about to return her license when the nanny threw her arms around his neck and hugged him tight. Ryder froze. He had no idea what to do. Her curls tickled his lips. Her sweet, light scent filled his nostrils. And her soft curves were impossible to ignore, even through his Kevlar vest. Then he heard the unmistakable sound of a dainty hiccup.

This wasn't good. He should have already peeled her off and been on his way to the door. But instead, Ryder found himself closing his eyes in delight. He felt his body uncoil and relax in the warmth of Miss Clarke's embrace.

She pulled back, her eyes wide. "Oh! I probably shouldn't have done that bit—molesting an officer an' all. Sorry."

Hiccup.

Ryder was relieved she'd been the one to break away—and, honestly, a little disappointed. He gave her the license and waited for the wireless printer to produce a pocket-sized version of the warning, which he then handed to her. "A memento of our evening, Miss Clarke."

She chuckled. "Please, call me Noelle."

"All right. If you call me Ryder."

That's when she unleashed a full smile on him. He couldn't look away. Her green eyes sparkled. Her cheeks were rosy, and her lips were a soft pink. And suddenly Ryder wondered how he ever imagined her a ridiculously cute, homesick girl.

Because Noelle Clarke was clearly a beautiful, grown woman.

She wasn't hitting on him, though. There was nothing coy in her expression. Noelle had simply dropped her guard for a moment and allowed herself to be seen. And he liked what he was seeing. A lot.

He needed to get out of there.

"Are you hungry, Ryder? Can I make you something to nosh?"

"I…well, thank you, but—"

"A toasty perhaps? Soup?"

He had no idea what a toasty was, but his empty stomach told him to go for it.

The nanny hopped down from the stool. "They have the best of everything here, so I can probably whip up whatever you might fancy."

Ryder nearly jumped when his police radio squawked. "Excuse me, please, Miss Clarke."

He headed toward the front hallway, glad he had an excuse to walk away from what he fancied—because he fancied her. The call was a traffic accident with injuries, and he turned to find Noelle leaning against the archway to the kitchen, hands folded primly in front of her thighs. She was such an appealing combination of sweet and sexy.

"I have to go. I do appreciate the offer, Noelle. I can't remember the last time I noshed on anything."

She grinned. "Of course. I know you're quite busy. Keeping the peace and all that."

Ryder nodded politely. He took two steps toward the front door, then turned around again. The nanny stood gazing at her sock-covered feet, shoulders curved in. She looked a little lost. And a lot lonely.

That's when it hit him—Noelle would be spending Christmas alone in this huge, empty house. All he wanted to do was wrap her up in his arms and take her home with him. Of course that wouldn't happen. Couldn't happen.

So why wasn't he already out the door?

"Are you squared away with the alarm, Miss Clarke? Do you need me to help you reset it again?"

She looked up, shook her head, and gave him a brave smile. "I've put you out enough tonight, and besides, I've taken care of it. I promise there won't be any more trouble. Thank you for everything."

She followed him to the front door. "Stay safe, Officer. And again, Happy Christmas."

CHAPTER THREE

Ryder moved silently across the carpet of his sister's living room and entered the kitchen without turning on a light. Glynnis was so on edge lately that the click of a light switch could send her bolting awake, unable to breathe.

He couldn't blame her.

Ryder put the milk in the refrigerator door and the bread on the counter, then gasped in surprise. His sister sat motionless at the kitchen table, illuminated only by an Asbury Avenue streetlight, hands folded on the tabletop.

"You scared the shit out of me, Glynn."

"Sorry."

"What are you doing up?"

"Couldn't sleep."

"Want to join me for a cup of tea, then?"

"Sounds perfect."

Ryder flipped on the dim light over the stovetop, put the kettle on to boil, and got out two mugs. He unbuckled his utility belt and draped it over one of the kitchen chairs, stretching in relief. That extra fourteen pounds of equipment always felt like a half-ton by shift's end.

"Any more presents that still need to be wrapped? I'm happy to do a few before I go upstairs."

"We're good." She smiled at him, her face half in shadow. "Hey, Ry?"

"Hmm?" He rifled through the individually wrapped tea bags, picking a mint for her and an orange pekoe for him.

"Do you remember Christmas mornings when we were kids? How we'd race down the stairs in our pajamas and just dive headfirst into the toys like crazy people?"

He laughed. "Sure do."

"I was just sitting here thinking…we had no idea how much it took—all the money, time, and attention that went into those few frenzied minutes. I mean, remember how Dad scattered around the half-eaten carrots as proof that Santa's reindeer had visited? And Mom arranged the cookie crumbles on Santa's plate? They thought of everything, just so we could be swept away by joy."

Ryder poured boiling water over a tea bag and placed the mug before Glynnis. It had been a decade since their parents were killed in a car accident, but, in moments like this one, the pain felt particularly fresh. His sister's expression showed that she struggled with the same sense of loss.

"We were completely protected, Ryder. Innocent. We believed the universe was full of magic, just for us, and our parents were these…I don't know…just these detached bystanders."

Ryder felt himself smile. "That's the benefit of being a kid at Christmas. It's all magic and no reality."

Glynnis looked up at him, her expression intense. "I want that for my boys. They've had too much reality this year."

"As have you." Ryder took his mug to the table and sat down opposite his sister. They remained in silence for several minutes, while Ryder's gaze wandered out the window. Snow danced in the streetlight.

"Did you have a good shift?" Glynnis cradled the mug in both hands and took a small sip of her tea.

"Not bad, actually." He knew what he was about to say would sound crazy, but he needed his sister's blessing if he were to do this. "Hey, Glynn, do you think we could squeeze in one more person for Christmas Eve?"

Her eyes widened above the rim of the tea cup.

"I met somebody today."

Glynnis stilled.

"I mean, I encountered her on a security alarm call. Two really. And I guess I didn't meet her in the usual sense, but now that I know she's there, well…I can't stop thinking about her."

Glynnis put down the mug, a smile tugging at her lips. "This sounds serious."

Ryder laughed, mostly at himself. "It's too soon to be serious."

"So? Who is she?"

He dunked his tea bag into the hot water a few times, searching for the right words. "A nanny. Very sweet and funny. Very British. Her name's Noelle." He glanced up to find his sister, grinning. "She's alone in one of those McMansions by the lake. The family's on vacation. I thought maybe she'd appreciate some company. Would you be ok with that?"

Glynnis titled her head, considering his question. "Is this an act of Christmas charity, Ryder? Or is she hot?"

"She's hot."

"At least you're honest."

"But she's all alone."

"Hmm." Glynnis took another sip. "Did you already ask the hot nanny if she wants to join us on Christmas Eve? I mean, she might be loving the alone time."

He hadn't thought of that.

"Mommy?"

Spidey stood by the refrigerator, hair sticking up on one side of his head. He yawned. "I heard Uncle Ryder laughing."

"Hey, bud. Let's get you back to bed." Ryder stood, sweeping Ethan into his arms. He was getting heavier by the day.

"Wait. Mommy?"

Ryder paused in the hallway so Ethan could ask his question.

"Is Santa going to bring us a dog like I asked? Is he? Are we getting a dog?"

"Let's head back to bed. It's late." Ryder carried Ethan down the hall, entered the second door on the right, and deposited him in his twin-size Spiderman bed. On the opposite side of the room, Seth snored in a toddler bed shaped like a racecar. Cole was in his room across the hall, probably passed out on top of his Chicago Cubs comforter, as usual.

"So, are we?" Ethan's eyes burned in the dim light. "Have I been good enough this year, Uncle Ryder? Good enough for Santa to bring us a dog?"

He reached down and smoothed the little boy's sweaty bed hair. What a question! Had he been good enough? This kindergartener had discovered his mother, half-dead on the living room floor, then had the presence of mind to call 911 and comfort his brothers until police and EMTs arrived. The kid wasn't just good. He was a stone-cold badass.

But a dog? Another rowdy beast stomping through this three-bedroom apartment was the last thing Glynnis needed.

"I'm not sure what Santa has planned, Ethan." He leaned down and kissed him on the top of his head. "But whatever it is, you can be sure that he knows all about you. He knows you're the smartest, bravest kid in the Greater Chicagoland area."

Ethan yawned again and closed his eyes. As Ryder tucked the covers under his chin, he noticed a small smile settle on his nephew's lips.

"Hey, Uncle Ryder?"

"Hmm?"

"I've decided I want to be a policeman when I grow up. Just like you."

"Not Spiderman?"

He shook his head, eyes still closed. "Don't be silly. There's already one of those."

Crack!

Noelle shot up in bed with a gasp, planting her palms on the duvet as she looked around. Her bedroom was awash in the blue glow of the telly, and the unmistakable soundtrack from Downton Abbey floated through the air. Siggy was on top of the covers near her feet, his ears perked, a low, deep growl rumbling in his chest.

Pulling herself from the fog of sleep, Noelle attempted to put the pieces together. Apparently she had nodded off with the television on. And apparently she'd snacked herself into a stupor, because on the bedside table was the empty wine bottle, a large bowl littered with buttery popcorn kernels, and a wrapper from a frozen ice-cream treat. Right. It was all coming back to her now, the details break-

ing through the haze. The DiPaolos were on holiday, and she was alone in the house. She'd set off the alarm by accident—twice. She'd met that smashing policeman. Good. She was up to speed.

But what was that sharp pinch on her bum? Noelle reached beneath her and unearthed what had been poking her flesh. It was the business card of Officer Shag-a-licious, on which he'd written his mobile number. She glanced at the alarm clock and saw that it was 2:45 a.m. She'd been asleep for at least an hour.

Noelle grabbed the remote and turned off the telly. She cocked her head, listening to the silence. Unless she'd been dreaming, a very loud noise had just woken her up. But if it wasn't a dream, what was it and why hadn't she heard it again? At least it wasn't the bloody security alarm. She'd had the sense to disarm the contraption after Officer Smashing's second visit, deciding she'd spend the next morning studying the operating manual in detail, then call the security company to walk her through setup. There was no way she would risk being fined, and there was no way she'd want another shrieking phone call from Pru.

"Oh, my God, Noelle! What the hell is going on? We just landed in Aspen and here I find yet another alarm notification. I knew we shouldn't have left you there alone…"

No. No, thank you.

"*Rrrrr-uuuhf!*"

Siegfried jumped to his feet on the mattress. He stared intently at the dark bedroom window, his lips peeled back, his growl more ferocious. There was nothing out there, of course—the bedroom was on the second floor. Siegfried had certainly chosen a strange time and place to pretend he was a guard dog.

"Lie down, Sig."

He didn't—total shocker, that. Noelle was about to go back to sleep when she heard the noise again.

Crack!

Siegfried shot off the bed and ran to the window, balancing his paws on the sill and barking like a mad beast. Noelle told him to quiet down, but the dog's body began to shake as his growling and barking intensified. She squinted. Had she just seen something moving outside? Wait! There it was again—a tiny, red, glowing dot beyond the black windowpane. She sat quite still in the completely darkened bedroom, barely breathing.

Her eyes adjusted enough that she could discern the outline of a man in the large tree outside her window.

"*OhmybloodyGod.*" Her heart pounded. "Oh, no. *Hell*, no!" Noelle jumped from bed and grabbed her mobile phone, quickly punching in 9-1-1. But before the call could go through, she hung up. What if she was only imagining this? What if the police came for the third time, only to find more of nothing? She would be the nanny who cried wolf and got fined for doing so. And the next time wouldn't be a warning, would it? How high did the fines go? Five hundred dollars? Seven-fifty? A thousand?

Noelle snatched the bent business card from the bed sheet. She ran into the attached bathroom and dialed the policeman's number. It rang five times before he picked up.

"Partridge," he grunted.

"There's a man outside my window!"

"Uh…" She heard him fumble around in the dark to turn on a light. "Who is this? Wait. Is this—"

"Yes, yes! It's me, Noelle Clarke! You said I could ring if I had a problem. Well, I'm having a rather large problem at the moment, as there's a man trying to—"

"Hang up and dial 911."

"What if he's gone when the bobbies get here? I'll be fined! He's in the tree outside my bedroom right this instant, staring at me!"

She heard him cuss under his breath. "Hang up and dial 911 immediately, Miss Clarke. Do not open the door until patrol officers arrive. Lock yourself in a safe place, like a closet or bathroom. I'm on my way." He hung up.

Noelle jumped when she heard the unmistakable sound of glass shattering somewhere on the first floor. With shaking hands she dialed 911 again, telling herself over and over that she would get through this, that she could keep a clear head, that she was British and she could bloody well keep calm and carry on! The operator answered.

"Come straight away please! A prowler's in the tree outside my bedroom and someone's downstairs!"

Noelle placed the phone on the vanity and put it on speaker, which allowed her to get dressed while she continued the conversation. The emergency operator asked her a whole series of questions—her name, age, where she was in the house, whether the doors and windows were locked, and if there was a security system. Noelle had answered each question while throwing off her nightgown, hopping into jeans, and pulling a hooded sweatshirt over her head. But when the operator got to that last question, she froze.

"I turned off the alarm!" She blinked, staring at her reflection in the bathroom mirror.

"Miss Clarke?"

"Oh bloody hell, how could I be such a plonker? But it kept going off! Pru is going to kill me!"

The 911 operator spoke slowly and evenly. She told Noelle to remain where she was and lock the bathroom door. But at that instant, Noelle heard Siegfried bark.

"Siggy!"

"Miss Clarke? Do not leave the bathroom."

She cracked open the en suite door. Siegfried stood on guard at the window, growling, his tail tucked between his hind legs. Oh God! If this daft creature somehow got himself injured…she couldn't let her thoughts continue in that direction. "Siggy, come!"

The dog ignored her. He barked louder.

Noelle straightened, determined to make her voice sound as deep and authoritative as possible.

"Siegfried, you ridiculous, arse-wipe wanker! Get in here this instant!"

For the first time ever, the Goldendoodle obeyed her command. He skittered wildly across the bedroom and ran into the open door of the loo. Once he was safely inside, she locked up and dropped to her knees, hugging the fuzzy git around his neck. Siggy licked her face.

"Miss Clarke!"

"Yes, yes. I'm here. I had to get the dog."

"Do not open the door again unless I tell you it's safe to do so."

"Absolutely. Of course." She stood.

"Officer Partridge just confirmed he's on his way. Two other units are en route."

"Brilliant."

A loud crash came from downstairs. Noelle froze.

What if someone was coming for her right this instant? She had to be prepared to defend herself, but how? With what? She glanced around the bathroom in a panic.

"Miss Clarke, are you there?"

"Yes, I'm here."

Her first year at uni, Noelle had taken a self-defense course. And now, at the only moment in her life when those skills would have come in handy, she could barely remember a thing the instructor had taught her. Something to do with gouging out the assailant's eyeballs, perhaps? Jabbing one's opponent in the throat? It was all a blur. It was if her brain had shut down as it flooded with anxiety.

Her heart pounded. Her fingers went numb. The moment felt surreal. Poor Siggy pressed his body against the far wall near the shower, clearly as terrified as Noelle.

Protection—she needed something to use as a weapon. She grabbed whatever struck her as useful. First, she snagged the stainless-steel nail file from the cluttered countertop. She snatched a leather belt with a metal buckle from a hook on the inside of the door. From under the sink she selected a spray bottle of window cleaner and a canister of foaming bubbles that promised to remove rust stains from the loo. It was better than nothing.

Noelle wrapped the belt around her waist, put the file in her back jeans pocket, and shoved the cleaning supplies in the oversized pouch on the front of the sweatshirt. Siegfried began whine.

She heard another noise from downstairs, closer this time.

Noelle was ready. She turned off the bathroom light, then carefully eased open the door. She peered into the dark bedroom but saw no movement at the window.

"Miss Clarke! Are you there?"

Oh bugger! She'd forgotten her mobile phone! She retrieved it from the counter and whispered her reply. "Yes."

"Officers are…"

"No!" Siegfried bolted out the bathroom door. Noelle went after him, her whisper desperate. "Sig! Come back. Please, Siggy!" She caught a glimpse of him racing down the stairs.

A moment later, an inhuman yelp echoed up from the foyer.

"Siggy!"

"Miss Clarke. Stay in the bathroom."

Noelle heard sirens. She spotted four flashing blue lights coming up the close. Emboldened by the arrival of reinforcements, she shoved the phone into her empty back pocket while keeping the call active, keenly aware that she was about to disappoint the operator in the worst possible way. With the bobbies in place to handle the situation, she decided there was no way she would lock herself away in the WC while poor, daft Siegfried tried to play hero. She moved into the hallway.

Honestly, this was the most cracking thing that had ever happened in her life!

She'd not taken two steps when the dog galumphed his way back up the steps, nearly knocking Noelle over on his way to the bedroom, where he dove under her bed. At least he wasn't seriously hurt. She moved stealthily down the dark hallway, pressing her back against the wall, sidestepping her way to the top of the stairwell.

"Police! Put your hands on top of your head!" A loud, masculine voice rose up the stairs.

She stopped.

"Do it! *Now!*"

Noelle placed her hands on her head as her knees threatened to buckle. And that's when she heard a scuffle on the marble floor below and realized the command hadn't been directed at her. She was so relieved she nearly passed out.

"Noelle Clarke? Are you up there? It's Glencoe Public Safety."

"I'm here. I'm here." She focused on catching her breath. Her heart continued to bang against her ribs.

The hallway light popped on, and a female police officer ran to the top of the steps. "Are you injured?"

"I'm fine."

Just then, Siggy reappeared. He slinked out from under the bed and slithered on his belly toward Noelle. He didn't seem physically hurt—just terrified. She lowered her arms and stroked the dog's head, noting the policewoman's badge read "Officer Lucinda Epps."

"Did someone actually break into the house?"

Officer Epps ignored her. "I need to clear the second floor, ma'am. Please go downstairs immediately. Officer Lowell will take your statement."

Noelle's eyes went to a gray-haired patrolman standing at the foot of the steps, hands on his hips. He nodded politely. "We have him in custody, Miss Clarke. You're safe. Come on down."

She eased along the steps, arriving in the foyer just in time to see a man in handcuffs being led out the front door. She couldn't help herself—she screamed.

"How many were there?" Noelle's eyes darted to the officer. "I heard glass shattering. Did they break something? Please tell me they didn't break anything."

He nodded. "There was just one suspect. He busted out a window in the garage."

Noelle squeezed her eyes tight and groaned. She'd been alone in the DiPaolo's house for less than half a day and she'd already bodged up the situation something awful. All of this was her fault. She should have paid closer attention to how to operate the alarm keypad, and she should never have disarmed the thing! She almost wished she was back in London, living with her mum and dad and making three hundred bloody lattes a day.

"Noelle."

A hand gently caressed her shoulder, and without turning she knew Ryder Partridge had arrived. She recognized his voice. She remembered his scent. But she wasn't prepared for what she saw when he stepped into view.

The starched bobby uniform was history. Ryder now wore a black fleece pullover, a pair of worn jeans, and hiking boots. His hair was a smidge untidy, which was her fault, since she was the one who dragged him out of bed in the middle of the night. Yes, he'd looked smashing in his uniform, but he was even sexier now. It was all she could do not to reach out and run her fingers through his light brown hair.

"Hullo." She spoke in a rather pitiful whisper.

"Are you hurt?"

Noelle shook her head, suddenly feeling shaky, perhaps even close to tears. Perhaps this was the effect of yet another adrenaline crash. How many could one girl handle in a day?

Officer Partridge frowned, glancing at the bulging pocket of her sweatshirt. "You sure everything's good?"

"Never better." A little sheepishly, Noelle unbuckled the belt around her middle and placed it on the large round foyer table. Then she pulled the nail file from her back pocket and removed the cleaning products from the front pouch of her hoodie, well aware that the entire process made her look like a complete nutter.

"Doing a little midnight housework?" The older officer could not contain his chuckle.

She shrugged. "I thought I should prepare for a worse-case scenario."

He let go with a good laugh, making some crack about the rash of intruders responsible for untidy bathrooms, but Ryder Partridge, her champion, shot him a look that promptly ended his fun.

Officer Lowell cleared his throat. "Okay. Yeah. Glad you're all right, Miss Clarke."

"I'll take her statement," Ryder said.

"Sure. Good night."

The older officer made a hasty exit out the front door.

Ryder returned his attention to Noelle. He slid his hands into the front pockets of his jeans and studied her. His expression was one of bewilderment. "Uh, just out of curiosity—"

"I planned to spray loo cleaner in his face and gouge out his eyes with the nail file."

Ryder seemed to mull that over for a moment. "All right. I'm almost afraid to ask, but the belt…?"

She pursed her lips, feeling defensive. "I thought it would work as handcuffs, if need be. You know, for a citizen's arrest."

He raised one eyebrow. "Of course."

Just then, Officer Epps made her way down the staircase and spoke to Ryder.

"Upstairs is clear. No sign of attempted entry. I'll do the paperwork and e-mail a copy to Northshore Security." She turned to Noelle. "You claimed you saw a man in the tree outside your window?"

"It wasn't a claim. I did see a man. He was looking right at me."

The policewoman smiled and shook her head as if she thought Noelle a simpleton. "It's unlikely anyone would try to climb that high in the dark, Miss Clarke. It's pretty icy out there, too." Then she spoke to Ryder. "I can't even be sure there is a direct line of sight from her room to that tree."

Noelle felt her spine stiffen at the insult. "Oh, but there is! I first noticed a little red glow. Then I saw the outline of a large man."

"You probably just saw your own reflection."

"I know what my own reflection looks like, officer, and the last time I checked, I do not look like a large man. I saw someone in that tree, and he saw me."

"Oookay."

"In fact, my life may very well be in danger now, since you arrested only one burglar here tonight. Am I right?"

Officer Epps looked to Ryder.

"You are aware that I could identify him in a line-up, right? At least his general shape. He might come back to make sure I can't testify against him."

Officer Epps laughed. "Might want to cut back on the cable TV, Miss Clarke."

Noelle felt her mouth fall open. She was just about to come back with a comment that was at once sly and cutting when Ryder cleared his throat.

"I'll check it out," he said to his coworker. Then Ryder took a barely noticeable step in Noelle's direction, making it clear that he was taking sides. Noelle couldn't help but feel vindicated.

"Gee whiz, Partridge." The policewoman patted him on the back and made her way toward the front door. "Such dedication. You're a credit to the profession, dude."

The front door opened and shut once more, shooting a cold draft through the foyer. Suddenly the house seemed too quiet, like it was holding its breath. A wave of shyness went through Noelle. She became unsure what to do with her hands. It was just the two of them now, and the dynamic had changed. Noelle was no longer just a false-alarm repeat offender, and Ryder wasn't on the clock. He'd come out there in the middle of the night because—

Because she'd called him?

Because he was concerned for her welfare?

If the policewoman's snarky comments were at all representative, every one of the police officers present that night had noticed Ryder's off-hours interest in the case—or maybe in Noelle herself. Unless she was misreading the entire situation…

Just then, Ryder took a step closer. He leaned in, wrapped Noelle in a gentle hug of reassurance, and rubbed her back. The contact lasted just seconds, but it was long enough for her body to flood with warm delight, comfort, and need. He pulled away, then leaned down to kiss her cheek.

"I'm glad you're not hurt, Noelle."

She stiffened, looking into his eyes. Her body quivered. Her cheek buzzed with awareness. Did he just kiss me? Well, on the cheek, but that still counted as a kiss, did it not?

"Where's Siegfried?" Her eyes darted up the stairs, then back to Ryder.

"He just went into the kitchen."

Noelle sighed with relief.

"But…" Ryder tipped his head and stared at her. "Siegfried? Someone named that doofus dog Siegfried?"

CHAPTER FOUR

Ryder pounded the last nail into the plywood, then tugged a corner to check the fit. "This will do the trick until the glass shop can get out here." He turned to see Noelle standing near the shiny Lexus SUV, under the garage fluorescent lights, hugging herself against the cold. Siegfried leaned into her leg, but Ryder couldn't tell if the dog was providing protection or seeking it.

"How much will it cost to repair, do you think?" Noelle's mouth pulled into a frown. "The DiPaolos will likely take it out of my pay."

Ryder returned the hammer to the well-stocked tool cabinet, so shiny and organized that he suspected it was mostly for show. "No more than a couple hundred bucks, but the family has property insurance, right?"

She closed her eyes and sighed. "I suppose."

"You'll need to let them know what happened so they can start the claim process."

"Ooh, I can't wait for that conversation." With a deadpan expression, Noelle launched into a nasally Chicago sendup. "For God's sake, Noelle! You've turned our French country dream home into a pile of rubble!"

Ouch. The impersonation must have been accurate, though, since Siegfried began looking around for his owner. That made them both laugh.

"So you're an actress?"

"A what?"

He shoved his hands into the front pockets of his jeans. "You said earlier that gadgets weren't your thing, and ever since, I've been trying to figure out what is. That was a professional-grade imitation you just did just now."

"Ha! No. I'm far more boring than that, I'm afraid. My master's degree in is English literature, Chaucer to be exact. He's a—"

"Medieval poet."

Her eyes snapped open. "You know Chaucer?"

"I wouldn't say I'm a fan but I know who the guy is—Canterbury Tales, right?"

"Quite right!"

"Yeah, that was required reading for my freshman lit class. I only remember one thing about it, though."

"And that was…?"

"It was like trying to comprehend Klingon."

Noelle leaned her head back and laughed. Ryder thought it was a joyful sound—rich and heartfelt—and when she looked at him again, her cheeks were pink and her eyes danced.

Such a beautiful woman.

"Chaucer was brilliant and bawdy, actually. A keen observer of human nature." Her body language changed, and though she widened her stance, she seemed taller somehow. Noelle gestured freely as she spoke. "His use of Middle English vernacular changed the course of language and storytelling forever. My master's thesis was on the female power dynamic of the Canterbury Tales."

So this was the thing that made the lovely Noelle Clarke tick. Ryder wondered how an English professor came to be working as a nanny, but that was a mystery for another time. Right now, all he wanted to do was kiss her.

Badly.

She must have mistaken his silence for boredom.

"I do prattle on. Apologies. I can get cheeky when it comes to Chaucer."

"No need to apologize for your passion, Noelle. Not to me. Not to anyone." Ryder placed a hand at her elbow. "Let's get out of the cold."

Immediately, Ryder regretted touching her. It only made him remember that he wanted more—much more—which brought him right back to his central question: what the hell was he doing?

For more than an hour now, Ryder had attempted to be honest with himself about his motives. Had he come here tonight out of concern for a citizen in danger? Had he stayed to help Noelle because it was the decent thing to do? Had he volunteered to take her statement to aid his fellow patrol officers?

Or, was he falling so hard and so fast for the funny, pretty, and passionate nanny that he would use any excuse to spend time with her?

"You're exhausted, no doubt." Noelle stopped near the kitchen island and turned to face him. "I can't thank you enough for your kindness today, Ryder. You've been wonderful. And I truly appreciate the careful step-by-step instructions on the alarm system. I feel quite capable now."

"So you're kicking me out?"

Her green eyes widened. "No…"

"Good, because there's a loose end we need to tie up before I hit the road. Grab your coat."

A few moments later, Ryder dug his hiking boot into the tree bark for leverage. He wrapped his hand around a winter-bare branch and pulled himself from the ground. After finding a series of footholds in the slippery sycamore, he reached a large branch on level with the house's second floor, then glanced down at Noelle. She stood in the snow, staring up at him, wringing her mitten-covered hands.

She called up. "You really don't have to do this. I know I'm not crazy, and that's all that matters."

He laughed. "No one said you were crazy, Noelle."

"Well, it was certainly implied."

She looked adorable down there in the flashlight beam, her red wool coat buttoned up to her chin, her loose blond curls a halo of sunshine in the darkness.

"This is your bedroom, correct?"

She nodded.

"How about you go back inside, turn off the light, and take a look out the window? Then tell me if this is where you saw him."

"Right! Just a jiffy, then!"

Ryder followed the red flashes of her coat beneath the tree branches, then watched her hurry across the snowy yard. He felt the smile linger on his face long after she was out of sight.

There was something refreshing about Noelle Clarke, and it wasn't just her accent. She had a wide-eyed happiness about her. Somehow, she'd managed to escape being jaded by life. It could be a cultural thing, since Ryder hadn't met many American women he could say that about, but he suspected it was simply who she was. But not all she was.

She had the analytical mind of a scholar. She was quick-witted. She was sweet to silly Siegfried. And she could stand up for herself when needed—it had been impressive to see her go toe-to-toe with Lucinda Epps. All these things only made him want to learn more.

Though he'd only met Noelle Clarke twelve hours ago, he'd noticed she could not hide her true feelings. One look at her face and he knew if she was embarrassed, angry, amused…or interested. He wondered what it would be like to have that kind of woman in his life, a woman who was exactly as advertised. It would sure be a novelty. And though he hadn't returned to Chicago to be in a relationship, what was the worst that could happen if he asked Noelle to join his family for Christmas?

They could discover they had nothing in common. That their attraction was situational. And there was nothing to build upon. So what? He already had nothing in the relationship department, so there was nothing to lose.

Right then, Ryder decided that before the sun came up, he'd ask Noelle to spend Christmas with him.

He twisted in his perch, returning his focus to the upstairs window. As he did, the beam of his flashlight caught a small flash of white in the tree branch. He leaned closer, holding the flashlight on his left shoulder. It was unmistakable. A fresh cigarette butt had been crushed into the bark.

Tap, tap, tap!

He turned to find Noelle raising the storm window and poking her head outside.

"That's it exactly!" Her face lit up with excitement. Siegfried barked in agreement. "That's precisely where he was! I swear it!"

"Oh, I believe you."

"You do?"

"Yep." Ryder grinned. "You know that reddish glow you mentioned earlier?"

She nodded, her eyes widening.

"Seems your prowler was in violation of the family's 'No Smoking' policy, and he left a calling card."

Noelle fetched a sandwich baggie from the kitchen pantry and handed it to Ryder. She watched him carefully transfer the cigarette butt from his gloved hand to the clear plastic, then zip the baggie closed.

"How about I make us a cup of tea of something hot while you fill out your evidence form?" She turned toward the stove and Ryder followed her. "Tea? Cocoa? Cappuccino?"

Noelle was used to his company by now. Having Ryder hanging about in the kitchen felt comfortable, natural. She would certainly miss him when he was gone.

An awful thought struck her. What if she never saw him again? What if he wrapped up his night of chivalry and walked right out of her life?

"Don't go to any trouble." His voice was close behind her now, softer and more relaxed than she'd ever heard it. And though she'd certainly appreciated the uber-manly, uniformed version Officer Partridge, she decided she liked the off-duty Ryder even more.

"It's no trouble at all. I'll just put the kettle on and…" Her prattling ceased the instant his hand touched her waist. She spun around to face him, breathing sharply.

There it was again, that flash of awareness as their gazes met. He slid his hand across her hip to the hollow of her back. She gasped. He nudged aside the hem of her sweatshirt and pressed his palm to her bare flesh. She quivered in delight. "Oh, my."

"If this isn't what you—"

"I want it."

Bloody hell. She was regretting her utter lack of feminine mystery when Ryder chuckled, a low and sultry sound of appreciation.

"I only meant that it feels quite lovely, really, and I don't want you to stop."

"Noelle, I have a confession to make."

She tensed.

"I'm single, if that's what you were wondering."

She relaxed a bit, studying his hazel eyes. There was bare honesty there, and a bit of mischief—a combination she'd always found irresistible in a man.

He moved closer, so close she could feel his body heat through layers of sweatshirt and fleece. "I wouldn't be standing here, touching you like this, if I were taken, Noelle."

"Quite right." Her throat went dry. "So what's to confess, then?"

"I've wanted to kiss you since your false alarm."

"The first one?"

"All of them."

Good heavens! Was she imagining this? Would she be waking up from this delicious dream any moment now? The oven handle against her bum led her to believe this was real. He was real. And he was waiting for her to give him the all clear.

"I've a confession as well, Ryder."

"Oh yeah?"

"I've been wanting to kiss you, too."

"Since the mistletoe?"

"Since you walked through the front door."

"Which time?"

"All of them."

Ryder's eyes crinkled in amusement as he moved slowly and with purpose. The hand at her back brought her closer while the other gently swept a curl from her cheek. He smiled down at her.

It was difficult to breathe. Never in her life had she been the intended target of such a spectacular smile. That smile made her feel special. It make her weak. It made her happy. But as Ryder's gaze slid from her eyes to her mouth, the smile faded. His jaw tightened.

Apparently, Ryder Partridge took his kisses quite seriously.

Oh, yes. Yes, he did.

The initial skim of his lips on hers was warm, smooth, luscious. The kiss was curious and tentative, each press and release a query. Did they fit? Was it right? Could they understand each other without words?

Noelle felt herself yield to the growing insistence of his kiss. When Ryder's lips began to move on hers with hunger, she opened to him. God, how she wanted this, wanted him.

She felt him harden against her, and the sensation sent a hot lick of lightening through her belly. His embrace tightened as the kiss grew hotter, slicker, and deeper. She threw her arms around his neck with abandon.

"Noelle." It was a moan against her mouth.

Suddenly, their legs were shoved apart. Their lips unlocked and the moment was over. "What the—?" Noelle looked down to see Siegfried's head lodged between their knees.

Ryder laughed. "I think he's jealous."

"I think he's an arse."

He brought a finger Noelle's chin, tipping her face to his once more. "That, Miss Clarke, was a kiss for the record books."

"Quite spectacular as far as first kisses go." She felt herself break out into a giddy grin.

"There's more where that came from—at least on my end—in case you're interested."

"My end as well—in case you're interested."

"Gack! Brruuhhf!"

They leapt away from the stove in the nick of time.

"I apologize, Ryder. Siggy's so—wait! You don't have to do that!"

Ryder had already torn off several squares of paper towel and made quick work of the partially digested plastic.

Noelle sighed. "Was that—?"

"Yep. Rudolph the roadkill reindeer."

"How unfortunate."

Ryder chuckled softly as he washed up at the sink and dried his hands. When he was done, he gathered Noelle into another embrace. She knew immediately that it was a goodbye squeeze. "I've got to get some sleep before my shift tomorrow."

"Today, you mean."

"Right. Today." He slipped his fingers into her hair, still cuddling her, still caressing.

Noelle did not want this to end. She breathed in his clean and masculine scent and tightened her grasp around his waist. She turned her cheek to rest on his chest. "Do you have to work over Christmas?"

"Nope. I signed up for double shifts on Thanksgiving and New Year's so I could be off on Christmas Eve and Christmas Day."

She closed her eyes. The sensation of his fingers in her hair was a decadent delight.

"Share it with me, Noelle." Ryder slowly stepped back and positioned her at arm's length, his expression one of gentle curiosity. "Would you? It's just my sister and her kids. Nothing fancy. We watch Charlie Brown, eat too many Swedish meatballs, and read *The Night Before Christmas*. In the morning the boys open presents. I'd like you to be my guest for any—or all—of it. Whad'ya say?"

Her mouth fell ajar. For a long moment Noelle could not find the words to respond. They'd only just met but he wanted her to share Christmas with his family? That was…how could…

Noelle shook the fog from her mind. "How kind of you to ask, Ryder, but I fear I'd be intruding. I mean, this is your family, your traditions. I would just be some random person off the street come to nosh on all the Christmas biscuits."

He laughed, touching her forearm. "I'm not being kind and you're not some random person, Noelle. I want you to be there. I like you, Noelle. A lot. But… maybe you have other plans."

She took a step back. Ryder held onto her hand. "No plans."

"At least think about it?"

"Tomorrow is the day before Christmas Eve."

"It is."

"I don't have gifts for your nephews! I don't know their ages or their interests! And your sister—I don't even know her name!"

"Glynnis." Ryder produced a pensive smile. "Cole is seven. He's into baseball. Ethan is five and obsessed with superheroes. Seth is three and likes race cars. You're all caught up. But please don't think you have to buy them anything."

"Well then." Noelle tried to think this through. Yesterday afternoon she was an overworked nanny on holiday, wallowing in the twin indulgences of solitude and silence. Now she was considering Christmas with a house full of children. How did that happen?

"I really don't think I can." Her eyes tracked to Siegfried. The Goldendoodle leaned against the kitchen island, watching them from behind a set of shaggy eyebrows, looking slightly nauseous. "If I leave Siegfried alone, I'll return to nothing but a few pine needles and an empty manger."

Ryder laughed. "Then bring him along. The boys will love him. So you are both officially invited, how does that sound?"

"I'll think about it."

"That's all I can ask." With her hand in his, Ryder walked to the front door. "I can stop by tonight after my shift …if you're still awake."

Before she could answer, Ryder spun her around and strategically placed her under the mistletoe. He cupped her head in his palm and gifted her with another perfect kiss. It was warm and silky, sweet and sensual.

Then Ryder tilted his head and claimed her mouth as his. Her legs turned to jelly.

Noelle had enjoyed her fair share of kisses in her twenty-six years, running the gamut from anemic to overkill. But never had she experienced kisses like the ones shared with Ryder Partridge. The two of them seemed to carry on complete conversations without making a sound. They could say everything without saying a thing.

Noelle heard Ryder loud and clear. This was a goodnight kiss, not a goodbye. This kiss under the mistletoe was a promise of what could be.

CHAPTER FIVE

Noelle woke at noon and set off on what she knew would be a reckless and wild excursion. She took the DiPaolo's four-wheel-drive to Westfield Old Orchard mall, on the eve of Christmas Eve, in the middle of an ice storm.

She had to be bloody mad.

Noelle hadn't been entirely honest with Ryder earlier that morning. She'd promised to consider his Christmas invitation, but the truth was, she'd already decided to go. How could she refuse? Ryder invited Siegfried to come along.

He must like her *a lot*, just as he'd said.

Finding a parking spot required a great deal of patience and the liberal use of curse words, but Noelle eventually found a more-or-less legal place to leave the Lexus. She spent the next few hours going shoulder-to-shoulder with thousands of her fellow shoppers, their voices a cacophony that echoed through the atriums and down the escalators. Noelle was forced to dodge baby strollers, senior-citizen walkers, and teens with their eyes glued to cell phones.

Her first stop was a toy store that appeared to have been ransacked by a Viking horde. She found a superhero wall clock for Ryder's middle nephew. It was out of batteries and had stopped at half past Aqua Man, but was marked half-off. She chose a box of little metal fire trucks and police cars for the youngest. And for the baseball fan, she picked out Chicago Cubs glow-in-the-dark wall decals, keeping her fingers crossed that the North Shore boy wasn't a nonconformist White Sox fan.

At a large department store, in a picked-over display of women's accessories, Noelle found a lovely abstract scarf in muted shades of burgundy for Glynnis. Because she didn't know the woman in the slightest, impersonal would have to do.

And for Ryder…?

Noelle wandered through the throng, the shops passing by in a blur as she made a mental list of everything she knew about him:

He was handy with tools.

He excelled at climbing trees.

He looked smashing in a police uniform.

He was totty, droll, cuddly, and smelled fantastic.

Ryder had even braved a required reading of *The Canterbury Tales.*

Oh, and he was an accomplished kisser.

The list of unknowns was far longer, however. Had Ryder always lived in the Glencoe area? Where had he gone to college? Why had be chosen law enforcement work? Why was he single? What other family did he have—parents, grandparents, more siblings? And what were the things most important to him?

As much as Noelle racked her brain, she couldn't figure out what to get him for Christmas, because when all was tallied up, Ryder was little more than a stranger to her.

"Oh! Apologies!"

She'd just smacked into a sullen teenager with a phone, who shot her an accusatory glare. "Whatever, dude."

A few moments later, she found herself staring into the shop window one of those franchise hair salons. The digital sign declared a "short wait" for the next stylist. Noelle calculated that it had been six months since she'd had her hair trimmed…why not?

An hour later, she left the salon with a head of smooth and tidy curls that just skimmed her shoulders—a bit shorter than she'd wanted but well done at a bargain price, nonetheless. She splurged and got

her nails done as well, choosing a Christmas-y red. But what to wear? Noelle wandered through boutiques and department stores until she found what she didn't even know she'd been searching for: a dusky red, long-sleeved knit dress that would look smashing with her black boots. And it was on clearance! She purchased funky earrings and a new pair of opaque black tights to go with.

Noelle drove home, braving the traffic and slippery conditions on the Edens Expressway, and was about to pull in the DiPaolo's private drive when she slammed on the brakes.

The postbox. In all of yesterday's excitement, she'd completely forgotten to check the post.

She knew it was there. She could feel it. And sure enough, she opened the latch to find the letter sitting on top of a pile of glossy mail order catalogs, bills, and junk mail. Without delay, she tossed the stack into one of the shopping bags on the passenger seat, and pulled into the garage.

Noelle let Siggy out to the garden and fed him dinner. She raided the mudroom cabinet stocked with rolls of gift wrap and bows, then set to work on the gifts. She turned on the great room's giant-screened telly for company, catching up on recorded episodes of a popular American singing competition. All the while, the envelope mocked her.

It remained unopened on a side table, propped against a reading lamp.

The return address read:

THE UNIVERSITY OF CHICAGO
DIVISION OF THE HUMANITIES
DEPARTMENT OF ENGLISH LANGUAGE
   AND LITERATURE
DOCTORAL ADMISSIONS COMMITTEE

She went back to the gift paper and tape, the sound of slightly-off-key crooning in the background.

Another singer came and went. Noelle glanced at the envelope again. It was plain white. Not overly thick, but perhaps containing more than one sheet of paper. But probably not. The English Ph.D. program received more than 600 applications per year and had a dismal two-percent acceptance rate. A rejection was almost guaranteed.

Yes, her personal interview had been smashing. Yes, she'd been quite proud of her writing sample submission, which had been the first twenty pages of her master's thesis. Yes, there was a chance—albeit a small one—that she'd get in.

And if she didn't, well, life would carry on. She'd finish up the second half of her assignment with the DiPaolos. Perhaps she'd move to another U.S. city and apply to another doctoral program. Perhaps she'd go back to London. Or travel somewhere exotic, like Asia or South America. Peru had always been on her bucket list.

"Really?" She chided the TV judges while arranging the pretty scarf in its gift box. "Four turnarounds for that awful bit?"

Out of the corner of her eye, the white stationery glowed in the lamp light.

She wrapped the baseball decals next, writing "Cole" on the nametag. She chose the "Old King Cole" spelling, since that had to be correct. Though she'd certainly heard a few bizarre American monikers—Phoebe's best friend was named Goji, after the berry—Noelle couldn't imagine anyone naming their child after a lump of carbonized plant matter.

Siegfried came near her perch on the sofa. His tail—which had always reminded her of an old-fashioned Ostrich feather duster—wagged enthusiastically. It knocked the admissions letter to the floor.

"Oh, Sig!"

He dropped his head in shame.

"You silly boy." She patted his chest, which perked him right up. "I know you miss your family." Noelle returned the letter to its place of honor and continued wrapping.

She would open it the letter. Eventually. Perhaps in the days after Christmas proper, a time already conducive to depression. But for now, the longer the letter remained unopened, the longer Noelle could hold onto hope. She wasn't quite ready for the crash-landing of reality.

She finished wrapping the gifts, turned off the telly, and stretched out upon the sofa, allowing herself the indulgence of a short nap. Now, if she could only decide on an appropriate gift for her new—what was Ryder Partridge to her, anyway?

Friend with potential benefits?

Temporary crush?

Everything she'd ever wished for?

With a loud sigh, Siggy collapsed on the rug beside her. Noelle closed her eyes, as thoughts of Ryder Partridge followed her into sleep.

He rang the doorbell several times before he heard barking, followed by Noelle's voice ringing through the marble foyer.

"Coming! *Ooomph.* Siegfried, you knob head! Would you get out from under my bloody feet, please?"

The door flew open and there she stood, dressed in a pair of black jeans, a soft gray turtleneck, and what looked to be comfy wool socks. Ryder noticed two things immediately. First, he'd woken her up, and he felt awful about that. And second…

"I like your haircut."

Noelle appeared disoriented. "Ryder! What time is it? Hi. Come on in."

Siggy jumped up, resting his paws on top of Ryder's thighs. "Hey buddy! What's the body count today?" He roughed up the fur on Siggy's neck then returned the dog's paws to the floor.

Noelle yawned. He noticed indentations in her cheek, as if she'd been sleeping on a zippered pillow.

Stopping by had been a selfish idea. "You know what? It's late and I should have called first, so I'll head out."

"No!"

She shook her head, curls skimming her sweater. "I'm awake now. Truly. I must have fallen asleep on the sofa…" As she turned and wandered toward the kitchen, she reached up and fluffed the back of her hair.

Ryder stopped in his tracks. How could such an everyday gesture be so *freaking hot*?

"Tea?"

"Hey, Noelle?"

"Hmm?" She spun around, her eyes sleepy.

"We can talk tomorrow."

"No! I'm glad you're here. I'm…" She gave him a shy smile. "I'm quite pleased to see you, actually."

He reached out for her, and Noelle sank into his arms, snuggling against his chest. Ryder closed his eyes in bliss as he rested his chin on the crown of her head. "You feel so good."

"You do, as well."

He breathed her in—something flowery mixed with citrus and warm female skin. "And you smell delicious."

"As do you."

Thank God he'd showered and changed at the station. "So have you thought about my offer?"

"Yes." Noelle peeked up at him, her lips curled in a playful smile. "It is with pleasure that Siggy and I accept your invitation for Christmas."

Yes! "I'm happy to hear that." Just then, he noticed the coffee table in the adjoining family room was piled with wrapped gifts. Several rolls of holiday paper lay on the rug. "I hope those gifts aren't for my family, Noelle."

She followed his gaze, and when she looked at him again she appeared hurt. "You don't want me to bring gifts?"

"It's just …you didn't have to spend your money on anyone. You weren't obligated to do that."

Noelle smiled sweetly. "Oh, but I wanted to! And anyway, my mum would disown me if I showed up empty-handed. Wouldn't your mum feel the same?"

Ryder thought back. He'd been a senior in college the year his mother died, but Noelle was correct—from the time he'd been a toddler, his mother had hammered home the importance of manners. "She would."

"See? Besides, I quite enjoyed the outing. It put me in the holiday spirit. I had to purchase and wrap my family's gifts back in May, before I left for the states." Noelle stepped from his embrace. "Let me tidy up a bit and light the fire. How do you like your tea?"

Ryder watched her flip the gas fireplace switch and scoop up the rolls of paper. As she carried them through the kitchen, she smiled and hummed something Christmas-y. *Angels We Have Heard On High,* maybe? Whatever it was, Siggy seemed to enjoy it. He clomped along at her heels, tail wagging.

That's when it hit him—Glynnis and the boys were going to love Noelle. How could they not?

How could *he* not?

She put the gift wrapping supplies in a mudroom cabinet and when she returned to the kitchen, she caught him staring. Two small lines crinkled her forehead. "Milk and sugar?"

He couldn't take his eyes off her. The past few months had been a fight for survival—his sister's physical recovery, the boys' emotional battles, and his own challenge to face every day on its own terms. The recent past hadn't been about what Ryder wanted or needed, or even preferred. It had been about how he could protect those he loved, and it had been a job he'd been honored to do.

But now here was Noelle, beauty and joy breaking through his darkness. She was a direct hit of oxygen and sunshine, and Ryder could feel himself coming back to life in her presence.

He'd been thinking of her all day. He'd already picked up her Christmas gifts. But should he tell her all this? He didn't want to close her openness or worse yet, scare her away. He would keep it light. Friendly.

"How about I make us some hot chocolate?"

Her lip curled in disgust, and he busted out laughing.

"Okay. It's official. You're the only person I've ever met who doesn't like hot chocolate."

"Oh, I like it just fine. I'm just not fond of those powder packets you Americans dump in boiling water."

"Ahh." He took a few steps forward to stand before her. Ryder gently caressed her upper arms, then slid his palms down her forearms to her delicate wrists. He loved how she felt in his hands—soft but strong, solid but curvy. He lifted the fingers of her left hand to his lips and planted a kiss on her knuckles.

She remained unconvinced.

"I'm talking the real deal here, Miss Clarke. Old-fashioned, Greater Chicagoland hot cocoa made from scratch. No powder packets involved."

She sighed. "Well, then. What ingredients do I need?"

"You don't need anything. Just point me in the right direction and I'll have it ready in no time."

Ryder spent the next few minutes gathering supplies—cocoa, sugar, vanilla and salt from the cabinet, heavy cream and milk from the refrigerator.

The sound of instrumental Christmas carols spilled from the family room and he turned in time to see Noelle straighten from her crouch in front of the sound system. She spun around and walked toward him. This wasn't the first time he'd admired the way she walked. It was an unhurried gate with a barely-noticeable swing to her hips. Noelle's walk was unforced and natural, the way all of her was. "The saucepans are in the sliding drawers under the island, second from the top."

"Perfect."

"Am I allowed to watch?" Noelle hopped up onto the marble countertop and swung her sock feet.

"Of course!"

Ryder began by measuring out dry cocoa and sugar into the saucepan. Next, added milk and cream in small increments.

"You never want to rush this part," he told her.

"Heavens no. Good things are worth waiting for."

"Abso-bloody-lutely."

She giggled at his first attempt at a British accent. "Ever been to the U.K.?"

"Nope."

"Maybe I'll show you around someday."

"I'd like that."

Ryder paused to take her in. Noelle's head was tipped slightly, her smile crooked, and her curls grazed her cheek. Their gazes met. Her green eyes locked with his, and they stayed locked for a long, long moment. Ryder remembered the first time this had happened. It had been when Noelle gave him the grand tour of the basement.

He'd never believed in that "love-at-first-sight" bullshit. But lust? Sure—instant lust had happened more times than he cared to remember, and each time it brought trouble. But never, ever love.

Anymore, he wasn't so sure what he believed.

"Is it supposed to bubble like that?"

"Whoops!" He lifted the saucepan from the flame. Vowing to pay closer pay attention to the task at hand, Ryder stirred until the chocolatey paste formed a gloss.

She inhaled. "It smells divine."

"Would you like to stir?"

Noelle hopped down and slipped into place between Ryder and the commercial-grade range. He cozied up to her back and reached his arms around her, feeling every swell and dip of Noelle's body against his. She fit just right, like she'd been custom made for him.

That was a new one, too. He'd never thought that about a woman before.

He leaned in, brushing his lips against her earlobe. "Beautiful."

She relaxed into him. "The cocoa?"

"And you."

Noelle added milk and cream until it reached the perfect consistency, then Ryder suggested she top off the concoction with a smidge of real vanilla and a pinch of salt. He poured the scalding liquid into two mugs, and for a finishing touch, Noelle added a healthy dollop of whipped cream to each cup.

They carried their hot chocolate to the family room. Noelle motioned for Ryder to have a seat on the overstuffed sofa and she nestled in next to him, tucking her feet underneath. They sipped in silence, appreciating the golden shimmer of the fireplace and the lights of the Christmas tree.

"Was I right?" Ryder wagged an eyebrow. "Is this better than the powdered stuff?"

Noelle leaned toward him and whispered. "Much, much better. But you've got something on your top lip, Officer Partridge."

He swiped at his mouth, then tried to lick it away. "Did I get it?"

"Hmmm, not quite. Let me help you." Noelle set her mug on the coffee table, then dispatched with his, too. She scooted forward, balanced on her hands, and raised her lips to meet his.

Her mouth was silky soft and chocolaty sweet, tender as it moved on his. With a demure slide of her tongue, Noelle pretended to search for the wayward whipped cream, giggling the whole while.

This woman was driving him insane.

"There wasn't anything on my lip, was there?"

"No."

That did it. Ryder slipped an arm under her knees and gathered her onto his lap. They both laughed as he dipped her playfully over the edge of the sofa, her head falling back. Noelle's green eyes flashed at him, and that's when the image flooded his brain: the saucy English nanny flushed and naked in his bed, moving beneath him as he made love to her.

Slowly, he lowered his mouth to hers, kissing her deep, and deeper still, delighting in how she reacted. She softened. She mewled. And when she wrapped her arms around his neck he pulled her onto his lap once more, cradling her as he kissed her over and over again.

"*Ryder.*" God, how he loved how Noelle said his name.

He broke the kiss to check her expression. If all he wanted from Noelle was sex, this would be where he carried her up the grand marble staircase and ravished her in her frilly nanny bedroom. But he wanted more than a hit and run with this woman. He wanted as much as she was willing to give.

"What are you doing to me, Noelle?"

Her lips relaxed into a pensive smile. "I hope the same thing you're doing to me."

"We can always blame it on the hot chocolate."

She chuckled. "True, and now you've got me wondering what other heavenly treats I've missed out on since coming to the U.S." Noelle took his hand in hers but didn't elaborate.

"So what does an English nanny do for fun in the North Shore suburbs?"

She stroked her thumb over his. "Not much, honestly. I don't mean to sound piteous, but I've mostly worked since I arrived, and in my spare time I take the train into the city to the museums, walk along the lakefront, or read. I'm afraid I'm not the world's biggest party animal."

They settled into a comfortable conversation. Noelle told him about her life in London, her friends, her job in the coffee shop, her family, and her motivation for working as a nanny.

"Cultural exchange, huh?"

"Yes. And adventure. And an expansion of my horizons. It was all in the brochure."

He relaxed, stretching his free arm across the back of the sofa. "And?"

She frowned.

"Did you get any of that stuff, Miss Clarke? Cultural exchange? Adventure? An expansion of your horizons?"

"Not until you showed up," she said, and he laughed. Noelle began to ask him about his life.

Ryder didn't dwell on the horrific details, but when Noelle inquired how he came to be a public safety officer in Glencoe, he told her the truth. He told her about his career in St. Louis, and how he was getting ready to take the detective exam when the shit went down with Glynnis and her ex-husband. Noelle looked stricken, close to tears.

"But…her little boys. Please tell me they weren't there when it happened."

Ryder heard himself sigh. "They were, unfortunately. They were asleep, but Ethan woke up and found her. Which is a damn good thing, because by the time the paramedics arrived, she had to be resuscitated."

"Jesus." Her face fell. Her eyes glistened. "I'm so, so sorry, Ryder. That's the most horrible thing I've ever heard in my life."

"Agreed." He looked down at her hand in his. "But Glynnis is a fighter. She's clawed her way back and even though she has some really bad days, she's doing well. She's doing it for her kids."

Noelle nodded.

"And when you meet her, try not to make a big deal of it if you can. It's not how she wants people to see her, you know?"

"Of course." A tear slid down Noelle's cheek.

"You have a tender heart, Noelle." Ryder reached out and brushed the tear away. "I didn't mean to take this to such a sad place, but you asked, and I gave you the truth."

She sniffed. "There are very few heroes in the world these days, at least none I've known personally. You're my first."

"I'm not a hero."

"Oh, but you are." Noelle lifted her chin and studied him. "You went out of your way to help me, just some plonker who couldn't operate a security system."

"Well, you were a very cute plonker."

"And you left everything—your life and your career—to be with your sister and the children. You're their hero, Ryder, and believe me when I tell you that you're my hero, as well, and I know I'm a daft cow for saying this out loud, but I'm…" She blinked, her green eyes wide. "I've gotten myself quite worked up over you."

He felt himself smile. "What does that mean, exactly?"

She shrugged one shoulder. "I suppose you could say I'm crazy about you. I think about you when you're not around. I'm afraid I've let my imagination get the better of me when it comes to you and me and what could be."

He reached out, cradling her hand in both of his. "I can sympathize with your predicament."

She looked surprised. "You can?"

"Hey, Noelle, I know we've just met, but I think I'm down for the count."

"And what does *that* mean?"

It means I've never met anyone like you—beautiful, funny, smart, and sweet. And I'm really hoping we'll take the time to get to know one another. Think we can do that?"

Noelle didn't say anything at first, but a smile broke over her face. "I'll try to work you into my *shed-yool*."

He laughed and pulled her into a hug. To think… just a couple days ago, he didn't even know there was a Noelle Clarke in the world, and now she was in his arms, in his life.

Out of the corner of his eye, Ryder noticed something odd. A single, white envelope was propped up against a table lamp on the opposite side of the couch. He squinted, trying to read the print.

It was addressed to Ms. Noelle E. Clarke and the return address was…if he was making this out right…the University of Chicago Department of Humanities?

"What's that, Noelle?"

"Hmm?"

"There's an envelope on the—"

"Nothing!" She launched herself from his embrace and snatched it, shoving it down between the couch cushions and then sitting her decidedly attractive bottom directly over it.

She pursed her lips. "It's just an envelope."

After a moment of uncomfortable silence, Noelle let go with a ridiculously dramatic sigh. *Oh, bugger it all!* She couldn't believe she'd forgotten about the bloody envelope and now it had become a *thing*.

Ryder was leaned back onto the pillows, his arm draped casually atop the sofa. The look on his face was a mix of amusement and worry, which was understandable, since she was acting like a complete nutter.

On one hand, Noelle wanted to be herself with Ryder—she wanted to tell him the truth. After all, he'd just shared his own heartbreaking story with her, had he not? He'd trusted her enough to answer her questions with honesty. And they'd both just admitted their affection for one another. So telling him would be the logical thing to do.

On the other hand, *no one* knew about her application, which meant that no one would ever have to be informed of her failure. If Ryder knew she'd applied, he'd ask her to open the envelope, like any normal person might want to do. Perhaps he would try to convince her that there were other programs, other universities, and that Chicago was daft for not accepting her.

But what if she, herself, wasn't ready for all that?

She stared at her hands for a few moments before summoning the courage to look him in the eyes. "The truth?"

He cocked his head. "If you're willing."

Noelle moved her gaze to the fireplace flames. She didn't want to see any hint of enthusiasm on his face, or encouragement, because that would make his eventual disappointment unbearable. She cleared her throat.

"I've applied to the doctoral program in English Language and Literature at the University of Chicago."

He did not hoot or holler, which was encouraging.

"My dream is to be a university professor. It's a complete long shot, but it's what I think I'm supposed to do with my life, and the letter inside that envelope will do one of two things: it will either award me a five-year fellowship with a living stipend, full tuition, a research grant, and health insurance, or, conversely, it will tell me to chivy along and not let the door knock me arse over tits on the way out."

Ryder still said nothing, which made her curious, so she peeked at him. His face was calm, but his eyes were shadowed with something akin to empathy.

"Well?" She crossed her arms over her chest.

"You're scared to open it."

"Damn right I'm scared! *I'm petrified!*"

Noelle didn't know why—if it was the lack of sleep or how preternaturally handsome Ryder Partridge was, sitting there so understanding and calm, or if it was the psychedelic properties of all that chocolate, sugar, and cream, but whatever the cause, she didn't bother to think before she spoke.

"I have always been my worst critic, Ryder. I am exceptionally hard on myself, and yet, I always reach for what should be out of my grasp. And the truth is I chose this nanny job because after all my research, the University of Chicago was my dream program, the perfect fit, and now…" She reached beneath her, pulled the envelope from the sofa cushions, and held it aloft. "My answer's right here, and I'm not brave enough to face it."

Ryder came to life. He leaned in to touch the side of her face. "You don't have to do anything you don't want to do."

"I don't?"

"Nope. But here's my question—can you live without knowing? Should I just go ahead and chuck that letter into the fire?"

"It's a gas fireplace, so no."

"All right. Then how about this?" He flicked the envelope with a finger. "If they've accepted you, is there a deadline to respond?"

"I have to accept or decline the offer by January tenth."

"Great. So one way or the other, you will open that sucker before January tenth. Deal?" Ryder held out his hand. Noelle supposed he wanted her to shake on it.

She sighed. "Deal." She slipped her hand into his but he clasped on to her tight, not letting her go.

"Noelle, everything is going to work out just fine."

"You think?"

"Sweetheart, I know."

It was quite late by now, and she walked him to the door. They made arrangements for Christmas Eve—Ryder would pick up Noelle and Siggy at three in the afternoon.

After one last, glorious kiss, she watched Ryder walk out to his police cruiser and back down the close. She shut the door and locked up for the night, then checked to make sure the security system was set.

She let Siegfried outside one last time and they climbed the stairs together. Her fingers stroked his fur. "Appears I've someone special in my life, Sig, just like that!" The dog looked up at her with sad, brown eyes. "Well, in addition to you."

CHAPTER SIX

Noelle took extra care getting ready. She applied a bit of eyeliner and lip gloss, then slipped on her new dress and earrings. Once she fiddled with her hair and pulled on her tights and boots, she was pleased with the overall result.

Ryder had said she and Sig were welcome to spend the night if they wished—quickly adding that he had a guest room. So Noelle packed an overnight bag for herself and added a plastic container with Siegfried's dog food, leash, toys, and water bowl. On top of the stack, she added the wrapped presents, then zipped the whole thing up.

Just moments ago, Noelle had finally settled on the perfect gift for Ryder. She had agonized over the decision but hoped he would love it.

Her chariot arrived a few minutes early. The look on Ryder's face when she flung open the door proved the extra mirror time had been worth it.

His jaw hung open. "Oh, my God." He let his eyes travel from her three-inch bootheels to her glossy lips, pausing shamelessly at a few places in between. "Noelle, you are the most gorgeous thing I've ever seen."

"And you look quite dapper yourself, Officer Partridge."

He was clean shaven and wore a pair of dark charcoal jeans, black boots, and a heather green V-neck sweater that played off his hazel eyes. He looked good enough to eat.

"Shall we?"

"Let me grab your coat." Ryder hurried into the foyer and held open her pea coat while she slipped her arms inside. He accidentally on purpose allowed his hand to linger a little too long on her hip, then brushed his lips against the side of her neck.

Together, they gave the security system a quick check, then locked up. Siggy was only too happy to jump into the back of the cruiser and Ryder held open the passenger door for Noelle.

She inclined her head toward the rear of the vehicle. "What if he chunders all over your back seat?"

Ryder answered her, perfectly straight-faced. "Won't be the first time."

The drive to Evanston took no more than fifteen minutes. A steady snowfall had already deposited several inches of fresh white fluff on the grass. Colorful Christmas displays lit up homes and shops everywhere Noelle looked, and she felt a rush of bittersweet emotion fill her chest. She wasn't homesick. She'd enjoyed a lengthy video chat with the clan earlier and felt as if she'd shared a bit of Christmas with them.

Her emotions were linked to the here and now—the fleeting beauty of pristine snow, Ryder's easy companionship, and the scary-wonderful promise of a new beginning.

Noelle reached out to squeeze Ryder's hand, and he squeezed hers in return. The spark between them would evolve in time, she knew, revealing whether it had the depth and strength for something serious. But she wasn't all that worried. In fact, the more time she spent with Ryder, the less she needed a name for what was unfolding between them. That was a welcome first for her.

It was the unopened envelope that troubled her. She'd tucked it into her overnight bag in the hopes that at some point tonight or tomorrow, she would be ready to open it.

Ryder pulled up to a charming two-story clapboard house on a wide boulevard. Unlike the DiPaolo's sterile monstrosity, it was one of dozens of modest but welcoming older homes, tightly packed along the street, their windows flooded with light and life.

Ryder attached Siegfried's leash and tossed the strap of Noelle's bag over his shoulder. He held her arm as they made it up the slippery walkway and onto the porch.

He looked down at her, his face shadowed in the dim afternoon light. "Are you sure you're ready for this?"

"Of course."

"It can get pretty wild in here sometimes."

"Ryder," she said, patting his shoulder. "I'm a professional nanny. I've got this."

That smile. It blanketed her in happiness. And the kiss that followed…Noelle's boots may have been on terra firma, but her heart went soaring.

"Sagfred is here!" The front door flew open, and a little dark-haired boy dressed as Spiderman began jumping up and down. "Can I pet him? Can I pet him?" Before Noelle could respond, he'd grabbed the leash and dragged the Goldendoodle inside.

"It's Sag-*freed*, doofus." That pronouncement came from an older boy, who held out his hand to Noelle. "I'm Cole."

"A pleasure to meet you, Cole. I'm Noelle."

He gave a knowing look to Ryder. "Yeah. We know."

A toddler in footie pajamas came hurtling toward the door.

"Go on in," Ryder told her, pulling on the door knob. "Seth will escape if we don't get this closed."

Glynnis came out of the kitchen and Noelle walked right toward her, grabbing both her hands. Glynnis was bony and pale, as Ryder had warned, but her eyes had the same calm strength as her brother's. Noelle liked her immediately.

"Thank you so much for having me."

"It's our pleasure—we've heard a lot about you."

The first half hour was chaotic. Seth would not leave Noelle's lap, which seemed to bother Ryder and Glynnis more than it did Noelle. Ethan tried without success to ride Siegfried, then settled for a bit of rolling about on the floor. Cole seemed fascinated with Noelle's accent.

"So you're English," he said, knowingly.

"I am indeed. I'm from London."

"I've heard of it. It's almost as big as Chicago, right?"

Siegfried got ahold of one of Ethan's army men, and a great chase ensued. Siggy seemed to be having the time of his life running from the boys. On one pass through the living room, he looked at Noelle as if to say, "*Finally. Someone who knows how to play!*"

Noelle helped Glynnis set the table and bring out the serving dishes. It was a menu made in American kid heaven. Meatballs and crescent rolls took center stage, with sides of glazed carrots, pasta with marinara sauce, fresh fruit cups, and a salad for the grownups. Everyone had a plastic goblet filled with sparkling fruit juice accented by a festive maraschino cherry.

Just as Ryder predicted, too many meatballs were consumed, especially by Siegfried, who had positioned himself on the floor between Cole and Ethan. Several times during dinner, Ryder reached under the table and placed his hand on Noelle's knee. It was at once intimate and kind—she knew he was checking to make sure she felt at home, but he needn't have worried.

After dinner, there was a wickedly competitive game of Parcheesi, followed by the traditional watching of *A Charlie Brown Christmas*. Ethan and Cole sprawled out on the carpet with Siggy. Seth curled up on Glynnis's lap. Ryder and Noelle were next to each other on the sofa.

Ryder whispered in Noelle's ear. "I've seen this at least once every single Christmas of my life. Have you seen it before?"

"Oh, yes, but in the UK, Christmas is all about Blue Peter."

Ryder raised an eyebrow. "That sounds painful."

Noelle laughed so loud that Seth shushed her.

She whispered to Ryder, "It's a kids TV show in Britain."

"Thanks for clearing that up," he said.

Once the cartoon had ended, it was time to set out cookies and milk for Santa, and carrots for the reindeer. And once the boys were in their Christmas jimjams and Siegfried had been let out to the garden, everyone settled in for a reading of *'Twas the Night Before Christmas.* Glynnis turned off all the lights save those on the Christmas tree. Ryder threw another log on the fire and picked up the hardcover illustrated book, clearly a well-loved family heirloom. He clicked on the attached book light.

"Uncle Ryder." It was Ethan. He stood up, walked over and slipped the book from his hands. He then handed it to Noelle. "I like the way you talk. Can you read it to us?"

Noelle got the okay from Glynnis and Ryder, and opened to the first page. She cleared her throat…

The sharp peel of Ryder's cell phone made everyone jump.

He rose from the sofa and cleared an obstacle course of children and dog on his way to the dining room. "Nobody move. Let me grab this real quick." He snatched the phone from the table. "Partridge."

"Oh, no." Ethan rolled his eyes for dramatic effect. "Now we'll *never* hear the story."

Ryder's gaze shot toward Noelle as he listened. "Right. Seriously? So he's in custody right at this minute? Uh, huh." Ryder gave Noelle a thumb's up, for what reason, she wasn't sure.

Glynnis sighed. "I hope he doesn't have to go in tonight."

Noelle's heart sank. She hoped the same.

"All right, Lucy. That was nice of you. Sure, I'll tell her." He laughed. "Bye."

"What was that about?" Cole asked.

"Police business. Nothing major." He ginned at Noelle. "Turns out a man who's been climbing people's trees in the middle of the night was just arrested."

Noelle gasped. *The cigarette man!*

"For climbing *trees?*" Cole was incredulous. "Geez, that's harsh."

Ryder returned to his spot on the sofa. "Well, he did some other bad stuff, but he won't be causing any more trouble."

"What brilliant news! Thank you!" Noelle leaned in and kissed Ryder on the cheek, immediately several pairs of eyes laser focused her way.

"See?" Ethan shook his head. "I told you there'd be kissing."

It was time to return to the story book. Noelle cleared her throat again and began to read.

" *'Twas the night before Christmas,*
and all thro' the house
Not a creature was stirring, not even a mouse…"

The boys sat in rapt attention, hanging on Noelle's every word, leaning forward to see the drawings she shared at each turn of the page. Seth sucked his thumb while he listened, his eyes popping wide when she got to the bit about reindeer prancing on the rooftop. When Noelle reached the end and closed the book, the room remained silent.

She saw that Glynnis had fallen asleep in the chair.

Eventually, Ryder and his sister got the boys to their beds while Noelle tidied the kitchen. More than once she heard Ryder explain that Santa would not come until everyone was well and truly asleep.

"But how does he know for sure?" Ethan asked. "We could be faking!"

Cole yelled from across the hall. "Oh, Santa knows all about faking, believe me!"

"*Cole!*" That was Glynnis.

When the talking ceased and a bed check revealed that sleeping had commenced, Ryder began carrying down Santa's stash, hidden away in the attic for weeks. In practiced silence, he and Glynnis arranged the toys and games and sporting equipment around the tree. Siggy, exhausted from the evening's festivities, snored by the fire.

When all was done, Glynnis gave Noelle a warm hug and thanked her for sharing the evening with them. "Will you be here in the morning? I think the boys are in love with you."

Noelle looked to Ryder. "Maybe. What's the weather like?"

All three of them went to the front window and pulled aside the draperies. The world was silent, blanketed in at least eight inches of fresh snow. Not a hint of pavement was visible on the residential street. Noelle turned to Glynnis. "Looks like we'll be here."

Ryder banked the fire and made sure everything was locked up, then gestured for Noelle to follow him. "My lair is this way," he said, wiggling an eyebrow. Noelle laughed. "Let me grab my bag."

She rounded the corner and came to a halt before the front hallway table. "Bloody *hell*!"

Ryder arrived at her side. "What's—" he touched her arm. "Oh shit."

At some point in the evening, when no one had been paying attention to Siegfried, the knob head had decided to help himself to the contents of Noelle's overnight bag. Kibble was strewn about the floor. Her toiletry bag had been chewed through. And the envelope—*the envelope*—was ripped open, bits of toothpaste-smeared paper scattered everywhere.

The only good bit of luck was that she'd placed the wrapped gifts under the tree upon arrival, so Siegfried had not destroyed those, as well.

Noelle put her face in her hands and cried.

It took Ryder about fifteen minutes to tape the pieces together. While he worked, Siegfried cowered under the dining table, somehow aware that this time he'd committed a sin far worse than beheading a wise man.

Ryder smoothed out the last page, folded everything into its original order, and slipped the papers back into the reconstructed envelope. It wasn't pretty, but it was minty fresh and readable.

"It's fixed, Noelle."

He found her standing by the revitalized fire, hands folded demurely at her front. She'd barely said a word.

Ryder slipped behind her, wrapped his arms around her waist, and pulled her near. She allowed herself to lean into him.

When she spoke, her voice was a hoarse whisper. "So now you know my fate and I don't."

"Yep."

"That's situational irony in its purest form."

"If you say so."

"You think I'm quite silly, I suppose."

"Not at all."

"I'm just trying to gather my courage."

"Is there anything I can do to help?"

Noelle spun around to face him. He knew immediately that she already had all the courage necessary. Her chin was set. There was a steely gleam in her green eyes.

"Tell me. Just tell me, Ryder."

"Wait. You want me to—?"

"Yes."

"Noelle…"

"Aaauughh. I didn't get in! I *knew* it. Let's go upstairs so my bitter hysteria doesn't wake up the boys."

Ryder laughed. He couldn't help himself. She was making it far more difficult than it needed to be.

"Don't laugh at me."

"I'm laughing *with* you. But you're right—we should go upstairs."

He grabbed her bag. He grabbed the envelope off the table. Then he grabbed Noelle by the hand.

They tiptoed through the kitchen and up the back stairs, Siegfried at their heels. He opened the door and tossed everything onto the couch, then turned to face her.

"You got in, Noelle."

She froze.

Ryder raised his hands to her cheeks. He steadied her. "You got in, you smarty pants, you. You've been accepted to the University of Chicago's English literature doctoral program."

Her expression went blank.

"Hello?"

"I got in?"

"You did."

"I got in."

"Yes."

"I got in!"

Ryder picked her up and spun her around, his mouth searching for, and finding, hers.

"I-got-in-I-got-in-I-got-in." The words came out in one long squeak against his lips. He kissed her harder, laughing, twirling her around. He felt her hot tears on his own cheeks. "I got in, Ryder!"

With his mouth on hers, Ryder carried Noelle to his bedroom, then gently deposited her on the bed. He was careful not to break the seal of his lips because she began squealing with excitement. "Shhh… shhh…we can't wake up the boys."

"I got in!" she whispered, grabbing his face, her eyes wide with surprise and joy. "Do you know what this means?"

Ryder looked down to see that Noelle's hands were absently tugging on his sweater, as if she were trying to undress him.

"I'm going to get my bloody doctorate! I'm going to be one step closer to a teaching post. Take this damn jumper off, would you?"

"My sweater?"

"Yes!"

Ryder didn't need to be told a second time. He yanked it up and over his head.

She tugged at his T-shirt. "Full tuition, a five-year stipend for living expenses, health insurance, and research support. Ditch this shirt, as well. Hurry!"

He hurried.

She went for his belt buckle next.

"You're undressing me, Noelle."

"I am. I'm going to be a bloody professor one day, but right now I need you starkers. I need to feel your skin against mine. Get these pants off."

He grasped the hand now fumbling with his buckle. "Noelle, are you sure?"

"Oh. Right. We need to go about this correctly." She tried to wiggled out from beneath him. "I should give you your Christmas gift first!"

He rolled off her, breathing hard, confused and still laughing. "Now? You want to exchange gifts *now*?"

"This won't take but a moment."

Noelle hopped from the bed. She unzipped one high-heeled boot, then the other, and tossed them aside. She removed her earrings and placed them one by one on his nightstand.

She looked around, just now aware of her surroundings. "I like your place. Lovely. Now, would you please unzip me?" Noelle turned away from him and swept up the hair from the back of her neck.

Ryder pushed himself from the bed, out of breath, still chuckling, in a state of disbelief. He staggered toward her zipper.

"Thank you." Noelle spun around and gave him a gentle shove back onto the bed. He bounced a few times, his mouth open in astonishment.

"Happy Christmas, Public Safety Officer Ryder Partridge."

She wiggled one arm out of a sleeve, then the other. With both hands, she slid the red dress down her body, past a spectacular red lace bra, down her trim sides, past a flat stomach, and over the spectacular curves of her red-lace trimmed hips, taking the black tights along for the ride. She wiggled the collection of fabric down her thighs, past her knees, then kicked everything to the corner.

"How do you like your gift?"

Ryder had to blink. He had to shake his head. "You mean—?"

"That's right. You get *me* for Christmas. *Me*, the naughty nanny professor." With that, she reached behind her back to unclasp her bra. The wisps of red lace slid down one arm then dropped to the rug, displaying two of the most perfect, creamy, round breasts he'd ever seen. They were topped with two cute pink nipples. The only thing left was a tiny, red triangle between her luscious thighs.

He'd been right. She had great legs.

Noelle walked toward him, coming to a stop between his splayed legs.

He groaned, bringing his hands to cup her ass, letting his lips slide down the center of her belly. "I think I fucked up."

She laughed, placing her hands on his shoulders. "Whatever do you mean?"

Ryder glanced up at her, knowing that he had to look like a…what was that term she liked? — *knob head?* "Your gift is pepper spray. A pepper spray key chain."

"What?" Noelle's curls fell around her face as she began to laugh. "You're telling me that I stand here before you, soul and body unwrapped for your pleasure…" she snickered, "…and you…you got me bloody pepper spray on a bloody *key chain*?"

"For your protection. It's more convenient than a big-ass can of foaming bathroom cleaner."

Noelle snorted with laughter and fell into his arms. He tumbled with her, in all her glorious, giggling nakedness.

"Don't you want to know what else is on the key chain?"

"A nail file?"

"A key." He rolled on top of her, leaving a trail of kisses down her neck, across her collar bone, and between the round perfection of her breasts. "The key to my place."

Her hands were all over him—his back, his ass, his chest. She nibbled his throat as she unzipped his jeans, then said, "This is the best Christmas… ev-errr."

"Abso-bloody-lutely."

They made love in Ryder's bed until daybreak Christmas morning. The hours were spent in exploration, in laughter, in whispered conversation. Never once did they wake the boys.

Outside, the snow continued to fall.

A Connecticut Yankee transplanted to Central Florida, Debra Jess writes science fiction, romance, and superheroes. She began writing in 2006, combining her love of fairy tales and Star Wars to craft original stories of extraordinary adventures and fantastical creatures. Her first published novel, Blood Surfer, *has won the National Excellence in Romance Fiction Award for Best Paranormal and Futuristic. Her follow-up novella,* A Secret Rose, *has won the Maggie Award & Golden Leaf Award for Best Novella. Her short stories have appeared in* Heart's Kiss *magazine as well as the* Fragments of Darkness *anthology. You can reach her at https://debrajess.com.*

SHAPED BY YOU

by Debra Jess

"Ack, he's naked!"

Miriam peeled open one eye from her supine position on the cold floor. Her gaze scraped past the unfinished ceiling of her loft to the object of her sister's astonishment.

"Yes, he's naked." She pushed herself up, only to have an empty wine bottle roll off her chest and onto the floor. It kept rolling until it hit the other empty wine bottles lined up against the wall, knocking them over like bowling pins.

"Is he supposed to be naked?" Rivka asked.

Miriam winced. Foghorn Leghorn had nothing on her eldest sister when she was excited. "That's how I sculpted him, so yeah, he's naked."

Her sister hung up her winter coat and walked over to the clay statue, her hand not quite touching the bulging muscles of his arms. "You've got chutzpah, that's for sure. I mean, does the mayor know he's naked? Is that how he ordered him? I thought you were supposed to sculpt a soldier for the new memorial?"

"A broch tzu mayor." Her anger scorched through her hangover.

"Well, you did sort of did curse him when we were all in high school and you had him arrested for stealing tzedakah money out of the charity jar."

Rivka had the memory of an elephant.

"Yeah," Miriam said. "Now he's the mayor and he's going to be the death of me."

Rivka circled around the statue, careful to keep her dress from brushing against the soft clay, admiring the fine details of Miriam's creation—and she had left no detail spared. The eyes were wide and ox-shaped, the nose smooth with a touch of a flare at the tip, the cheekbones sharp, the lips were plump and perfect, and a light dusting of chest hair to keep it all real. As for the rest of him—

"It's been seven years and the mayor's juvenile record was sealed. Are you sure he's targeting you?" Rivka asked, interrupting Miriam's musing.

"Yes, no—I don't know." Miriam started picking up the empty wine bottles to keep herself from staring at her creation. That's how she always thought of her sculptures—they were her creations to share with the world. Except this one. This one she created for herself. "He declared a budget freeze three days ago. Which means I won't get the first payment for the soldier the city council asked me to design for the new memorial until April. If I'm lucky."

"What?"

Miriam winced again as she dropped the bottles into the blue recycle bin. "Yeah, a week after I'd already ordered the clay and started the sculpture. I have one package of clay left in the chest."

"Sounds more like bad timing than a vendetta against you."

"It wouldn't be so bad, except two of my private clients haven't paid me for the commissions they hired me for this past summer."

"You're kidding? Have you put them into collections?"

"Of course, but I can't force them to pay." The tears started at the corner of her eyes. As long as she was on a roll, she might as well confess the rest. "My landlord is also doubling my rent January first. I had to scrape the bottom of my savings account just to make this month's rent. The whole gentrification of Main Street has made it a hot property. Even the tchotchke shop downstairs is going out of business. I'm going to get kicked out of my home."

Rivka hugged her just like when they were little girls, arms secure around her shoulders. "It'll be okay. We'll fix this."

"No, no, no. There's nothing you can do." Miriam pulled out of her sister's embrace.

"I'm a lawyer, there's always something I can do. Do you have your rental agreement?"

Miriam sighed and pointed to the small kitchenette she'd taken out a loan to build when she first moved here. "Top drawer, next to the sink."

This loft had been her dream—open, airy, with huge windows that overlooked the main street below. It had been a series of offices until she'd renovated it. She could even see the town green where the statue was supposed to be installed. Secretly, she'd hoped to buy out the tchotchke shop herself and convert it into a gallery for her smaller sculptures.

She'd always been the family rebel. Instead of following her sisters into college, gotten a career-focused job, gotten married, and having kids, she put her sculpting before everything else. Now, everyone would know she was a failure in art, in business, in life.

"All right." Rivka shoved the rental agreement into her purse. "I'll look this over in the morning. In the meantime, let's get you cleaned up and get out of here."

Miriam frowned. "Where are we going?"

"To the Chanukah party at the shul."

"Oh, come on—"

"No arguing. You need to get out of here. Breathe some fresh air. Give Ennis a call. He can join us."

"He won't."

"How do you know, unless you call?"

"I do know, because we broke up three days ago."

"What?"

Again with the voice, that pitch. Miriam looked back over at her sculpture. It had been so lovely to carve him out of clay in an alcohol-induced haze and forget about how badly she'd been screwed in less than three days. "Ennis showed up here with a Christmas tree."

"But, didn't you—"

"Yes. I told him I was Jewish, and he said it was fine. He didn't care. Religion wasn't a big deal to him. We'd been having fun together. He's a painter and enjoys the art museum as much as I do. Then he showed up with the Christmas tree and insisted I had to have one. I mean, the mezuzah on the door wasn't a big enough clue for him?"

"Oh, Miriam." Rivka dropped her purse to pull Miriam into another hug.

"I thought he understood. He never questioned why we never went out on Friday nights, or why I never ate ham, or unpacked my menorah. He just showed up with a Christmas tree figuring it didn't mean anything." The tears wouldn't stop. "We had a huge fight about it. In the end, he couldn't understand why I wouldn't want one. He said I could call it a Chanukah bush—we could celebrate both religious holidays. I said no, so he left, and he hasn't called me since. He chose the tree over me."

"What a putz."

Miriam laughed through her tears and pulled her head off her sister's shoulder. "I'm never going to find anyone."

"Nonsense. We'll find you someone. A nice Jewish boy—"

"I've dated all of the 'nice Jewish boys' in town. They don't understand me either. They treat my sculpting like it's a hobby. They either want me to get a *real* job or stay home, barefoot and pregnant." The hiccup caught her off guard. "I'm going to have to, you know. Get an 8-5 job sitting behind a desk all day."

Rivka pulled a tissue out of her pocket. "You are definitely going to the party tonight. Go wash. We'll light the candles and still get downtown before all of the latkes are gone."

Miriam followed her sister's instructions with all of the cheer of a worn-out wallflower. Rivka managed to find the one party dress she owned while she put on a little makeup in the half bath next to the kitchenette. Her bedroom was just a corner next to the front windows with a lay-z-boy, a bookshelf, a futon, and a television.

Rivka circled the statue again while Miriam dressed. "Well, he's certainly well endowed. And what a shayneh punim. What are you going to call him?"

"The Perfect Man." Miriam didn't even have to think about it. "He listens to everything I say, he doesn't interrupt, never criticizes, and he's hot to boot."

Rivka laughed. "He's certainly is. The alter kockers at the foundry are going to have a field day when they create the cast for him. Once he's set in bronze, he'll be a knockout."

Miriam tugged on her winter boots before she stood beside her sister, both of them admiring the man—her perfect man. Miriam couldn't help herself—she reached out to gently pat her perfect man on his all too perfect tuches—she didn't want to disrupt her handiwork. "All right. Let's light the candles and get out of here before I change my mind."

They chanted the prayers and lit the first candle with the shamash. At the last minute, Miriam remembered to turn on her TV. The city was safer than most, but it didn't hurt to let anyone sneaking around think that someone was home.

She spared one last look at statue standing vigil in the middle of her loft. He really was perfect from head to foot. In her imagination, he would hold her in his arms as they danced across the floor and in her bed. She would be his source of love, joy, strength, and desire. He would love her without trying to change her. Her perfect man would see her as perfect too, and not ditch her in favor of a blinged tree.

Not for the first time in the past three days did she wish with all her might that he was real.

The wind blew, and the snow fell from the dark sky. Locals turned up their coat collars and rushed through the sudden onslaught of white on their way to their cars. Visitors laughed and reached up to touch the snow as the flakes enlarged and raced past their faces and down the street. It was as if they had never experienced such a rapid change in the weather before. Perhaps, they hadn't.

If any of them truly paid attention, it would appear that the only building affected by the rapid change of weather was the one with the souvenir shop on the first floor. The lights from the second floor were dark except for what appeared to be a glow from the windows.

The rest of the street beckoned shoppers with bright colorful lights strung across doorways and wrapped around lamp posts, showcasing everything from cafes to shops to arcades to banks. None of these buildings were touched by the weather, so it came as a shock when a bolt of lightning screamed from the sky and torched a transformer in front of the darkened building.

The lamps shattered up and down the street as the lightning spread, touching the loft and dancing across the roof.

Inside, the walls shook. From the shelf where Miriam kept her tools, a small oil lamp fell to the floor, spilling its contents. The oil pooled until it touched the drop cloths surrounding the statue, then spread across toward the kitchenette.

A second rumble shook the walls. This time, the menorah fell, the shamash candle's fire touching the oil and setting it aflame. The flames traveled along the oil to touch the drop cloths. The fire spread, until the flames kissed the statue's feet, climbing higher.

The clay should have melted, deformed, which might have spared the rest of the loft by smothering the fire.

Instead, the statue blinked.

Sick dread greeted Miriam the second she opened the door to her loft, her arms heavy with a sack of Chanukah leftovers. The faint smell of smoke pierced the freezing air. The lights from above, which she'd thought she'd turned off, created harsh shadows from her bookcase and supply shelves. The TV chattered in the background, but she ignored it because the windows were wide open, when she was sure she'd locked them, and the space where her perfect man had stood was empty.

Someone had broken in and stolen her sculpture! All of the grease and sugar from too many latkes and sufganiyot congealed in her stomach. She'd have to call the police. She'd have to call her family. She could see the headlines now: Goniffs Run Loose in Street with Naked Statue. Everyone would laugh, and she'd never get the clay back.

Her sister would once again try to be supportive. She'd nudged Rivka all night to stop her from telling all who would listen about her rent and clients.

"Stop embarrassing me," Miriam had hissed. "No one else needs to know about my tsores. I'll find the money somehow."

Maybe it was because she grew up in household where everyone was in everyone else's business. She thought she could hear whispers behind her back, but maybe the voice was only in her head: *She's the youngest sister and oy, an artist. How is she supporting herself?*

She dropped the food on the flimsy card table that doubled as her dinner table, the plastic tablecloth scorched around the edges. The menorah lay next to it, the red and blue candles melted onto the scratched unfinished floor. It was her own fault. She should have put the menorah in the sink where it couldn't fall. She wanted to clean up the mess but decided it would be best to call the police first. She walked over to the empty stand where her statue was supposed to be and pulled out her phone.

"Please don't."

She screamed and dropped her phone. The deep voice came from the corner of the loft, lit only by the TV screen. A man was sitting in her favorite—okay, her only—comfortable recliner. He stood, the shadows from the bookcase playing with the fine definition of his abs as he walked toward her. Miriam backed away because not only was this guy huge, he was naked.

Her back against the art supply shelf, she reached behind her and found her sculpting knives. This guy might have her outclassed in the size department, but she'd at least draw blood before he got his hands on her.

"I'm not going to hurt you."

"Of course you're not. I'll hurt you right back if you try."

He smiled, which paused her plan of attack. Why did he look familiar?

"I'm sorry I scared you. I wanted to air out the place before the fire triggered the alarms and sprinklers."

He stood there for a second, blocking her way. Waiting for her to say something? What did you say to goniff? She tightened her grip on the knife.

"Let me turn off the TV," he said. "Then we can talk."

Talk. Talk to a naked guy who'd broken into her home, set it on fire, sat in her recliner watching her TV, and had stolen her statue while still remaining in her loft? Right. There wouldn't be any talking tonight. There would be yelling, maybe even shrieking, and a lot of it. Once she got her voice back. Once she stopped staring at his—

"Here. Why don't you sit down and relax. You've had quite a shock."

He motioned her toward her recliner, like it was perfectly natural for a nude thief and probable rapist to make his victim feel comfortable in their own home. Her brain said *run*, but her legs walked over the chair and she sank down on the soft cushions anyway. The cushions were still warm from his body.

Instead of looming over her, the guy sat on the edge of her futon a few feet away, his long legs pulled up to his chest to hide his—

Stop thinking about that.

Why?

Because he's a thief and he's going jail.

But he has a perfect p—

Posture. He has perfect posture, nothing else.

She flipped on a lamp over her shoulder, ostensibly to get a better look at his face.

"Who are you?"

He smiled again but looked down as if shy. No longer in shadow, she could see his face. He had wavy dark brown hair, brown eyes, high cheekbones. A plague on the sense of familiarity dogging her. She should have been looking for a way to escape, but his legs were so long, he'd catch her before she made it to the door.

"I don't have a name yet."

"What do you mean, you don't have a name? Everyone has a name. What kind of shmegegi doesn't have a name?" If she could get his name, she could let the cops know—*if* her phone wasn't smashed to bits by this gorgeous specimen of a man and *if* she could grab it and convince this guy she needed to use the bathroom where she could call 911.

"You haven't named me yet."

"Me? What kind of nonsense is this? Why would I name you? Why would I even know your name?"

"You should. You sculpted me."

She glanced over at the empty space where the statue had used to stand. Then back at his face. The wavy hair, extra thick on the top, just like she'd styled it.

"This is—" She closed her eyes. "I drank too much. I knew it. A three-day bender—I fell asleep and never woke up. I'm unconscious and I'm imagining this whole conversation. You're not alive, you're not here, and I'll wake up tomorrow and you'll be a statue again."

"I hope not. I like being alive." He was a baritone to boot.

"Yeah, me too. Being alive, that is."

They stared at each other.

"It's late," he said. "And, I can see that you're tired. Why don't you get some sleep? We'll try this again in the morning."

He stood up, his full glory right at face level. Miriam had to admire her own work. If this was real—which it wasn't. It couldn't be real. A living, breathing golem. She wondered what his skin felt like, but she wasn't about to touch him. Touching a dream would make this perfect man disappear along with her logic. If she had to choose between logic and a dream, why not choose the dream?

You chose the dream of living in a loft, creating art. Now you're going to lose it all because it was a stupid dream. You can't handle your clients or the mayor or your landlord. You should have gone to college like your sisters.

He held out a hand to help her stand, but she deflected the gesture.

"Look, I can't sleep here with a strange, naked man in my room. Why don't I go get you some clothes at least? I won't be long, just a few minutes."

Her purse lay on the kitchenette counter. She managed to squeeze past him without touching him and grabbed her phone, which has fallen on the drop cloths, and her purse before making her way to the door. He watched her, his eyes following her every move.

"I'll be back soon, with clothes. Don't go anywhere. Don't touch anything. Don't—just don't leave."

Call the police.
Dial 911. It's not hard.
Your phone is still working.
You should call the police.

She didn't call anyone. The local 24-hour Shop-Mart didn't offer much in the way of fashion, but it was cheap and it provided the basics: jeans, sweatshirts, underwear, socks, and shoes. It wasn't like she had to guess at his size. She knew his exact size. She'd formed his body with her own hands, molded his feet so they matched, scraped away clay to make his fingernails even and round, smoothed the definition of the muscles along his biceps and thighs.

The beep from the teller reminded her to remove her credit card from the machine. At least her card still had some wiggle room, but not much. It wouldn't matter, she kept telling herself, because this wasn't real. She wasn't shopping for clothes for a golem, spending money she didn't have for a guy who wasn't real. Tomorrow, she'd check the computer for open calls. Then she'd remold the clay for a new commission. Whatever the client wanted, that's what they'd get. No more naked men for her.

"Merry Christmas!" The cashier called as Miriam grabbed the plastic bags.

"You too," she replied. It was automatic at this point. Correcting people all the time made her weary and most didn't want to hear it anyway.

Back at the loft she fully expected to see everything back in its place: no fire, no melted candles, no golem. She was wrong. Her perfect man had closed the windows and sat in her recliner watching *Die Hard*.

"I have clothes."

He stood up and looked in the bag. Piece by piece he removed the clothes, admiring everything, even the underwear. "These are perfect. Thank you."

"You don't even know if they fit."

He looked at her with a gaze that hooked her soul. "I know they'll fit."

What she'd been thinking earlier, her hands on him, forming him—he was thinking it too.

"I'll change in the bathroom. Why don't you get into your pajamas and get into bed?"

Her stomach froze over. "Um—"

"I'll sleep in the chair," he said, guessing her question before she could even ask.

"Okay." She watched him walk all the way to the half bath, the rolling muscles of his backside heating her up again. What else could she say? He was here. He was hers. She was responsible for him and she hadn't even given him a name yet. She should kick him out, but it was cold and snowing and he was—well, he wasn't naked anymore, but still…the thought of kicking him out made her feel as if she were kicking out a kitten.

She needed sleep. And a therapist, but she could only afford sleep right now. Real or not, if he was as perfect as she thought he was, he'd give her the eight hours she needed.

Though the alcohol had left her system from the rush of adrenaline the night before, she still slept like a cat in sunlight. Next thing she knew, she was awake with her golem—now dressed—sitting in the recliner reading one of her art books.

"You're still here?"

He looked up, surprised. "Did you think I would abandon you?"

"I didn't think you were real. I still don't think you're real."

He closed the book. "You were dreaming of me."

"I've dreamed of you often enough before I created you." She stretched and pushed off the covers. "It wasn't until I was too drunk to care that I actually constructed you."

"I'm glad you did." He leaned over the chair's arm, getting closer but not too close.

"I don't understand any of this."

"What do you need to understand?"

She thought about that. "English? I mean, you're made from clay. How do you know English?"

His lips twisted in concentration. "You talked a lot of while you were sculpting. I learned enough of social niceties and to hold a basic conversation. You also played music. While you were out with your sister, I read each of your dictionaries and thesauri. I read the rest of your books while you were sleeping."

Miriam looked over her shoulder at the bookshelf against the wall. She had an ereader somewhere, but art books were still best to keep in print, as was her Chumash and Siddur. The bottom shelf contained a few history texts and her favorite-oy-romance authors. If he read those then, oh boy. Her body heat rose along with the sun.

If he noticed, he didn't say anything. Instead he reached out to help pull her off the futon. "Why don't you take a shower. I'll get breakfast started."

"You know how to cook too?"

He reached over and pulled a cookbook from her bookshelf. Right. This was getting too real, even though it couldn't be.

A super-hot shower scalded her to consciousness without the need for coffee. She didn't bother with makeup but used her flat iron. If this guy was perfect, he wouldn't care what she looked like, right? She still changed in the shower room, though, pulling her best jeans and nicest sweater out of their drawers. Modesty might be pointless if her perfect man had already seen her drunk and stupid while she was sculpting him, but it mattered to her.

Had he, though? Seen her naked?

Back in the kitchenette, the sweet smell of latkes frying in the pan reminded her of the leftovers from last night. Her fear of him trying to create a gourmet meal out of her meager offerings dissipated. He'd warmed up the latkes, dabbed them with sour cream and apple sauce, added two jelly sufganiyot, and a tall glass of orange juice.

He portioned out a second dish. He eats! His Adam's apple even bobbed up and down as he swallowed.

"This is amazing. The flavors and the textures are just incredible." He sipped the juice. "I can't believe how sweet orange juice is."

It took her a second to realize he'd never eaten anything before. "I'll let the Sisterhood know you enjoy their food."

He eyed the rest of the latkes on the counter. She shoved them at him. A guy that big would need a big meal. He scooped some onto his plate, but also onto hers. She didn't argue. He didn't seem to mind if she stared.

Not only didn't he mind, he even did the dishes. What did she do to deserve all this? The more pressing question: what should she do with him now?

"Maybe we could go for a walk?" he asked.

She loved walking in cold weather, when there was no wind and snow was piled high. It also didn't cost anything, like a movie or the cafe next door. Was he a mind reader too?

The town square had the usual assortment of gazebos, benches, small gardens at either end, and, of course, memorials with statues. The oblong walking path encircled the whole ensemble, about a half mile in whole. Her winter coat and hat kept her warm enough, but her perfect man only had an extra sweatshirt to keep him warm. She hoped it was enough.

There were so many questions she wanted to ask, but now, walking around the path she had tread hundreds of times since she was a child, she didn't want to ask them. Did she really want to know more than she did? He said she created him, but she wasn't stupid enough to think that other than giving him a body she had anything more to do with it. She knew Who had given him life and questioning that wouldn't end well for either of them.

Still, maybe if she avoided the big existential questions, the Big Guy won't get too offended.

"How long can you stay?" she asked as they rounded the town green closest to the post office. "I mean, you look like you're in your mid-twenties. Will you live a normal lifespan?"

"I don't see why not. No point in being here if I'm anything other than a normal human."

"So, no superpowers? Beside super-fast reading and learning comprehension."

"I don't think so. I won't know until I try."

"Will you get sick? I mean, I bought insurance through the state's exchange, but it won't cover you unless—"

"Unless—"

Whoops. She really should have kept her mouth shut. "Unless we get married."

He was quiet for a minute, the sound of their boots crunching snow breaking the silence. "Do you want to get married?"

Could a woman have an even less romantic marriage proposal? Is that why she sculpted him? Not for giving the city the middle finger and showing the world that she was a great sculptor, but because she was lonely? Because she was jealous of her sisters and their families? Because she wanted someone who thought of her first, last, and always?

"I don't know."

They kept circling the town green. Four, five, six times. He asked her questions. So many questions. What type of material had she used to sculpt him? What brand of wine did she drink? Who was her favorite artist? She answered, and he listened, never interrupting her, never arguing with her. It was exactly how she had described him to Rivka: not just the perfect man—he was the perfect gentleman.

"What's that building over there?" He pointed to west, where the rising sun hit the solar shingles of an attractively designed roof.

"The art museum."

He stopped. "Can we visit?"

"Now?" She checked her watch. It was almost noon. They'd walked far longer than she had intended.

"Unless you'd rather go back home?" His brown eyes invited her to say whatever she felt. Home. Her loft. His loft, too? But, she loved the museum. She had splurged for a one-year membership. A mistake, when she should have been saving her money. She'd been a fool, but as long as she had the pass, she might as well use it, even if she had to pay for a day pass for him—her creation without a name.

"Sure, let's go. It's not as far away as it looks."

He held her hand the entire time they walked to the museum, as if this were a dream date. Maybe it was, because Miriam still had difficulty believing her statue had come to life. If it were a dream, though, would her hand warm while clasped by his? Would she feel so secure when they crossed the street together and he jumped so his body stayed between her and an oncoming car? She explained stop signs to him once they got to the other side.

They couldn't visit every floor or collection in one day, but they saw enough to satisfy the itch she got if she didn't visit at least twice a month. For once, she could talk about what she knew about the exhibits to someone who really listened, and wasn't just humoring her.

"Looks like they're getting ready for a new collection," he said, pointing to a stanchion rope draped across a door to one of the rooms.

"The sign says Regional Decorative Arts." She sighed, wistful. She couldn't afford to renew her pass next year. "That would have been lovely to see."

He leaned close to whisper in her ear. "Maybe you'll see your art here some day."

She blushed at the rush of heat from his breath on her skin. "They do have a small collection of local artists. I'm just not quite ready yet."

Truth was, she'd avoided the local artists collection this time, not wanting to see what she could have been, if not the city's budget mistakes. She could approach the museum with some of her smaller pieces, but the city's memorial would have given her a real name in the art world, and put her in a spotlight.

They strayed into the cafeteria for lunch. Her pass got her a discount, but even so, the cost of a couple of sandwiches reminded her of the problems she'd been trying to avoid.

She watched him take a small bite of his turkey sandwich. The vendor made them fresh every day, so the lettuce made a crisp crunch as the thick tomato tried to squeeze out the other side.

"I think I like turkey," he said, after chewing and swallowing. The simple enjoyment of each bite of food reminded her of how little she'd thought about the food she ate, especially over the last three days. Looking at her own chicken salad sandwich, she tried to drum up her own enthusiasm. No, there was no enjoyment there. She preferred to watch him eat, her heart filling with a joy she hadn't felt in a long time.

"The thing is," she said, putting the receipt in her pocket instead of eating. "I'm about to lose the loft. I have a stack of bills and the rent that won't get paid

because of the city's budget freeze and prior clients that won't pay. Most of my commissions are small, they paid for the basics. The city job was supposed to cover everything through the end of the year and boost my career. Now, I'll have to move back home. My parents are tolerant, but not tolerant enough to let you move in with me."

He turned thoughtful, using the napkin to wipe a spot of mayonnaise on his upper lip. How she wanted to be the one to lick that same spot herself. Oooh, there was that pesky lust again. She needed to cool it, or she'd embarrass herself.

He must have noticed though, because he reached over to stroke her cheek. Just his touch brought it all home. She could be herself around him. She could let her emotions free to fly wherever they would take her and not hide inside the responsible adult everyone expected her to be all the time.

She could fall in love in less than a day, and he wouldn't think her odd for doing so. But, did he feel the same?

"I could always get a job."

"Doing what?"

He shrugged, his massive shoulders looking as if they could carry the weight of the world for her. For a moment, she believed he could. "I'm not sure. We should check the want ads and see what's available."

Her laugh sounded as bitter as her tears. "You don't even have a name yet, never mind a social security number. You'll need both to get a legitimate job."

He frowned. "Lots of people work without documentation. I saw it on the news."

"Yeah, and they're getting deported, which is why they're in the news in the first place. If you get caught, where would the government send you? You'd go to jail and stay there."

He couldn't answer that. "Maybe I could be an artist too?"

"It's not that easy." She'd answered this question a lot over the years. "I've been creating art since I was a child. It takes a lot of hard work. You can't just sculpt something and expect someone else to buy it. It's taken me years just to get to the point where I could afford my own place. Or, at least I thought I could." Her tears started again. "That's why I'm going to miss next month's rent. That's why I had to accept leftovers from last night's party. I gambled I could make this work. That I could be just as successful as my sisters without having to follow in their footsteps, always be in their shadows."

He wiped her eyes with a napkin and encouraged her to eat her sandwich and drink her juice, but she still had no answers by the time they'd finished. Only after they returned to the loft did she remember to turn on her phone. She always turned it off when she visited the museum. Messages immediately flashed across her screen.

"Oh, no."

"What is it?"

"Messages from my sisters." This many messages usually meant there was an emergency, someone was sick or injured. She didn't even bother to listen to the recordings. She called Rivka first.

"Who is he?"

Miriam pulled the phone away from ear. No point in insulting her by asking *he who?* "He's a friend."

"Don't toy with me. Sarah saw you two walking together this morning."

Sarah was one of her other sisters, the school principal. The high school was half a mile from the town green.

Rivka kept talking. "And Orna said she saw you cutting through the parking lot heading to the museum. She almost had one of her nurses run out and get you, but then she saw you walking with a man. She called me right away."

Orna was an OB-GYN and her office was in a small complex between the main street and the walking path heading toward the museum.

"He's—a model. He's the model I used for the statue." True enough in an odd way. He was the model of her perfect man, the model she'd kept in her head and in her dreams since she was a child.

As if realizing he wasn't going to be able to help with this conversation, her perfect man winked at her before heading toward the kitchenette. He put the kettle on for tea while Rivka squeed.

"What's his name?"

"His name?"

As if speaking to a five-year-old, Rivka repeated. "Yes, what do you call him when you are talking to him?"

Her mind raced. The entire day, she hadn't called him anything. As if sensing a problem, he looked over his shoulder at her.

"Aish. His name is Aish."

"Fire? Who names their kid Fire?"

"I don't know, I didn't ask." Her defensive shields made her voice harsher than she intended. "Aish Tevet."

"Tevet? Like the month?"

She could hear the scratch of a pencil. Her sister was plotting something or else why would she write down his name? "Yeah, like the month."

"Not criticizing. Maybe his grandparents were hippies. At least he's Jewish." More scratching from the pencil.

While her sister plotted, Aish turned to face her with a thumb's up sign. He liked his new name. Miriam's stomach unwound until Rivka started talking again.

"Okay. You're both having dinner tomorrow at my place. The whole family is coming over, so we can meet him. In the meantime, I got your contract reinstated. You should get the first installment by tomorrow."

Miriam almost dropped her phone again. "What? How?"

"I bullied my way into the mayor's office this morning. You know, he's completely redecorated that office from the last time I was in there? So, I said I would be performing a line-item review of the budget for the rest his administration. I want to make sure the money he was saving on your contract was being used for city services and not for ordering new office furniture."

The air in Miriam's lungs froze over. She should have been happy, ecstatic. From the kitchenette, she could hear the teapot whistle. Rivka, of course, just kept talking.

"He scrambled and swore he would find the money for your contract before January 1st," Rivka continued, unaware that she'd just made Miriam's world so much worse. "How much you want to bet he's going to single handedly find the city's missing money and unfreeze the budget before the new year as well? Anyway, I can't do anything about your landlord or your clients, just yet. It'll take time, but you just get that naked statue dressed and ready for the foundry. Once he's installed on the green, everyone will think you're brilliant."

Miriam managed to stammer a thank you before she disconnected. She looked over at Aish, amazed at how quickly his name had become a part of him. She'd named him. She'd given him form. She hadn't given him life though, so where did that leave her, his future? Them?

"What's wrong?" Aish guided her over to her recliner so she could sit.

"My sister has managed to get my contract reinstated. I'm going to get the first installment check tomorrow."

Aish looked confused and she couldn't blame it. "That's good isn't it? You can pay the rent and some of your bills."

"No, I can't. I don't have a statue anymore. I'll need it to buy more clay and I still won't be able to pay my bills."

Aish pulled away from her. "There's an easy way to fix that."

She watched as he pulled back a curl of hair from his right temple. She saw the Hebrew lettering hidden there spelling the word *truth*.

"No." She stood up to face him.

"Yes. It's the fastest way to save you. You don't have much time. If you erase the first letter, the aleph, I will turn back into clay."

"You'll turn back into clay because without the aleph the word becomes *death*. I'm not killing you."

"You have to."

"No, I don't."

"Miriam…"

"Don't look at me like that."

He looked away. Good.

She took a deep breath to calm her pounding heart and to turn herself away from temptation. "I don't want to hear another word about turning you back into clay. You're a man now. More importantly, you're my man, and I'm not giving you up that easily."

He looked back at her, sorrowful now. "If you're not giving me up, how are you going to get enough clay without using the check? How will pay your rent?"

Miriam returned to the large chest holding her supply of clay and pulled out the last package. "I'm going to pray for another miracle."

Miriam did as she promised. She called her sister and begged off the family dinner because she needed to sculpt. Rivka was disappointed, but kept the guilt to a minimum, so long as Miriam promised to bring Aish to dinner next week. Then she prayed, and then set to work. For the next four days she sculpted, pausing only for Shabbat, then continued until the last day of Chanukah. Every time she returned to the chest, there was another identical package of clay sitting there. It didn't matter how much she used, there was always more clay.

Aish stayed by her side, making her meals, cleaning her kitchen, doing her laundry, going to the bank to deposit her check, and even reminding her to light the Chanukah candles every night. She worked sixteen, sometimes seventeen hours at a time. She styled the last bit clay into the collar of the third not-quite-as-tall, not-quite-as-handsome, but fully clothed soldier.

She stood back to admire her work. She figured by giving the city more than they expected, it would ease the sting of the city budget having to pay her in the first place. Maybe she was destined to create something incredible, but this project was not it. She would figure it out, however, with Aish by her side.

"You did it." His arms circled her waist.

"I did." She turned around in his arms. "I couldn't have done it without you."

"I have something for you." He pulled an envelope from behind his back. "Happy Chanukah."

She took the envelope and slid her nail under the sealed flap. Two cards fell out. The print and icons unmistakable. Aish had somehow managed to find time to run to the museum and renew her pass. He also bought one for himself. Did that mean he was going to stay with her?

"Oh, Aish. This is incredible. How did you—"

He smiled that same shy smile he'd graced her with whenever he was up to something. "I'll be working as a cashier in the cafeteria for the foreseeable future."

"But—"

He pulled out a social security card from his pocket. "I prayed with you. You got your miracle. I got mine. The *why* can wait until tomorrow."

She kissed him. Really kissed him, not the light pecks on the cheek he'd been doling out as rewards for sleeping and eating when he asked her to.

She pulled away from the kiss. "We'll talk about tomorrow, tomorrow. Right now, I just want to be with you. My man of fire and of clay. I love you."

"I love you, too, my woman of heart and soul.

Copyright © 2018 by Debra Jess.

Find Gracie Wilson in the trees enjoying nature's wonders, traveling to see the latest animal conservations, or at aquariums all around the world. This girl loves nature and all animals. She has many pets and is always adding new additions. The more the merrier in her mind. Sitting under the shade reading a book, letting the world around her pass by, while she is safe in her bubble of imagination. Well that is where she'd love to stay. She is a #1 Amazon Bestselling Author from Ontario, Canada. She is a first generation Canadian living in Ontario. Her family is from Scotland, so finding her in the hot sun for very long is unlikely, but give her rain and thunderstorms and she's golden.

SONG OF THE BRAVE

by Gracie Wilson

Here I am sitting in this empty room wondering what the hell am I going to do. When I glance down I can see the letter with "Charlie <3" written on it. I haven't been able to open the letter, but I haven't been able to put it down either.

Marley walks over and shoves me with his head, moving my hands from my lap so he can lay his head down on me. I reach out, rubbing his head.

"Marley, what are we going to do?" I ask.

He just looks at me with his big blue eyes and nudges my hand. The one with the letter in it. I know he can't possibly know what this letter is, but a piece of me feels that he's telling me to listen to Lacey.

I take a deep breath and open it.

Charlie,

I didn't want this to be your life a second time. For that I am so sorry. I just wanted to give you what your momma would have wanted, had she been here to look after you. The only thing that gives me peace is that with my passing you will be forever safe. I know you don't want to keep this gift, Charlie, but I'm asking you to please do as I say:

Take this money, take Marley, and continue our adventure. Go meet Lexa! You've put off meeting her long enough because of my health. I won't have you waste one more minute. I've enclosed a letter you are only to read after New Year's Eve, and after you meet Lexa. Open it right after the drop.

Don't let me down Kido, Momma and I are watching. Take the money, my Charlie girl. Live the life you deserve. The life I want for you.

And Charlotte…I love you, and that's why I want to take care of you. Please let me.

Forever your biggest fan (minus your momma, as we are tied in our parental pride).

Be Brave,
Lacey

The tears running down my face are those of both happiness and great sadness. Turning twenty-one and being on my own was not something I expected. Life has a way of kicking me in the ass when it thinks things are finally coming together. When I was fourteen, I sat my single mom down and told her I didn't like boys. No, she didn't freak out. She told me she didn't care who I loved; she was my mom and I was her baby, forever. My news changed nothing.

Two days later I was in class when the principal and guidance councilor came to get me from class. I knew as soon as they said my nickname—"Charlie", not Charlotte—it wasn't good news. I wasn't a-get-in-trouble kid. I didn't even know the principal knew my name. Standing in that hallway, hearing that my mom had been in a horrendous accident on her way to work, and that she didn't make it, made my whole world stop.

Children's Aid showed up to "claim me" since I had no family and I was put into a foster home. It wasn't a good one either. As soon as I could, I left. I was seventeen living in the dorms, in the first year of my undergraduate degree, with a mountain of student debt to my name.

It was then that I met my English teacher, Miss Lacey. She was this older woman who had such an amazing life story behind her. She actually fostered dozens of children but left the system when she realized it wasn't for the children, it was all a "money grab," as she would say. I can't disagree with her either. I had written something about my mom in a paper and included bits of my teen years. She wrote on the paper to come see her during office hours. I was a nervous wreck because I didn't know what to expect.

"Darling, how do you get through each day?"

I was shocked at her words and didn't know how to respond at first. "I like girls."

Don't ask me why I said that to this woman, but it was the only thing I could think to say to her in that moment.

"And I like nobody. Well, except my dogs," she said, and I couldn't help but laugh. Her carefree nature reminded me so much of my mom.

When the semester ended, she retired; we became family. She moved me out of the dorms and into her condo with her and her dogs. She also stopped letting me take out more loans, much to my dismay. I didn't want someone paying for me; she was older and needed to save her money. It was only then I found out how well-off Lacey was.

She was also a closeted author, not that anyone knew that. She wrote everything and anything she could, under many pen names and was well published. I only found out when she grabbed her iPad one day and opened her bank account app to show me why I should not protest her help. To say I was shocked would be the understatement of a lifetime—she'd paid off my student loans in full.

She died in November.

Once again I lost my whole world.

Lacey had been very sick and we'd had nurses coming in to take care of her while I was at school or studying. She wouldn't let me take time off to be there for her because she wanted me to graduate.

Over the years she had became a mom to me. She took care of me, and didn't care I was attracted to women—and just like my mom, I couldn't save her. All the money in the world couldn't.

That was a scary thought, since so many people work themselves to the bone for wealth, hoping it gives them all they need in life. But life can't be bought, not in this circumstance.

I rubbed the scruff of Marley's neck as he whinnied, sensing my mood. "I miss her too, bud."

I had only just started to love the holidays again with Lacey. Those three years I had with her would never be enough for me. Just like my fourteen years with my mother had never been enough.

Today was the reading of Lacey's last will and testament. I was left everything, including Marley, her Great Dane. Not that it would have mattered—Marley was always going to stay with me. But I also got the condo and all her writing residuals. Overnight I was a millionaire.

Sitting in this condo all I can hear are the remembered laughs. You see, we had a plan for this coming holiday. We were going to buy an RV and go to New York for the holidays and watch the ball drop together. Lacey had wanted to make up for the cancelation of my trip in October…

Marley lifted his head and nudged my other hand, the hand clutching the second letter. I'm tempted to open it, but I look up instead. "Fine, I won't, but if it all goes to shit I'm blaming you, Lacey." And then I laugh. I laugh until I cry, because one of the last things Lacey said to me was not to look up and talk to her but to seek her in hell. She thought that's where all her naughtiness was going to land her, and that the devil would lock her up because she'd stage a coup.

Not a chance. That woman was straight from the heavens.

I reread the first letter again, stopping at Lexa's name. Lexa is this insanely gorgeous woman I'd met on a dating site Lacey put me on. It was something for us to do when we were huddled up in bed watching movies when she had her bad days. For being in her seventies, Lacey was clever and technology didn't stop her like most her age. She thrived on it. Marley even had his own Facebook page, which I've been keeping up.

Lexa and I were *supposed* to meet at Halloween. I was going to fly to New York and visit her for the first time. Lacey was going to meet with her publishers about the publication schedule for the next two books she'd finished.

However, like always, the world kicked my ass. Lacey got worse in October and we weren't able to make the trip. She tried to force me to go without her, but I wouldn't leave her. I told Lexa why I couldn't come, and she's been one hundred percent supportive. She talked to Lacey up until the day she died.

When Lacey was buried, Lexa said she'd come to be with me. "I might not be able to help you settle her affairs, but I can be a support for you."

But I just couldn't. You see, I know exactly what Lexa looks like. All she's seen is some photos where you couldn't really see my face. Lacey was worried about the internet, so when she first made the account for me she didn't want to out me as a lesbian; she knew how cruel people could be. So here I sit in December trying to decide if I'm seriously going to do this. Am I going to hop in my truck with Marley and go on an adventure to New York City?

"Marley, what should we do?" Marley runs to the door and grabs his leash. I chuckle realizing that he thinks I'm going to take him out and that's what he really wants. With one quick glance into the bedroom Lacey spent her last moments in, the decision is made.

"New York, here we come!" I say and Marley jumps around with his leash in his mouth.

I rush into my room and start throwing shit in my suitcase. Mostly black dresses but I throw in this deep hunter green dress that Lacey and I ordered for New York. For Lexa. I'm probably forgetting something, but I know if I sleep on it I won't go. I will come up with a reason not to. What if I was wasting Lacey's money.…

Take the money, my Charlie girl. Live the life you deserve. The life I want for you, plays in my head. Lacey's last words are the final push I need.

I go to the bathroom to get my toothbrush and other necessities, throw them in my suitcase, zip it up and run into the den where Marley's food and travel bags are. I toss as much as I can inside the bags and he springs all over the place with excitement. It's nice to see that again because he's been so sober since Lacey passed away. He was just as lost as I was.

"Truck," I say and he runs to the door, turns around and sits in his spot to get his leash and harness done up. "We are going to do what Momma wanted, Marley." His tail wags the entire time. "Even if I'm scared shitless."

I lock up the condo, dragging my bags and dog behind me as I walk into the lobby, spotting Rupert, the doorman. "Marley and I will be gone until the New Year. Hold the mail, please."

"Yes, Miss Charlotte," he says, and I give him a knowing grin.

"If I have to tell you it's 'just Charlie' one more time, you are gonna get a telling, Rupert.'

"Yes, Miss Charlie." He chuckles.

I give him an evil grin before I chuckle too. "I'll take it," I say, walking out the door he holds open for Marley and me.

My stomach sinks lower and lower. How did I think I'd be able to get through this and just drive to New York like it wasn't the most insane thing ever? My steps slow until I'm no longer walking towards my truck.

Marley's leash goes tight and he turns to see that I'm just standing in the middle of the parking garage. I must be white as a ghost. He watches me closely for a moment then pulls his head to the side, gently tugging me forward.

"All right," I chuckle, "I get it." The half-grin on my face feels playful for a change.

The truck beeps and starts with a click of the remote. It is all black, the wheels are raised a bit, and it has tinted windows. When I open the door for Marley, he jumps up into the driver's seat with no issues and continues on into the passenger seat. I open the cab, push my rolling suitcase and Marley's bags into the back, then shut and lock it. I make my way back to the front of the truck, reach up for the grab bar and pull myself in beside Marley. When I glance out the window and see Lacey's silver Lexus, my heart drops. This was supposed to be the trip of a lifetime. One I would never forget—that's what Lacey promised. Even when she was so weak in her final days, she continually told me she was so sorry she couldn't come, too.

Marley's whimpers pull me from those memories. He stares at me like he's asking where we're going. I grab my cellphone, open up my contacts, and find Lexa's name saved into my favorites. She has continued to message me even though I haven't answered her since Lacey's funeral.

The last words of Lacey come to mind. "Love is love, my dear. Everyone deserves to be loved. Don't let the fear of being different sway you. They are the problem, never you."

Lexa, I'm coming to New York. I won't arrive until New Year's Eve. I don't expect you to be free, but I wanted you to know that Marley and I are going to finish what Lacey and I planned. My heart stops as I hit send.

My phone buzzes, almost immediately, and I slowly glance down at the message from Lexa. *See you at the ball drop.* I don't respond. I know this was always the plan but seeing those words send me into a frenzy. My breath escapes and I feel the world closing in on me once again.

Ruff.

When I take a peek at Marley, he's just sitting there, staring out the front window. With one last deep breath, I put the truck into gear and we begin our journey. The drive to the Buffalo border doesn't take too long but the closer I get to the United States, the faster my heart beats. When it's our turn to pull into customs, I'm barely keeping it together.

"Citizenship," the man in uniform says.

My passport. I reach into my bag, fighting to keep the tears back that are begging to be released.

"Canadian," I say quickly. The man studies my face.

"Do you have records for the dog?" I nod and hand him Marley's proof of vaccination with my passwort. "Is this your animal?"

Marley tilts his head to the side, watching the man as he stares at me.

"Yes." I gulp, trying to swallow these emotions rising in me.

"Where are you going? How long will you be gone for?"

Word vomit happens, "We're taking a road trip to New York City, because that's what Lacey wanted. Marley and I are going to be stopping along the way, but we will be returning on January second. We're all supposed to go and I was supposed to meet a friend there but I'm too nervous and Lacey is dead."

Shit.

Tears cloud my vision. The man's eyes widen at my blurting of all the wrong words.

He takes one more glance at Marley and me before getting up from his seat. For a moment it's like the entire world has stopped. I'm about to end up in jail for being a nut.

The man opens his half door and steps out. "I'm sorry for your loss. Have a safe trip," he says, handing my passport back to me along with Marley's records. He has a small smile and I wish I could return it but I'm a hot mess. If I open my mouth again it's going to be just like the last time.

All I can do is nod.

Tomorrow is Christmas Eve and as much as I'd like to avoid it I know I can't. The roads are much different in the United States and I've had to change my speedometer over to miles to make sure I'm not speeding. That's all I need; another word vomit session with a police officer.

Eventually Marley lies down and falls asleep in the seat next to me. He seems so peaceful, without a care in the world. I debate stopping as the sky grows dark but Marley is sleeping. I worry if I don't keep going I will come up with a reason to stop and turn around.

When the signs for New York City come, it all begins to feel real. I'm actually doing this. For me, but also for Lacey. I hadn't even thought to book a hotel.

There's a small parking lot so I turn. It's bumpy and Marley wakes.

"Rise and shine."

Marley perks up, noticing we've stopped moving which excites him.

On my phone I search for nearby hotels. Not many allow pets. Ten calls later I still don't have a place. All I say is, "Great Dane" and they refused us. The Langham is the only pet friendly one that doesn't have bug and rodents as potential roommates.

When I press that call button I panic at the lack of options.

A woman answers. "Let me just check to see if we have availability. Room preference? Number of guests?" Her voice is sweet but I know how quickly it can change once she knows about Marley.

"One, with easy access to take my dog outside." I keep my voice level so she doesn't suspect I'm nervous.

"We only have suites available and the cost of those can be quite large. You are looking at $1356 per night including the pet meal package." I drop my phone and quickly I'm scrambling to grab it.

"Hello?"

"Yes, Yes I'm here. That's fine," I say with a shaky voice. This trip is special, I keep reminding myself. Pulling out my credit card I relay the information to the woman. I have to remind myself that money isn't a problem for me anymore and that Lacey wanted me to do this trip.

"I'm actually almost in the city so I will be there soon for check in."

Once everything is set, I drive over to The Langham.

"Marley, I'll be right back," I tell him, patting his regal head fondly.

After I check in, they tell me that they can deliver anything we need—just call down. And bonus: I got a room on the second floor that allowed access to the back stairwell for Marley.

"Do you need help with your bags, Miss?"

"No, no. I'll do just fine, thank you."

Rushing to the truck, I grab our bags. These rolling cases really are a lifesaver. When I open the door, Marley jumps out and we make our way inside. When I run up the stairs, I'm praying each step not to crash into anyone.

I open the door to a whole new world. This is clearly a classy joint but it's strange to think I will be living among those that think this is normal. Marley follows me in quickly and jumps right on the California king bed, pushing around the pillows before laying in the middle. He watches as I unpack his bad and set up his pee pad.

"I don't know if I'm going to be able to sneak you out whenever you need to…you know. It's just in case."

He looks away. I chuckle. He hates this thing, but when Lacey got sick I didn't want to worry if I couldn't leave her and he needed out.

Once Marley is sorted, I unpack my things, turning to see the dog looking at me plaintively. I get it. Time to order room service.

The days pass surprisingly quickly, despite my nerves. We've been able to sneak out three times a day since coming here, going for a walk before the birds rise, so Marley can stretch his legs. Christmas Day was a hard day because I had no one to call. Lexa texts me, saying Merry Christmas, but like always I keep deleting the texts I start writing out to her, stressed about our meeting in a few days. All I did was watch movies with Marley and eat in bed.

But, today is New Year's Eve and I want to puke. I almost left yesterday to rush back home. Meeting Lexa in a few hours is causing me to panic. This will be me finally admitting what I've always said—that I want to date girls. And now, one in particular. But I've never acted on it before, hence the nerves.

Putting on the final touches, I pull the dark hunter green dress on, and then look at myself in the full-length mirror. The girl staring back at me is someone I don't recognize. The dark hair falling down my face in loose curls, the brown eyes that have seen far too much sadness, and a smile I haven't been able to show to the world. When I walk over to the safe, I open it for my ID. I also grab the second letter from Lacey.

With one last glance I see Marley curled up in bed, not minding my soon-to-be absence. I quietly shut the door hopefully not disturbing him. The stairs aren't too bad and I'm wearing nice dress boots with my outfit; I'm not a heels kind of girl.

The bellman asks if I need a ride and I nod as he walks out to hail one, and just like that I'm in the cab on my way to meet Lexa.

"This is as close as I can get you. They shut down a lot of the roads around Times Square." Looking at the time on my phone, I begin to worry she will think I haven't shown. I toss money to the man and rush out of the cab, not minding where I'm running but just heading in the same direction the crowd is moving.

Lexa had texted me a meeting place, explaining it would be a great place to stand and watch. It's ten minutes 'till midnight.

Despite the close press of people, Lexa isn't too hard to spot. She's wearing a black dress coat with a distinctive red scarf that we'd sent her in October for her birthday. Her long brown wavy hair is moving in the wind, her smile reaching her beautiful blue eyes. She's more gorgeous than any of her photos or video chats ever suggested. I pause and she does the same, not ten feet away as if she can sense me too.

"Lexa." I call out and our gazes meet for the first time. My breath catches. I hug myself, unsure what to do next. This is my first time meeting someone romantically. Online dating horror stories don't give much hope, but now looking at Lexa it's as if I knew all along this is where I needed to be tonight.

Slowly she walks to me and I can see her fidget with her clothing, pulling on the hem of her jacket as if she didn't look like an angel already.

"Hi Charlotte."

"Charlie," I correct instinctively and my face grows warm at the thoughts of her and all that's to come. "I was worried you wouldn't show."

"Of course I showed."

"I wasn't sure what you would think of me. You know, when you saw me. What if you didn't like what—"

"I have a bit of a secret," Lexa interrupts gently. "Lacey sent me a photo of you in November when she took sick. You and Marley were cuddled up on the sofa. She told me that you might disappear a bit after she died, and to not take it personally. That she would get you here one way or another, but she didn't want you to be able to run before I knew what you looked like." She shifted nervously, smiling gently. "I'm sorry if she shouldn't have done that, but it was so sweet. She wanted me to be able to spot you; reassure you."

I want to be angry, but this is so something Lacey would have done and I can't blame her. She was looking out for me, as always, and I *had* thought about running. "Don't be sorry Lexa, it was unfair of me to not to send you photos when I knew it was safe, that you were genuine." I twisted my gloved hands in front of me. "I wasn't trying to be deceptive. I was just insecure and hiding."

"Charlie, I know this." She grabs flailing hands, stilling them, both calming and thrilling me. "It's hard, especially when you are also embarking on your first same sex relationship. But I don't care if you looked like the photo or not. That doesn't make you the person I wanted to meet. The person you are in here"—she reaches up and taps her temple—"and here"—she reaches down to place her hand over her heart—"is why I wanted to meet, and be here to ring in a New Year with you." Taking a step towards me, she tugs me closer to her and I hesitate. My whole body tingles at the proximity and I'm unsure what any of this means.

Lexa pulls me through the crowd and when I glance up I can see the ball preparing its descent. The press of warm bodies count down the seconds. When we've gotten as close as we can Lexa turns back to me with an infectious smile on her face that I can't help but return. "I'm so glad you came, Charlie."

I want to say something but all I do is nod.

"Lacey said you'd come, but I worried you wouldn't."

The mention of Lacey pulls at my heart strings and Lexa must notice that change because she squeezes my hand in reassurance.

The last ten second are now on the countdown, everyone around cheering, and pairing up for the final seconds. Lexa gentle pulls me close to her and I worry abouts what's to come.

The crowd roars as the last second hits and the ball finishes its descent. Lexa leans forward but changes course, kissing my cheek instead. The pain in my heart must show on my face because Lexa's face falls when she sees mine.

"I'm sorry. I didn't want to pressure you."

I don't know why but those last words from Lacey are playing in my head. *Be Brave.* Without allowing myself to think about it I lean forward, and Lexa move closer until we're an inch apart.

The moment seems to freeze and I notice what she's doing. She's waiting for me to close this final distance, to be sure I know what I want. I lean into her and for the first time in my life I feel normal. Like I'm not the odd one out. I'm not forgotten.

Her lips are soft and gentle, but I knew they would be. My hands slide out of hers, finding her waist, pulling her slowly until she pushes up against me. The crowd around us disappears and I can't think of anything but this moment with her. When I pull away slowly I'm nervous at her reaction, but she watches me with such a happy grin that my nerves settle.

"Don't be sorry," I say and she drops her head, suddenly shy herself. My hand finds her chin, bringing her gaze back to mine. "Thank you for waiting for me, Lexa."

She doesn't say anything at first, then: "Letter time."

Her words shock me. "You know?"

She snorts, delightfully to my ears. "If you didn't show tonight, I had strict instructions to go to the condo. Also, that there was a letter to be opened tonight—*if* you saw me."

Her eyes continue to study me, watching a torment of emotions play over my face. Excitement. Loss. Guilt. Hope. Love?

I put my hand in my front pocket and pull out the small envelope with my name written across it in Lacey's handwriting. My eyes glance over to Lexa and she nods for me to open it.

My Dearest Charlie,

If you waited to read this like I asked and are in New York at Times Square, then Lexa should be there with you and my secret is out. I'm sorry I

went behind your back in helping her to reach out to you, but when I knew my time was coming, I worried you would use this as another excuse to shut yourself off from the world. That's not what I want, Charlie, and your mother wouldn't have wanted that either.

You have so much to offer this world and Lexa isn't a bad place to start. She cares about you. She must if she's there with you, now, and I don't doubt she is. You deserve to be loved, my Charlie, girl, and so much more.

I know this couldn't have been easy, but now you've fulfilled my last dream. You can finally be free from all that fear of rejection. Don't push Lexa away, I think she will be an amazing addition to your life.

And, Charlie, know that no matter who you end up with, or what you end up doing in life, that I will forever be proud of you.

Take care of Marley for me, and Lexa. She loves you so.

This is your song, Charlie. This is the Song of the Brave.

Love always,
Lacey

The tears well up, breaking free. I let my hair fall in front of my face, trying to hide my reaction to Lacey's final letter. Lexa slowly puts her arms around me, gathering me close. I let go for the first time since the funeral and all these feelings come pouring out of me.

After a few moments, I gather myself again, pulling away. The crowd is still in party mode, but I'm spent, and I say something I hadn't planned on. "Would you like to meet Marley?"

Lexa perks up and claps her hands together with a smile of excitement. "Of course, I'd love to. If you're sure."

I've just invited her to my hotel. My heart races. I'm not sure I'm ready for the more intimate elements a relationship with Lexa will mean, but I know I'm ready for her to see Marley. Lacey would have wanted me to introduce them and I can't say I'm upset she wants to come back to my room.

I nod, and we walk out of the blockaded area to hail a cab. Lexa grabs us a taxi that just dropped off a group.

"The Langham please," I say as we scoot into the back of the vehicle. It takes us an hour to get to the hotel due to the post celebration traffic. I hand the man money before Lexa could and smile. She chuckles and slides out after me.

"This was the only place I could come with Marley, and they think he's a small dog, so we'll have to be quiet."

Lexa just nods, her eyes dancing, continuing to follow me. When we walk past the main desk, I smile at the woman working and grab Lexa's hand reflexively. Lexa smiles and to my surprise so does the woman at the desk. My date has heels on, so I decide to take the elevator. I wave my key over the panel to activate the elevator and press number two. The elevator roars to life and when the doors open on the second floor Lexa walks out first with me closely behind her.

"He might get a little excited," I warn her.

Lexa seems worried but she just smiles in a reassuring way.

"He's a baby, I promise."

As soon as I open the door, Marley wakes to see I've brought a friend. He jumps off the bed and crowds Lexa for attention before we've even closed the door behind us.

She steps back and Marley must sense something because he calms and sits, waging his tail to show his excitement. She eventually reaches to pet him and his head falls into her hand, causing her to laugh.

"Maybe you'd like to get out of the dress?" My heart jumps—Shit! That is not what I meant!—and I worry I've offended her. "I meant in case you're worried about Marley wrecking it."

Lexa's hand lays on mine, calming me instantly. "I know what you meant, Charlie."

I pull out a selection of nightwear and hand them to her to pick. She grabs a purple nightdress that I'd gotten from Lacey as a part of my birthday last year. She turns and quickly heads to the bathroom, closing the door behind her.

Before she can come out, I quickly pull off my dress, putting on a red nightdress that I also got from Lacey. I'm brushing my hair when Lexa comes out of the bathroom, holding her clothes as if unsure of where to put them. I rush to help, placing them on the dresser. Marley jumps up onto the bed and

we both just look at each other, waiting to see who will make the first move.

Lexa hops on the bed then waits. I could have gone around and sat with Marley between us but I choose to sit beside Lexa. She relaxes, a tentative smile lighting up her eyes.

A little shy, heart thudding, I turn the TV on and it's a replay of New Year's Eve celebrations around the world. Several minutes pass without us saying anything. Marley has been sitting just as silently, until he places his head in Lexa's lap. I can't help but melt, even though he eventually loses interest and jumps down to go lay in front of the door.

"Sorry. I know he can be a lot to handle…and I'm—"

"Perfect," she says, interrupting me. I go to correct her, and she places her finger against my lips, hushing me immediately. "You're perfect, Charlotte."

Before I can stop myself, I pull her to me, quieting her with a soft kiss. Again, she doesn't deepen the kiss and I worry I'm doing something wrong.

"Charlie, it's not that I don't want to. I just…are you really ready for this? Us?"

"Lexa, shut up and kiss me."

She doesn't wait for a second command. Before I can say another word, Lexa has me pinned to the bed, with her on top of me, holding me with her gaze. She waits, and I nod, although I'm not sure it was needed.

The pressure of her weight against me should make me nervous but instead it grounds me, keeping me here and not in my memories. Her hips start grinding against me gently, sensually, as her soft kisses and touches raise my temperature. Our clothing scrunches up, exposing more skin. For a moment, she pulls back, and my heart sinks, then she kisses me with even more passion, enticing me to respond in equal kind.

Slowly, I move my hand, placing it on her bare left thigh. She pauses then watches my hand as I slide it up until it's resting at her hips. I tease the edges of her panties as I slide my hand across her backside, pulling her forward. When I slip my fingers into the edge of her panties, sliding my hand around to the front of her, between us, closer to her center, she moans. Her surer hand moves on top of mine when I hesitate in my inexperience, to guide me in further, encouraging me.

I get lost in the moment, in her warmth. I'm not sure who is more aroused.

She spins us until I am lying on my side next to her, my hand sliding out of her panties as we resettle. She cups my face tenderly, catching her breath. Slowly, I pull the nightdress up so that her svelte stomach is fully exposed and my breath catches. She's gorgeous.

Lexa watches me carefully as I slip my hand under the night dress, dragging it upward. When I reach the wire of her bra, I try to hide my lack of knowing by not hesitating again; I slide my hand under the material, cupping her breast as her breath hitches at the contact.

"Is this okay?" I say, trying to keep my voice from shaking as I slide my finger across her nipple, which hardens, causing my insides to come to life for the first time. I've never had this feeling before and I don't want to stop. Lexa still hasn't answered me, caught in the moment, but her eyes haven't left mine.

My hand moves down her stomach again. I sweep my fingers across the edge of her panties, looping a single finger inside, waiting for the go ahead. Lexa nods, and I slowly pull down her panties as she lifts her hips off the bed to help me.

My hands are shaking. I'm tempted to make a run for it, except Lexa's smile relaxes all those fears.

She cups my face, pulling me into a long sensual kiss as my hand moves down again. As soon as I feel her warmth, the rest of the world falls away. Lexa's breath speeds up and I take that as a good sign. Slowly my fingers begin to move against her, back and forth, circling her arousal. Her mouth opens as she whimpers and I use this to deepen the kiss, her body showing all the signs that she's just as into this as I am.

She pulls me closer to her with each heavy breath she takes. I stare at her with awe and wonder. I must be doing something right because within a few minutes she is coming undone beneath me. The exhilaration I felt, knowing I gave her pleasure, almost undid me. I'm already so close to the precipice.

I don't know what to say, so I move my hand up to rest it on her stomach, hoping one of us will find the words as the awkwardness sets in. "I hope that was okay. I've never done anything like this, Lexa."

Without hesitation and before I can do anything to stop it—not that I would want to—Lexa leans into my neck, kissing her way down to my collarbone. "It was amazing. *You* are amazing."

She pushes me back until I'm on my back again, unbuttoning my nightdress until she can slide my breast out of the cup of my bra. She looks at me like I'm the most amazing thing she's ever seen and lowers her head, pulling my nipple into her mouth.

It's not long before I'm the one gasping in pleasure. I may be inexperienced, but I know Lexa is right for me. I've never wanted to do anything with a man; I've never felt this with anyone else who'd taken interest. Which is why I always knew she was different—that we were different. Love is Love, as they say.

Lexa's hand continues to work on my nightdress, unbuttoning me until my body is completely open to her hot gaze. When her hands slide teasingly, lovingly, down to my panties, I thought I'd be apprehensive. Instead, I'm eager.

"My turn, Charlie."

Copyright © 2018 by Gracie Wilson.

Tina Gower grew up in a small community in Northern California that proudly boasts of having more cows than people. She raised guide dogs for the blind, is dyslexic, and can shoot a gun or bow and miraculously never hit the target (which at some point becomes a statistical improbability). Tina also writes contemporary romance as Alice Faris. She won the Writers of the Future, the Daphne du Maurier Award for Mystery and Suspense (paranormal category), and was nominated for the Romance Writers of America® Golden Heart®. If you love The Lipski Partner Axiom, you should check out The Outlier Series by Tina Gower where you can read all about Kate, Becker, and the rest of the Accidental Death Predictions team.

THE LIPSKI PARTNER AXIOM

by Tina Gower

CHAPTER ONE

Seventy-two percent. If it had been a test score in my advanced placement physics class, I'd have cheered over the accomplishment, but as an injury prediction notice it benches me from the beat right in the middle of Yuletide season. The busiest, craziest time of the year for a cop and I'll miss it.

My bra strap digs into my insision sight and I scratch at it to keep the annoying fabric from irritating me further. Except I don't want to call attention to it—my father, Detective Hank Lipski, scares the shit of of most of my co-workers, but it still doesn't keep them from razzing me. I don't want to deal with the half-sarcastic questions on how I'm doing.

"Tough luck, mini-Lipski. And right after coming out of wing removal surgery. That must bite." Morales, a friend, takes a sip of his over-sweetened coffee. The guy likes the frilly stuff. Special milk, extra shot of vanilla. I'm not even a werewolf, and I could smell that shit from two lockers down.

"So, uh, if you don't have plans tonight…" Morris, my current partner, holds up his own injury report. "Looks like we're both benched. We could grab a bite and maybe head to the bar after?"

I do my best to hold in a groan.

Morris's non-stop attempts to flirt are annoying, and the fact we're paired together because he's also a gremlin (though not an angel mix like me) and we both come from cop families is equally aggravating. I stick out like a sore thumb with Morris always chanting how perfect we are together. As cops. Reminding him our partnership only goes that far is like crushing a puppy daily. The guy is relentless, though.

I crumble the notice in my hand and roll my shoulders back. Shoving my locker closed, I don't acknowledge Morales's comments or Morris's overtures. Instead, I go on a mission.

"Grayson!" Morales calls after me. "Lipski!" he tries again when I don't answer. "Don't do anything stupid!"

"So, are we meeting at the festival?" Morris yells out. He struggles to get his pants back on behind the changing partition so he can follow me. I speed up so he can't. I don't put it past him to stagger out half-dressed in front of the entire precinct, just to catch me.

I had a mission, and it included wrangling a certain Jackal and pressuring him for information. As luck would have it, I saw his little brown bushy tail as he sneaked into the break room on my way into work. He must have just posted the injury prediction notices fresh from the oracles and slithered out to retrieve his donut before heading back down to Health Predictions—government employee bodily harm division. Nothing more than a glorified pencil pusher. No longer preventing fated forecasts on the streets like me. No longer a lowly police officer.

I catch him as he lifts a donut to his lips. His eyes widen, knowing he'd been trapped. My lips twitch, I might have shown a little more teeth than I'd intended.

"My father put you up to this." I put both hands on either side of the door frame to keep him corralled. Shifty little thing, Eze Clevon, but as long as I focus right on him, he can't use the illusion magic on me that would make him appear as a small, sleek black-backed Jackal—though he's actually a huge and rough guy. One of the benefits I inherited from my troll-gremlin father: magic resistance.

He swallows, setting his donut down carefully. "Nope. I'm afraid not."

"He said he didn't want me out there on Yuletide, especially since I was recovering from surgery. A *voluntary* surgery the department *insisted* I do, so I could, you know, work as a police officer as I'm trained to do." I rub the top of my shoulder, the incision where my wing appendages used to be itched.

Having those little extra tendons and muscle where wings would have grown generations ago, was a status symbol among angels, the decision to remove them was an emotional one, and I'd done it with no complaints because the department required it for all their field officers. One wrong tug and those wing buds could pull on the tendons in my back in such a way it could put me on desk duty for the rest of my career. Damn angel physiology. Two little three-inch body parts no longer part of me and for what? So I could be iced during the biggest crime spree of the season?

"Grayson—"

"That's Officer Lipski to you," I force between my locked jaw, emotion threatening to spill over in an embarrassing display.

Eze clears his throat and holds up his hands, inching forward. "Grayson," he says again, this time with more insistence.

Okay, we could play that game, if he wants.

Eze had been my first partner before he abandoned me soon after we graduated from the academy; he transferred to predictions instead. We spent a few months as rookies and then boom, like a two-by-four to the ass he flattened me by announcing his career change to the entire department. He'd had a math degree with applied predictions, but he never mentioned it. Not until he was cleaning out his locker months after we both first started.

And the thing that sucked? We were an unstoppable team. Could anticipate each other's moves and emotions. It was a dream pairing. A pairing that made other teams extremely jealous. A once in a lifetime partnership. I couldn't help but take it personally. Especially since he made a point to avoid me after he transferred. My gut still had bruises from where he'd emotionally punched me.

And now I'm stuck with Morris.

My captain had dismissed my hurt as over-the-top. He'd asked if there was something more Eze and I weren't telling him. I shut the hell up after

that and shoved all that anger down below where it's been festering with questions ever since.

Eze must see that all bubbling to the surface as he softens his expression and says, "I didn't do the math on this one. I just delivered the numbers."

I let out a long breath, forcing myself to calm. Eze had no reason to lie to me. Deep down, regardless of the hurt, I knew he wouldn't deceive me—well, except for not letting me know beforehand about his career change. He barely interacted with me, so why did I assume he'd somehow orchestrated this all himself? Call it gremlin intuitions—which, don't get me wrong, usually were forged in delusional fires, and hunches that were not to be trusted. Basically, gremlins are prone to paranoia at times: this could be one of those times, considering how badly I'd done in the past keeping my feelings out of anything that had to do with Eze Clevon.

Even now, as he stands there, I'm drawn to hug him like I'd done countless times over the years when things got too intense while we were training. His touch would ease me, sooth my rough spots.

"Okay," I nod. "You know I live for these shifts. I'm going to miss all the action." I plop miserably into a chair. It squeaks as if echoing my protest.

Eze, donut still poised mid-air, shifts his gaze around the room, undoubtedly searching for someone else to take over the messy emotional part of this conversation. So much for my magical hug.

In disgust, I shove the donut box closer to Eze and roll my eyes. "Why am I even talking to you? You don't care. You left the police force and chose for predictions."

You left me.

But that last thought is silly. Eze and I were only work partners. Nothing else.

I scoot out of my seat before I embarrass myself. Crying over a lost shift or a lost partner—it didn't matter. I couldn't afford to show any weakness. As a daughter of a cop, and several generations of my family in law enforcement, I had to prove I belonged here, maybe more than anyone else. My employment couldn't be attributed to favoritism and nepotism. It had to be because I belonged. Period. The only way I'd get that is if I earned it.

But I have to be out there, working, to prove it.

I have one last option before I completely give up. I'm already bounding from my chair and out the door when the last-chance-thought enters my mind.

Eze follows behind me, donut abandoned. "Hey, Gray. What are you doing?"

"Nothing. I have the day off," I say, hoping he'll shake off. "Maybe I'll work on my tan."

"In the middle of a snowstorm?"

"Yeah."

There is an awkward pause, then: "I did care, you know. I do," he calls out, as I take the stairwell knowing he won't follow.

Stairwells, Eze, and I don't mix. It had been this exact stairwell where he'd told me he was leaving the police force. And the place I'd told him I'd lost all my respect in him for not telling me he'd been thinking about leaving.

I shake off those old ghosts while I jog down each step, a little guilty I'm about to use my father's connections to get me that out of jail free card.

CHAPTER TWO

"No. Absolutely not. Hank will kill me, revive me and kill me again and again until I realize my mistake." Becker glares at the predictions sheet. "Who else is on the list?"

I hadn't really paid attention. I'd been more upset over my own prediction and subsequent elimination on the roster tonight. I shrug.

"If you're the only one, maybe…but if you're not." He shifts, frowning harder. "I gotta call Kate."

I huff an exasperated sigh. "Seriously? Any prediction leads you to believe she's in danger. This is *my* prediction, not hers, wolf."

He fixes me with a stare. "Relax. She'll have more insight into the prediction and a lot more experience with interpretation." He sets my predictions sheet on his desk and snaps a picture, hitting send, then hits the dial button, shifting the phone to his ear. "Yeah, I need Kate Hale." There's a slight pause. "Yeah, it's Becker. I have her direct number, but you all harp on me when I don't do things official on an actual case…. Whatever, Yang." He snorts and then brightens when Kate must have come on the line.

There's a short discussion over my prediction. Becker eyes me as they analyze the numbers over the

call. Kate might have even sneaked into the database and checked the death roll for tonight. If there are injuries, there could also be accidental deaths, or homicides—both events Kate would have access to as the head of Accidental Death Predictions.

I sit back patiently…okay, *not* patiently. I'm fiddling with all the items on Detective Becker's desk. He allows it, probably because he sees me more like a pup that needed protection than a cop.

Beck had been more like an uncle to me growing up. When he'd lost his pack to a senseless act of violence carried out by an extremist anti-fate group, our family adopted him—though we were a poor substitute for the kind of structure Beck needed in a pack, but he'd found Kate and she filled that role for him. We still saw each other as family.

The door to his office opens, and I twist around in my seat to see who it is and glare. Eze ducks his head in, our gaze meets, his eyes shift to Beck on the phone, and makes a move to slink back out.

Beck puts his hand over the receiver and waves Eze inside. "Clevon, wait right there." He then turns his attention back to his mate on the phone. "Yep. Got it."

Becker hangs up and points to his computer. "Lookie what we have here." His printer comes to life as if on command. He snaps out the new report and sets it on the desk between us. "Clevon, come closer. You can't hear a pulse from the cheap seats."

"I'd rather play omega on this one."

Becker snorts. "Denied. Sit."

I snicker. Wolf sayings are usually amusing when bantered between shifters. Though neither Eze or Beck can actually shift. Eze's shifting is more illusion magic. Beck lacks the ability through generations of wolf packs interbreeding with other non-shifting species, though he is fairly pure-breed and holds more animal qualities than human. Eze's senses are limited compared to my surrogate uncle, but he still has a few tricks up his sleeve in the form of advanced hearing and scent.

Eze folds his big muscular body into a chair next to mine. He keeps his arms crossed and his eyes narrowed. Becker ignores his obvious non-verbal protests. I observe a few beads of perspiration on Eze's temples, and I'm all too aware of his body so close to mine. My pinkie is less than an inch from his elbow.

As if he can sense my unwelcome thoughts, Eze gaze wanders to mine, and for a second there's something there, something foreign, a yearning? So, subtle I think I might have made it up because in the next moment Eze's attention transfers to the newly printed report.

Desperate for a change in topic to keep me from closing in on those inches of separation between Eze and me, I snatched the newly printed report, still warm from the printer. I blinked at the general predictions notice, reading the details. My attention snags on one line: a riot. I would have been hurt in a riot tonight.

I set the report on the table, assuming Eze already knew this information and chose not to share it with me earlier. "Just because I'm not going to be there at the prescribed time and event didn't mean that crime won't occur."

In fact, it very much would continue to take place it would just be a different group involved. In most cases, the culprit would have been predicted on already, but that's not what the report indicates.

"Multiple officers are involved in this one, Grayson. Don't take it personally. They've got to assess what staff member combinations will result in the least number of casualties and a captured perpetrator."

"But they don't even have a lead. The predicting oracle says, 'vision unclear.'" I scan the paperwork to be sure I didn't miss anything.

"Sir," Eze shifts in his seat. "May I ask what you needed me for?"

Becker zeros in on my ex-partner. "Yeah, it appears she's not going to sit this one out. Your job is to babysit."

"I do *not* need a babysitter," I protest.

"You can take it or leave it," Becker insists, still looking at Eze.

Eze looks pained. "Sir, that is an unnecessary breach of protocol—"

"There is no way in seven hells I'm going to allow Eze to follow me around all Yule—"

"It's not for 'all Yule.' It's for one night of Yule," Becker says to me, then he refocuses on my soon-to-be bodyguard. "And you delivered the prediction. Don't you want to run point on this investigation?"

"Yes, but I didn't make *this* prediction. I crunch numbers. I'm not a field agent—"

Becker grunts. "Which is a shame, considering your talents as a police officer are being wasted behind a computer."

Finally. Something we agreed on.

Eze's jaw clamps closed and his stare burns right into the center of Becker's chest. He won't question Becker's assignment any longer. Jackals often serve at least a two-year stint in the military after finishing an accelerated schooling program, and Eze is no exception. His first instinct is to obey and protect, both of which he is being ordered to do today.

"You have fun at the Yule festival—as a civilian," he says to me, the last bit pointedly, then smiles at Eze, "And you'll take this case, accepting the extra help Grayson'll provide, and we'll consider ourselves even."

I lean forward as if I've gotten away with something and should leave while I'm ahead, but it feels like there's some catch to this arrangement I'm not yet understanding. "But my father will kill you, you said. I don't—"

"Leave Hank to me."

Eze sinks lower in his chair, mumbling something, but since both Becker and I have advanced hearing we catch it: *How in the hells does this make us even?*

Becker grins wider as his response. Me? I'm stuck wondering what in the gods names did Eze do to be indebted to Ian Becker.

CHAPTER THREE

I'm halfway to my car when I hear the familiar rhythm of a pissed off Jackal. There's part of me that knows I should be remorseful for pulling Eze into this somehow, not that I had anything to do with it; I'm the innocent bystander. Becker made the call, and he outranks both of us in our respective departments. All it took was a few short conversations with our superiors, and we were good to go.

I didn't stick around for the visit he made to my father. There was a lot of yelling, and my hearing is too sensitive to volunteer for that show.

Anyway, I don't feel any guilt. Eze and I make a good pair. It only rankles a little that he doesn't feel the same anymore about that aspect of our now-dissolved partnership.

I whirl around to face him, stopping him short. "Let's make this easy. We'll meet at the Yule festival tonight. I'll text you when I'm on my way, with an approximate location."

"I promised my mother and my brother's family that I'd be at the First Fruits Festival after I got off work. My nieces are going to be devastated."

Right. He usually decorated one of the deities with his nieces, where festival attendees would bring their offerings. As a respected Jackal family, they represented one of eleven houses along with the lions, descendants and followers of various gods of Africa, and others.

I let out a long breath of air. "Okay, we can go there first. It's usually wrapped up by the time the Yule celebrations start, right? We hit both last year while on duty as cadets-in-training, remember?"

His deep frown stays in place.

"Gods, don't look so put out. Was I really that awful of a partner that it's this painful to be around me again?" I sling my duffle over my shoulder and stomp the rest of the way to my car, my truck opening with a chirp when I press the button on my keys. I throw the work stuff I won't be using tonight inside.

"I took the bus," he says.

Yeah, well, how's that my problem? I want to say, but I know what he's implying. Being partnered with someone all through the academy and then through initial training and then partnered while on the force really works as a get-to-know someone. "I got seats. Lots of spare seats…" I open my door as if I'm not going to wait too long for him to make up his mind. But we both know, I'd stand here a few hours while he dithers over his choices; I'm hopeless when it comes to my loyalty to Eze. He can either go home on his own and trust that I'll meet up with him as I promised, or he can follow me now and completely fulfill the assignment he's been given.

I continue waiting. My shoulders sag. "I know this really sucks. I know I'm like the princess of the force and all. My dad's a cop. Your police liaison in Health Predictions is a close family friend who'll basically end you if you screw up. And so, you have no choice but to partner with me. Again." A little of my tough shell breaks as I consider what I'd been afraid was the issue all along: maybe I wasn't as great a partner for him, as he had been for me. Maybe he'd been humoring me and inwardly screaming for get-

ting stuck with the cop who'd be made of glass. One wrong move and everyone would be pointing at him for the blemish.

Eze's frown disintegrates from his face, in its place is a mask of concern. "Gods, Gray. That's not it at all. You are an amazing cop."

I'm mortified, realizing I had voiced my fears out loud. "Then why?" I nearly choke, forcing the question out that I'd asked myself over and over.

He remains frozen, his lips slightly open as if contemplating the correct answer to tell the class. The one the teacher most wants to hear.

It's an awkward pause, one that will result in no good, I can tell by the wild fear in his eyes. So, I chicken out. Maybe I'm not ready. Instead, I slide into the driver's seat and wait for him to hop in the car.

He must sense I've given him a little longer to answer and eventually joins me. Quietly we head to my place, so I can change for the evening.

CHAPTER FOUR

My apartment is fairly sparse. Most people expect a mess to match my frenetic personality, but I do have a sense of order. Hank Lipski might be my father, but Angela Lipski *is* my mother. And anyone who's been to our family home knows: my mother brings organized to a whole new level. Hello label maker and color-coded bins addiction. I'm not that extreme, in my place, but I do like opening my closets and seeing everything in its place.

I set my keys on the counter, and Eze hesitates at my door. I glance behind me to see what his hold up is, but it's as if he's frozen at the threshold. "You should come in, I'm going to need a second to get supplies, get ready. You know—undercover cop stuff. Gotta look like a proper civilian tonight."

He clears his throat, looking around. "Uh, yeah, I've just never seen your new place."

Right. It's been six months since we've spoken, other than in passing or on official police business, and around that time I'd been living with my parents to keep costs down until I was done with the academy and had a couple paychecks banked. "Well, here it is."—I sweep my hands to reveal my place. There's not much to it. A room. A bathroom. A kitchen nook. It's a studio, so everything is an open floor plan except the bathroom—"Go ahead and have a look."

He surprises me when he does starts to survey the room, but instead of looking at my furniture—sparsely furnished as it is—he inspects the windows and the security system. Typical Jackal.

I leave him to his paranoia and pick out a nice outfit for tonight that won't restrict me too much if we need to run, but is also flattering. I pick a shimmery shirt that drapes lower in the back to show off my new wing tattoo that covers my scars, has a longer hem in the torso and fits snugly over my stretchy skinny jeans. Boots over the pants—stylish, but sturdy. My gray-brown hair goes up into a loose bun with a few curls bouncing down. Gray-brown is my natural color, a little genetic gift from being an angel, but also a gremlin-troll. It's unique and where I got my name. I don't mean to be vain, but it's my favorite quality about myself.

There's a brief moment where I glance into the mirror and wonder how Eze will see me in this. I brush away that unwelcome thought. Eze is not my boyfriend. We're *not* romantic. My anger is only due to our partnership breaking up unexpectedly, nothing else. I repeat that mantra until I sinks in, which is only a few dozen times.

A light coat of make-up finishes the look, and I move around the room to toss a few things into my duffle. Some hexes, anti-hex potions, a variety of salts, a couple of handy spells from Kate's cousin, Ali. I'm usually not much of a use in the magic department because I've not yet mastered the ability to get a lot of these contraptions to work due to my immunity to magic. Most of it fizzles out at my fingertips like a match in a windy rainstorm. The few I threw into my bag are the ones I seem to be able to use with some success and a few I'll have to talk Eze through using for me if we need them to be more effective.

I think I have what we need, so I head to the freezer where I keep a few of Ali's fate-blocking cookies—again, another tool that won't work fully on me but might as well bring them. I'm tossing a sack of cookies into my duffle when I notice my front door is wide open and Eze is out on my front porch glaring down my neighbor.

"Hey, man, chill. I saw her car and was just seeing if she was home," the troll says and attempts to break free from where Eze has cornered him.

Eze tightens the space between them. "Most people knock, they don't peek into a window."

"Whoa," I interrupt the interrogation. "Eze this is Benj. He feeds my geckos, Pike and Ringo, when I'm working a lot of shifts in a row."

Eze waits a beat as if processing the validity of that information and then angles his body so Benj can slink by, which he does clutching his backpack in front of his chest as if it were a shield.

Benj and Eze are around the same height, but Eze fills that space with more dominance. Benj is leaner and like a puppy who never grew into his paws, Eze more like a well-conditioned athlete.

Benj reaches into his bag for the mason jar I set on his dining room table this morning when I thought I'd be working back-to-back shifts.

Eze holds his hand out, preventing the exchange. "Not so fast. Slow."

Benj's gaze flicks between us. "It's crickets. For Pike and Ringo. In a mason jar."

Eze doesn't take that explanation. "Hands up where I can see them."

"You're being ridiculous," I tell him, but Benj complies immediately, moving slow. I hold back a laugh. "Eze, it's fine. He's a friend."

"Friend." Eze practically chews on the word as if it's the bone of his enemy. Then he snorts as if he didn't like the taste. He digs through my neighbor's bag until he finds the jar in question and holds it out to me.

Our fingertips touch, igniting a warmth low in my belly. Tension I didn't know I'd been holding melts from my limbs. Except I don't get an opportunity to enjoy the feeling for long. Eze snaps his hand back as if one of the crickets bit him. He stumbles from the ground lacking his usual grace and shoves the bag into Benj's arms.

Benj glances from me to Eze. "I, uh, guess I'll see you later." He reaches in for his usual hug but stops short when Eze's low growl rumbles from behind him.

Benj backs out of my apartment, fumbles for his keys and unlocks his door in record time. His apartment is next to mine, so it doesn't take him long.

Eze gestures towards Benj's door when it closes. "I don't like him."

"That's too bad since you'd get along with him. He works in experimental forecasting. They calculate predictions so far into the future they become prophecies."

Eze glares at Benj's apartment. "I hate him more now."

"Really? Honestly, what do you have against Benj. He's harmless. *You have gone out of your way to avoid me before today, so why should you care?* I add, although I am too chicken to say that out loud.

"He's attracted to you."

I scoff. "Nah." Then I sober up at Eze's serious expression. "Wait—really?" I arch an eyebrow. "How do you know? You're not a werewolf, and you can't smell attraction."

"Jackals and werewolves have more in common than you think." He gestures to my bag. "You're ready?"

"Yeah, but—"

I put the mason jar down, follow Eze out of the apartment, but he heads to the car before I can ask him why Benj being attracted to me is a terrible thing. I mean, I don't like him back, and Benj has never acted on his attraction. I don't think he will; he's very respectful.

Eze is sitting in the driver seat when I get to the car, and I frown in confusion. I bend down, holding back a grin as I meet his gaze through the opened window. It was just like when we had been partners. "So, uh, thanks for driving." I pass the keys to him.

He takes them with a grunt. "Force of habit."

Eze had always driven on all our shifts. Mostly I let him because I liked to be the first out of the car when we'd have to chase down the assailant. Eze would always catch up, which is why I needed a head start.

I hop in the car. I expect him to start driving and be on our way, but Eze keeps his eyes ahead. "You got inked."

Out of habit, I twist a little to look behind me, but it's useless, I can't see my new tattoo except through an elaborate mirror set up. Two angel wings start at my shoulder blades, furrow up to the tops of my shoulder, and gracefully spreads out down my back. Feathers drape in an artistic pattern, some colored

in, some left as impressionistic outlines. The artist used a silver ink for some of the shadow and color. He said it would be like my "signature" unique artsy touch because of my name.

"Yeah." It's all I can manage through the emotion of the surgery memory. Gods, it was two little appendages. I didn't even blink when their removal was mentioned as a suggested voluntary requirement for the police force. I'd known my entire life it would be happening if I continued in my pursuit of this career. Except, I'd been a mess about it since.

I thought I'd done a good job keeping my voice neutral, but Eze—I can never seem to hide from Eze. "You sacrificed a lot to be a cop."

I bristle at this. "I want this life. I'd sacrifice anything." I flick my gaze away from him and stare out the window, holding back what I really want to say: to lash out over him not sacrificing enough. Not wanting it enough to stay partners.

But he says, "I know the feeling."

I snort. My anger wells up, threatening to spill. When it becomes too much to remain contained in my body—when I know if I don't vent the steam I'll explode—I snap. "You have no idea what sacrifice is. You gave up being a cop and went for the easy career."

He lets me spew my toxic accusation, taking the insult with not so much as a flicker of hurt crossing his expression. After a few minutes, while I'm breathing heavily to gain back my control, he nods. "I've made sacrifices, Gray. For something I want more than anything. I sacrificed."

I shake my head, willing for the nonsense of what he's saying to deflect off me. A year ago, when we'd both graduated we confessed to each other that we wanted to be on the beat more than anything. What had changed for him?

I think he's going to double down and defend his explanation, but he pulls out his tablet instead. "Predictions in a city crisis event update every half hour. Let's see what we're dealing with now that they've got all the new players in motion. Maybe this whole thing has blown over."

It takes a few clicks for Eze to find the revised reports. But I can tell by the iron set of his jaw that the news isn't good news. The sudden shift in mood sweeps me in, and I motion for him to pass it over to me. He hesitates for a moment—I don't have clearance to analyze forecasts, nor am I even privy to their reports and raw data. This is an event unfolding based on predictions of what *might* happen, and so it's tricky. We can't take anything as certain.

He tips the screen my way after sighing. "It's just a new list of names on the injury list, except this time we have civilian casualties."

I scan that list in case anyone I know is on it. And I see a name that sends chills through my system. Annalee Lipski. My sister.

Shit.

CHAPTER FIVE

Eze must see the name at the same time I do because he flips the tablet closed and tears out of the parking lot and with no questions. We head to my folk's house. We might even speed through a few yellow lights along the way. Eze knows this puts us at risk of getting flagged by the Traffic Predictions department, and they'll send out a patrol along our path to catch us and prevent our erratic driving, but as an actuary, he also knows all the moves to keep them off our tail.

We reach Mom and Dad's house in record time. I burst through the door in time to witness Annalee screaming about the unfairness of life and slamming a few doors. She's still in high school, and her emotions run deep. It wasn't so long ago that I can't relate.

Dad's barreling voice rings out from the kitchen. "We don't have control over the predictions, but I'm not going to send any of my daughters out there to be harmed. Not even a scratch." He walks into the foyer, making a beeline for me. His gaze burns. "And that goes for you, too!"

I rear back at the force of his tone. Eze catches me as I stumble into him. "Me?"

"Don't act innocent. I revoke my permission for you to work on the case Beck arranged for you. I won't have either of you out there tonight." Dad paces like an angry lion who's had his dinner delayed by a few hours.

Mom sits on the couch with her arms and legs folded in ridged protest. Nobody's happy with this new development. Yule is everyone's favorite holiday.

Missing the festival would mean missing the biggest event of the year in Angel's Peak.

"Are *you* going out tonight?" I ask my father, keeping my tone casual.

"Don't make this about me. I'm a police officer. I have a job to serve."

I arch an eyebrow. "I'm a police officer, too, Dad."

My mom sighs. "Grayson, honey, he's not going to make sense for a while. Just leave him alone until he calms down."

Eze clears his throat. "I, uh, have a question."

Nobody acknowledges him, but also nobody stops him from speaking. My mother finally tips her head in a gesture for him to continue with his inquiry.

"Where does your family usually congregate? At the Yule ceremony?"

It doesn't take much thought at all. "We pretty much take up camp around the Yule log. There are a few benches there. They have a bar there and…" I realize what he's getting at. "You think we can find the catalyst if we find the place?"

He nods. "It stands to reason you would have asked to patrol the area you'd be most familiar with and could visit with your family. Since there had been injury and casualty prediction notices on you and your sister…"

He's right. I had been working out a way to do exactly that. "So before, in the first prediction, I would have been with them when the fight broke out—"

"You were likely somewhere near." He makes a motion as if his brain is working faster than his verbal skills and for me to finish his thought.

"I could have been protecting my sister. No, I *would* have been. I could have prevented a lot of casualties," I point out.

My dad snorts. "I wouldn't go too far with these theories." But my overdramatic comment composures him and I can visibly see him lightening up, though he continues to pace the room.

Eze points, eyes wide as if I've guessed the winning number. "Yeah. I'm not suggesting a whole 'save the world' theory, but Grayson's presence mixed with others would have meant the better outcome."

Dad stops pacing and frowns at our little exchange. He presses a fist into his palm, his teeth grind. "Eze, with me." He gestures for my ex-partner to follow him into the library where he's installed soundproofing to keep the rest of the gremlin-trolls in our family from hearing what he's about to say.

I follow behind, even though I've not been invited. Dad doesn't bar me at the door. He knows better. He didn't raise obedient little girls. We're all warriors, and it's his own gods damn fault I won't fall in line where my own fate is concerned.

The door closes behind us.

Eze holds up his hands as if showing he's come in peace. "I know what you're thinking, but Grayson isn't on the casualty list any longer—"

"Because she had her shift taken away," my dad interjects.

"I was going to go anyway, though," I clarify. "Remember, Beck's orders. I'd have still shown up on the list if I were in immediate danger. I'm not a target."

"*If* you were protecting Annalee, then it means we were—are—targeted in some way," my dad says, running his hand over his skull.

"These are all just theories, until it happens," Eze reminds us both. "But we can have information that we can pull together and find the catalyst, if we talk with others on the list."

"Then we should compare both lists and see if we see any patterns. If the fight breaks out in our usual hangout, then we would know others on the list." I might have come to that conclusion if my eyes hadn't glued to the one name I recognized right away: Annalee's.

"Let me talk to her. Talk to all of my sisters. We would have all been standing together maybe we can think of someone we all have in common."

After considering it for a while, my dad finally relents, and we file into the living room where we call a family meeting to order.

My four sisters each peek out of their room. Annalee hastily wipes the tear tracks from her face, holding up her chin in defiance.

Eze brings up the list of those injured from the riot and the previous list that is now deemed obsolete. We all bend over to see if we can find any commonalities.

Annalee shakes her head. "I don't know any of these people." She looks up to plea with her parents. "Can't we just not go to our usual hang out area? Leave early?"

There no possible way Annalee read all the names that quickly, but I understand her desperation. She probably has plans with friends tonight, a girl she likes will be there, and I'm sure she wants to flirt and be a teen while she still can. College is ever looming in her immediate future.

"What's Doug's surname?" my sister, Cassandra, asks. Her brows furrow, concentrating over the list.

Most of my family know people's first names, but not their last. Troll culture doesn't really pay much attention to family lines—it's more of an individual's accomplishments that are praised. Angel's pay attention to family ties, but it's considered rude to ask—it's assumed you would just know if someone were important or not. Why is social interaction among some cultures so complicated?

Piper, the next oldest after me, watches Annalee with some kind of silent communication between them. I nearly comment, but Annalee speaks up first.

"We can't miss Yule because some idiot is hells bent on creating drama," Annalee tries again when nobody answers her first complaint.

"It's more than drama at this point. People are going to get killed tonight. Note that your name is on the second list." Eze frowns at the list as he looks it over a few more times. "I know a few of these names." He points to a few toward the top listed. "They'll be at the First Fruits festival. Some city officials that open both ceremonies. And the stage is near the Yule log. We can start by questioning them."

"There are a lot of heated debates going on right now," my mother comments. "It stands to reason they're going to have some clues for the catalyst of the event."

I glance at Piper, but that expression she had before is gone. It's as if I imagined the exchange between her and Annalee.

"Send me both lists, and we'll keep checking it over for any names that might jog our memory," Dad says.

A tentative plan in place, Eze and I gather our things, but my father stops him as we're rushing out the door. "You won't leave her side. Understand?"

"Dad," I huff at how embarrassing it is to have my father doubt my ability to take care of myself.

Except Eze goes completely still and solemn, an expression he reserves for serious circumstances.

Come to think of it, this version of Eze has been more keyed up than the Eze I knew. The Eze who was my partner had been laid back. Chill. This Eze had yet to crack a smile.

He's attention zeros in on my father with laser focus. "I will not leave her. You have my word, sir."

Dad narrows his eyes at my ex-partner. "It's starting to make sense now."

Eze's expression morphs into confusion.

"You're the one Becker was talking about." My dad arches an eyebrow and straightens as if surprised, but then understanding dawns as his shoulders lower. "Oh." His gaze flicks to me and away as if he doesn't want to give away some secret.

I press my lips together, realizing there is some secret exchange that I've been somehow deemed unworthy of knowing. First Annalee and Piper and now Dad and Eze. "If this has to do with the case, I should be informed. I can't go in blind, with no—"

"It doesn't." They both respond. Quickly. Too Quickly.

"I wouldn't withhold important case information," Eze adds with more confidence, after a brief pause where he and my dad exchange a look. "But I *will* tell you." He glances at my father again. "Later."

My father nods, agreeing to whatever terms they seemed to have concluded in their silent negotiation. Now that Dad has sniffed him out…for whatever secret they're now holding.

My father runs through several more precautions for us to consider before I "Dad" him enough times with frustration and then we're sent on our way. Finally.

CHAPTER SIX

First Fruits is a celebration that happens in the later afternoon, and although it's just after lunch, we're somehow already late.

Eze and I chomp down a few Ghoul sandwiches from Banshee Bites in my car as he runs me through the plan. Since we're not listed as the main team on the case, we can't exactly demand an official's time—so we looked up the schedule and find a potential opportunity to chat with one of them in particular, at a booth. Re-election is coming up. Those serving on the council are canvasing full force this year. Frea

Cobweb, a Fae running on the more liberal ticket, is scheduled to be at her booth in the next ten minutes.

Lucky for us she's early and sitting with another candidate up for re-election, Mortimer Muckslinger. Both politicians sit close, facing each other, their eyebrows tight together as if discussing an important issue. Eze and I walk up together, waiting to be acknowledged.

Frea glances up, noticing Eze—which is understandable. He's a big guy. Muscles. Tall. A presence that is gentle, yet commands attention. Some would call it charisma. I just call it Eze. There is nobody else in the world like him. And he was my partner. Working with him again these last few hours will only make my Eze-yearning ten times worse when I need to inevitably say goodbye to him again. He will slink off into his office desk job, and I'll go back to fighting crime on the streets.

A sinking fear hits me. Could that secret he and Dad were referring to have to do with Eze finding out I sliped into romantic feelings for him? He'd mentioned having a few tricks when he sniffed out my neighbor, Benj's, attraction. Oh boy, I'm going to need to head that one off if it's true. He's got to know I'd never act on them and make it difficult for him. Or had I already in some way? Is that what pushed him away. Ugh.

Mortimer and Frea twist their bodies to acknowledge Eze, waiting for him to address them. No one thinks I have enough presence to wait for me to address them. Typical.

With a look I let him know that I think he'll handle these two on his own. He nods, agreeing. I slide off to give him space to work his investigative magic, except a gesture from him indicates he doesn't want me to go too far. Ah, that's right. His promise to my father.

So, I pull up the two lists of injuries from tonight's riot and compare. One extra name popping out this time that I'd scanned over before. *Alan Morris.* My current partner. Ah, crap. How did I not notice his name before? It must be that, like his advances, I am always in reject mode with him. With a sigh, I pull out my phone to check in with my annoying sidekick.

Morris answers on the first ring. "Why Lipski, I didn't know you cared. Calling to confirm our dinner plans? Perhaps a mistletoe interlude?"

"We don't have dinner plans, Morris."

He sucks in a dramatic breath as if I've pierced his heart.

I'm firm. I won't apologize for that. No way am I ever going to leave any wiggle room for him to sneak in and believe he has a chance. "I'm calling to ask you a few questions about the Yule festival tonight."

"Yeah, injury list. Bummer, right?" There's a muffled crumpling on the other end of the line like he's eating something while talking to me. "A group of us on the injury list were going to buck orders and hang around the event site. When those fuckers decide to riot we'll be there to put. Them. Down. You know what I mean, Gigi?"

"It's Grayson or Officer Lipski." But I wonder exactly how he knows the nickname my little sisters call me. As a baby, Cassandra couldn't pronounce Grayson and called me Gigi. It stuck. I'm going to interrogate my siblings until I find the leak.

I turn back to the issue at hand. "I really suggest that now that you've been tagged on both lists so far that you steer clear tonight."

"Disagree," he says as though he wouldn't give my suggestion any merit or thought. "The riot is bigger than the first prediction. They made it worse by benching us. Way I see it, they need us. More manpower we have at ground zero, the more likely to snuff out any disobedience."

"Unless we can prevent it," I say and then bite my lip. I don't want to invite Morris in on what Eze and I are working on. Partly because if it gets too big then it might be hard to manage, and also because I want to keep Eze to myself—I mean, I don't want anyone else to get credit for this investigation. If we succeed, this will look great on both our records. Morris, the attention hog, will demand more credit than he's due, like he does with all our big breaks since I've been partnered with him. Since we're both cop's kids we get lumped together more than I'd like.

"Prevention? Naw, this thing is bigger than that now. They've shipped that sail…or drove that bus? Whatever. I say we hit this civil discourse with some Angel's Peak Police Department power. You in?"

"I don't think so," I say and decide I'm not going to get through to Morris. I called him out of obligation. He *is* my partner, and I didn't want to see him hurt. Who knows what kind of idiot they'd pair me

with next. My choices are limited to the new hires. Or is it that nobody measures up to Eze? The idea I'll never have it that good again causes my heart to ache as I watch him lean into the conversation with the politicians.

"…so is that a yes?" Morris asks, still talking, even though I've mentally left this conversation before it started.

"Uh, no. I'm sorry…what?"

Morris sniffs into the receiver. "I was asking for what info you got. Sounds like you're on to something there. A little freelance investigating? Maybe I want in on your little adventure. I'll keep it between us. Partner privileges and all."

"I don't have anything," I say as firmly as I can. Aside from all the complicated feelings welling up inside me concerning Eze, Morris gets too drunk in his off-time to really trust him. Even if we did decide to let in one other officer on our case, it wouldn't be Morris. He's probably drunk as Bacchus when he gets injured tonight. That's likely the biggest reason he's on that list twice.

Eze ends his conversation, saunters toward me, going slow, noticing I'm on the phone. He's always been a gentleman and keeps his distance even though like me he can hear a little better than a human can. Unlike my dad and Becker, Eze and I always followed usual etiquette, pretending neither of us has any special ability. We did capitalize on our strengths as a team though. Just to the outward world we appeared not to. I don't know why we bothered. It's as though we grasped at one thing that kept the professionalism of our pairing intact.

"I gotta go, Morris." I quickly hang up before he starts talking again and then can guilt me later for cutting him off.

My gaze meets Eze's as he arches an eyebrow, as if in question. I answer, "Morris is on the list twice. He's my partner so I thought I'd try…" I trail off, shrugging.

He nods, clearing his throat. "Gotta take care of your second." Then his eyes lower to where his hands are awkwardly rubbing at his pants. Yeah, he must have realized his mistake right as the words fell from his mouth. When he left me partnerless, he wasn't taking good care of me then.

I'd pushed my surgery up to sooner than I needed because I couldn't stand shifts without Eze anymore. The surgery pushed that pain off a little longer.

"Grayson…" Eze tries. He swallows. He rubs his palms along his sides.

"What did the council members say?" I interrupt the apology I know was coming and I'm not sure I'm ready for. Did I really want to know why he left me?

He squints as if acknowledging my change of subject, but not letting me get away with it. "Okay, but we do need to talk about us."

The way he says us causes a shiver along my spine and settles in my gut. "Business first." My voice cracks at the request.

Eze motions for me to follow him through the festival. We head in the direction I know we'll find his family, walking slowly. "After speaking to the two members, I think I have one theory over the initial catalyst to the fight breaking out. It appears a major debate took place earlier this morning and one member left in a tizzy along with all his followers. LaDonna Merry wants to tighten magic laws within the city limits. Her platform is claiming it will make the streets safer."

"We have a high magic user population. That's not going to fly for a lot of people, even if it is needed."

Eze taps his nose.

I frown. "So now we have a catalyst."

"A probable catalyst," he corrects me.

"Okay, sure." I text my dad and Becker to let them know this new development. "It's one of her followers and not her. If it were her personally that instigated a riot, she would have received a specific forecast warning."

"Or it's a magic user, and they dampened their intent to cause harm so an oracle couldn't forecast their plans."

He inclines his head. "Also likely."

"We need to track down LaDonna Merry and see if she has any other insight. If she's concerned about safety in the city, then she's going to hate the idea that her debate sparked so much controversy that it caused a riot."

"Let's hope she's concerned. If the schedule is to be believed, we only need to wait here for another half hour and she'll show for a speech after the fertility god presentation." Eze guides me to an alcove, and through the clearing I see his family laughing and talking with each other. His nieces are running around with streamers of ribbon and twig crowns woven in their hair. The love surrounding them is evident. No wonder Eze spends all his free time with them. When we'd spent time with them early in our cadet days, I felt as though I got a peek into their warmth and wanted to be a part of it in a way that meant we'd have to have been more than work partners.

My stomach flips at the memories, and as if Eze can read my thoughts he puts his hands out to keep us from joining them just yet.

For a moment I'm worried he's about to tell me I'm not welcome into his family gathering, and my gut switches from flipping to falling. He must know how I feel about him.

But instead, Eze's gaze finds mine, and he looks guilty, ashamed.

"I have to tell you something. Something I promised I would tell you."

Here it is. The *thing* everyone has been dancing around. Becker seems to know. Now my father too. And now I'm allowed to know the information. It scares and terrifies me—because I know by his face that this is a secret that will change us forever. Permanently. Not just a break like the one we had when he changed careers, but a final chapter that will explain the entire saga.

Eze glances at his family happily enjoying themselves. "They know," he says, as if this is part of the explanation.

But then I realize, it kinda is. Eze wouldn't keep secrets from them. Jackals are not as wily as people assume them to be. With their family and friends, they are loyal and trustworthy. But enemies? Beware. So whatever he's about to tell me means he must have to share it, if he's inviting me into his inner circle again.

"After your surgery a prediction came in. A breaking and entering," he says and takes a deep breath as if that is finally off his chest. "Okay, well…yeah." He dusts himself off as if ready to join the festival now.

I furrow my brow, confused. This isn't the life-altering secret I'd been expecting. I snatch the back of his jacket to keep him from running off. "Whoa. Hold up there. What do you mean? I never got a prediction."

He swallows and nods as if, right, sure, he should give me a little more information. "You implied I never protected you after we weren't partners anymore. That's not true. I took care of it."

"You…took care of it," I say each word slowly, attempting to make sense of what he's said.

He nods, grabbing my hand. "There wasn't a breaking and entering, right? Taken care of."

"But I didn't know about it. I wasn't alerted. I was in danger, sitting at home curled into a blanket, eating cheese puffs and weepy about my wings…" I squeeze my eyes shut at revealing the emotional memories from those nights after the wing removal surgery. More so emotional because Eze had abandoned me during a time I thought he'd be there to support me. "So it didn't happen? How? What did you do?" My eyes widen. "Oh my gods. Did Becker hurt someone?"

Becker totally hurt someone.

He frowns. "No. And why would you think it would be Becker maiming on your behalf."

When he says it, I realize—"Oh shit. You hurt someone?"

He sighs. "Nobody died." Eze rubs his hand down his face and peeks through his fingers. "I might have taken the prediction instead of filing the report. I might have stayed up all night outside your apartment to catch the assailant. I might have been caught by Becker doing all these things. He might have let me off without an infraction."

I hold back a laugh. Not because I disbelieve the events but because, well, it is hard to believe parts of the story. "How did Becker know to find you?"

He glances down. "I don't know." But the tone of his voice reveals that he did know. "The important thing was that there wasn't a break in on your apartment."

"You and Becker caught the assailant?"

"We, uh, more likely lowered the probability by scaring away anyone planning an attempt."

I let that sink in, the fact my ex-partner had my back when I thought he'd abandoned me. I'd been hard on Eze, and now I felt the guilt of the anger I'd had directed toward him for the last several months. I take a deep breath, knowing it needs to be said. "Eze, I'm really sorry. I've been so hard on you today…"

He shakes his head. "Stop. Don't."

I put my hand on his arm to keep him from interrupting my apology. His gaze narrows on where our skin touches. His expression shifts to something else. Something more recognizable. Heat.

His eyes flick up, and then all that simmer is focused on me.

"Oh." My brain demands that I take my hand away as if I've touched a burning stove, but my heart—it's always known what it wanted—won't let me.

Our bodies lean into each other as if pulled by some force beyond both of us. If I'm honest with myself, these moments happened during our shifts, and we'd play it off as nothing to each other. Deep down I knew. I knew what we were playing at. And I thought Eze had been oblivious to it.

I was wrong.

His body is now a hair's distance from mine. His head tipping and tilting to accommodate the right angle for something that would have been forbidden if we were still working together.

"Uncle Eze!" The squeal interrupts us both.

We jerk back on to our respective sides of the alleyway, nervously fixing clothing and contemplating our life choices.

"Hey, Q," Eze says and crouches down with open arms in time to catch his running niece. He flings her into the air.

Quara hugs her uncle as if she's not seen him for ages, rather than the few hours it's likely been. Eze's family all live together in an old Victorian that's been converted into separate apartments for each family. It's a lot like Becker's new pack set up—common for shifters.

Quara places a hand on either side of Eze's face. "Your scratches are back." The three-year-old furrows her brow in concern.

Eze smiles wide. "I didn't get a chance to do my second shave." He thrusts forward and rubs his cheeks on the girl's upper arm.

She giggles in delight. Eze's sister, Margo, trots over to us. "Quara, I told you to wait by the float. The parade is about to start."

"But mama—Uncle Eze!" She points at her favorite uncle with apparent disbelief that he could bring her any trouble.

"Sorry I'm late," Eze says as he sets the toddler down.

His other niece, Amara, joins them, straightening her glasses and waiting patiently by her mother's side.

"Well, there's still time. Lot's to do. We have a few more flowers to pin, and the officials keep threatening to pull us from the lineup or force us to roll out half-finished." His sister walks as she talks, and we have no choice but to follow.

A basket of flowers is thrust into my arms, and I'm put to work.

CHAPTER SEVEN

A few minutes and a successfully decorated deity later, Eze and I climb off the float only be pulled back up again by Margo.

"No you don't! You helped, it means you take part in the glory." She leaned in closer so only Eze and I could hear her. "Don't leave me alone with Mom and Dad. They have to stop and talk with *everyone*. Seriously, how many *good* friends do we really have? At my last count, the entire neighborhood."

"We really can't," I say to let her down easy. "We've got this investigation going on, and we're trying to catch a person of interest before they leave the festival."

Margo's shoulders drop. "Oh, all right."

Eze looks distraught over the disappointment. "I'm sorry, I was late. That left all the work to you. You are really the better sibling." He's not buttering her up. Eze is nothing if not genuine when it comes to loving his family and being a productive member of it.

I interject a solution. "You took point on the last interview. I can do this one on my own."

"I shouldn't leave you," Eze says.

Margo's eyes widen. "No. I didn't mean to split you guys. It's so good to see you again, Grayson. You and Eze together, yeah?" She nods enthusiastically, then seems to realize she's cheering a little too hard for our partnership and what that support must look like. "I mean for your *friendship*. It's great for that. I always thought you guys would make great… *friends*." She smacks her hand to her forehead. "I'm going to go count the roses on Luamerava's chest."

She takes off from the awkward conversation. Lucky.

"I can call Becker," I say, continuing our discussion.

He shakes his head. "You know…" He pauses in thought. "If we ride the float to the end of the parade, we'll be the first to arrive at the city center and can be right at the edge of the stage for the speech, catching LaDonna as she's leaving rather than right before she goes up."

Okay, that makes logistic sense. "But we don't have a lot of time to spare. We should narrow down who and what we can before the event occurs. If she has insight into who might cause the riot, then we'll have more of a chance to prevent it if we have the name sooner."

"True, but I'm not allowed to leave you unattended. Becker won't be able to get here through traffic, which is a nightmare about now." He runs his thumb over his bottom lip.

It's a little distracting considering a few moments ago I would have had a chance to kiss that mouth had we not been interrupted. So, it must be the insanity of hormones that cause me to backpedal. "You know, maybe we do it your way."

Plus, a person is running around the city who had plans to break and enter my home while I was laid up after surgery. Sure, these occurrences are usually random, and the person likely had no preference whose home he or she was breaking into, but the idea that it was fated to happen leaves me unsettled. The violation felt is no less real even though it never happened.

Being with Eze is safe. His presence warms me.

And that's how I ended up on a First Fruits Festival float waving to the crowd.

CHAPTER EIGHT

The speech is thankfully short and being able to watch it makes it easier for Eze and me to gauge the reactions from the crowd. LaDonna Merry hammers home her ideas to shut down several magic establishments and tighten laws and loopholes that allow unsavory magic users certain freedoms, yet will leave white magic—magic in the use of good—untouched.

"Extremist!" someone shouts from the crowd.

"Hate speech!" another cries.

As pro-magic myself, I was a bit worried after finding out her stance, but hearing her speak it doesn't sound at all extreme. In fact, they are laws we've needed to look at for a long while.

"Can we get an ID on the hecklers?" I lean over to whisper to Eze.

He's already got his tablet up and sending out requests to any officer on duty in the area to pull those protesters aside for questioning.

I ease back into the railing we're leaning against, waiting for the speech to end. The plan, according to her security detail, is that she will exit the stage in our direction and we've been given permission to intercept her and pull her aside for questioning.

Which happens right about…*now.*

LaDonna exits the stage to lackluster applause and booing, yet holds her head high. She hasn't said anything too radical, but I have a guess as to why she's getting the reaction she is. LaDonna is a member of the magic user community as a bruja. As she explained in her speech, she comes from a long line of Latina women who practiced alchemy. Once a huge figure in the education of magic to the public— giving it a positive face. Now, some see her stance as a turncoat. Others claim she's gone off the deep end. They wouldn't be as harsh if it were coming from a Druid, or another line of historically powerful magic users rather than a mere bruja—even though they've been proven to hold equal power when tested.

Either way, she's startled to see both Eze and me at the foot of the stairs and glances to her security as if reaching for a safety net. I realize we're out of uniform—she's not to know we're police. Still, it's upsetting to see someone trying to do good be shaken. I know immediately she'll have something for us and nobody else has taken her seriously.

Eze steps back, well aware his larger stature will be viewed as looming rather than reassuring to this smaller woman. I greet her instead.

"Ms. Merry," I begin. "We wanted to speak with you about recent threats made against you." I show her my badge.

She takes a visible breath and follows us to a tent behind the stage. We settle in, and she gestures for us to sit.

"I will save you the time," she says. "Due to the heightened security for tonight's Yule celebration, we canceled our second speech. The debate this morning should have been my first clue that the atmosphere for reasonable discussion tonight wouldn't be possible."

"You canceled it?" I check the schedule, but her name remains as one of the speakers tonight for a second debate with the other council candidates.

"Right after the first prediction reports," she clarifies, explaining why she doesn't appear on the second report as an injury.

Eze frowns. "The reports escalated—"

She sighs. "I thought by removing myself it would lessen the impact of the riot and maybe some of those protestors would leave knowing I wouldn't be there, but that doesn't seem to be the case." She presses her fingers to her temple as if staving off a headache there.

"Any protestors in particular?" I ask.

The expression on her face tells us she has a few names in mind. "Get a pen and paper ready."

CHAPTER NINE

It takes us a few hours, in several interrogation rooms to keep the suspects separate and unable to collude on their responses, but we're able to pull in all the suspects between Becker, my dad, plus Eze and me. Through the process, we find out a few potential rioters are hard reads. Not quite fateless, meaning the oracles can't predict their futures or forecasts, but that it's extremely difficult and their forecasts come sparingly. It explains why our culprits went unnamed in each prediction. On top of that, they'd been messing with some questionable fate-blocking spells. Reason enough to suspect they'd been planning a riot.

The clock strikes seven, the sky is black with flecks of stars, and it's right around when most families will be arriving at the Yule festivities. The first of the new oracle predictions arrive.

It's official. No more riot. Eze and I sigh in relief for narrowing down the threat before the event could occur. We bask in the glow of accomplishment. As a team? We still got it. High fives all around as the countdown begins to the time the event was fated to occur, but really the threat is now so low even Dad relents and allows Annalee and the rest of the Lipskis to attend Yule.

Eze pulls me aside at the station. We escape down a long corridor and into the stairwell. Yep, that stairwell. The one where we left things between us in shambles.

He takes both of my hands in his, and we face each other. Eze's gaze stays on me, and there is a long, meaningful pause. I think I know what's coming, but I want to prove I can be patient and wait for Eze to acknowledge my hopes.

"Grayson," he says. "I never ever intended to leave you. When we were partnered I admired you. In a lot of ways, you were the perfect partner as a cop. And then as time went on, I saw myself imagining more."

"I wish you'd said something." I squeeze his hands in mine.

His brow furrows. "And say what? I'd have risked our partnership, and it would have changed things between us. If you felt the same way, it would mean the end of us working together. You know the city has strict rules. We'd never see each other. I never expected you'd hate me for it and then I couldn't find a way to make it right. I messed it up and I feared messing it up more by explaining my motive."

It's true. Kate and Becker faced the same challenge, and they were only police liaison and actuary working on cases together in Accidental Death. With Becker now in Health they could work on a few cases that overlapped, but the two departments rarely interacted. Enough to keep H.R. at bay.

"You're right. Human Resources wouldn't allow us to remain partners." Truth is that if Eze had shared his feelings while we were still partners, it would have put us in a bind no matter if I returned those feelings or not. "But why did you do it all without asking me first? Kate and Becker came up with a solution together. You cut me out of that."

"You wanted to be on active duty. The fact you'd cut off body parts to do it was evidence enough how serious you were. I only wanted to be on active police duty because I'd be with you. It wasn't a question when I realized that. I'd wanted to tell you that day when I announced my transfer to becoming an investigative actuary, and I chickened out. I thought, maybe it had been a fluke. We were in close proximity for several years of our life. Working, sleeping, eating—everything together. You know how Jackals can be when they den."

I nodded. Jackals had pack tendencies like any other shifter. Just because their shifting was more based in magic, didn't make them any less animal in other areas. They created close bonds with family and with us spending a lot of time together, those emotions could be triggered. Confusing our relationship where he was concerned.

"So it's like a sisterly thing?" I lower my shoulders, trying to hide my disappointment and humiliation. In the alley, I'd really thought…

His eyes widen as he realizes my interpretation. "Oh no." He coughs and can't seem to meet my eyes for a moment. "I assure you there isn't anything sisterly about…*this*." He clears his throat a few times and analyzes me, as if trying to figure out the right words to convince me of what he means, but instead he pulls me close. I feel the evidence of his explanation by the very un-sisterly hardness between his hips as he presses into me.

My gaze flies to his. Jackals aren't exactly wordy, but they're not usually so bold either. At least Eze isn't.

"Distance didn't make anything I felt for you go away. It made it a lot worse. I'd been really good at keeping you from noticing me coming up with excuses to be near you. I volunteered to bring the health reports upstairs to the station each morning if I knew you were on shift. Morales knew and would tip me off to your schedule. I'd been working up the nerve to the right icebreaker, but you hated me."

I cringe. "Oh gods. I was so angry. But it's because I felt the same way about you and I couldn't admit it…why it hurt so much for you to leave." The words hurt as they come tumbling out of my throat. The memory of the pain the separation had caused. "I had no idea you would ever see me that way, so I guess I assumed our work partnership was all I would get and that had to satisfy me." I'm breathing faster, my heart beating to a quicker tempo.

"It didn't satisfy *me*." And then he does it, his lips crush to mine as if he can't wait any longer.

My mind is in shock, but my body gets on board with the plan much quicker as my temperature heats. He slows, and our lips play and explore and tempt. My hands can't help but explore his muscular back and arms. He vibrates as if straining to keep himself held back. We'll have to work on that. I'm an angel, but I'm also a troll-gremlin, and none of those heritages are made of glass.

I pull back slightly, but only enough to break contact for a second to suggest: "We should be there. As much as I'd like to keep following this thing with us to a logical conclusion—and we will—we also have a case that's left partially open until the event time passes. Let's officially see our best case through." I lay my head on his chest, wishing that we could speed up to that time. I want to be with him, but I know both of us too well; we'll be antsy until this thing is fully done. Or more accurately: we can't go to bed until this case is put to bed. Wink, wink.

He sighs. "Yeah, you're right." He brings my hand up to his lips and leaves a soft kiss on my knuckles. "Grayson Lipski, may I have the honor of being your Yuletide date?"

"I'd be honored," I say.

We both leave the stairwell, *our stairwell*, and head for the elevators.

"We just need to stop by Health for a final report—"

My phone buzzes with incoming text messages. I turn the screen to show Eze my excited family heading to their usual Yule hangout. *See you soon*, the texts say.

My dad bursts through the station doors. "There you both are. We can't miss the celebration. All your hard work and you can't miss Yule!"

My dad slings his arm around me, and I'm as good as kidnapped for the evening.

"Tell you what," Eze says, calling out to me as my dad sweeps me into the elevator, too elated and happy to realize what he's interrupted—or maybe he knows and wants to torture us. "I'll meet you there."

I barely get out my affirmative when the doors ding closed on us.

CHAPTER TEN

"Look at this one." Annalee points at the children's drawings from the yearly contest lining the streets. "This one is the best," she proclaims.

I read each one as we pass with a dopey smile on my face, wondering how long Eze will be.

Yule is fireworks.
Yule is cotton candy.
Yule is a warm hug.

My sister, Piper, and I walk along the alley leading up to our family's "spot"—our area near the bar booths where we've all congregated for years. Everyone knows that *that* is the Lipski's bench. Other cops come to chat for a bit. My mother's cousins will often flirt with the new recruits. A tradition I rolled my eyes at until they did it to Eze and then I took a stance at how humiliating it had become now that they were "older." But angels are graced with great skin that seemingly slows the aging process. My mom, at nearly fifty, could still pass as mid-twenties. And, yeah, I get the "is that your sister" comments constantly.

The bench is in sight, and Annalee and Piper grab my arm at the same time, preventing me from our usual hangout.

"Mom and Dad's anniversary," Annalee says as if that's explanation enough.

"Oh, shoot." I smack my hand to my forehead. "You'd asked me to reserve the hall. I'll do it on Monday. Everyone is closed for the holidays anyway."

"That's not all," Piper says and twists her fingers together while biting her lip. "Annalee has something else."

Annalee's eyes grow big as if she's been thrown to the wolves. "Piper, you promised! It had nothing to do with the riot anyway."

"I promised not to tell dad. Grayson should know. She'll help you without going batshit." Piper pins me with a look as if I better not make a liar out of her.

"Know what?" I grab each of their hands. "Come on. We're sisters. No secrets." An old chant we used to employ when we knew one of us needed a shoulder without judgment.

"It's…Morris." Annalee says, and all her air comes out in a rush as if it took a lot of effort to admit it. Her cheeks grow pink instantly.

I frown. "Morris?"

She nods and wipes a tear from her eye before it can threaten to fall. "He caught me…" She glances at Piper as if reaching for support.

"It's okay, Annalee," I tell her. "Did he catch you doing something you think I'd be disappointed to know about?"

She shakes her head. "It was a kiss. Just one."

"Whoa, with Morris?" I'll kill him.

"No. No. No. No." Piper gripes my arm as if I'm in danger of running off. "Don't get the wrong idea here. Well, sort of. I mean, Annalee was kissing Razeala Armitage. Morris witnessed it and has been lording it over her."

"That's not very nice of him," I say and vow to remain patient while they explain the details. "So he's blackmailing you? To who? Mom and Dad wouldn't—"

"They didn't. I told dad right away, thinking it would take away his ammo, right? So Dad gave me the whole embarrassing safe sex condom talk. Again. Even though we won't even need a condom. I like girls!"

We all cringe. Dad's condom talk is infamous. He and mom have a slide presentation. Slide. Presentation.

"Then I told Morris," Annalee says. "But he says I owe him a mistletoe dance tonight. He's making it out like a joke every time I get insistent that it's inappropriate, but…"

"It's gross," Piper says, finishing our younger sister's sentence.

It *is* gross. Infuriating. Disgusting. I cross my arms and glare into the crowd, and as if I've materialized Morris into existence, there he is, standing by the bar and eyeing out family bench as if he's waiting for us.

"Ladies, thank you for letting me in on how much of a jerk my partner has been. We'll file a report against him."

"A report?" Annalee gasps. "I don't want to get a cop in trouble. They're so needed on the force to keep our town safe."

Piper squirms looking equally uncomfortable.

"He's been inappropriate with me too. I'll start by telling him to stop and then I'll file for a different partner. It's the only way to distance him from me and, by extension, our family. But I can't do any of that without a report. He needs to learn these jokes are unacceptable."

Both girls, looking grim, realize it's their only course too. They tried cutting off his blackmail attempts, and it didn't work. They tried telling him to stop, and he didn't listen. He'd gotten plenty of warnings.

I hook my arms with both of my sister's, and together we provide a united front to march to our usual family bench.

Except Morris cut us off before we could make it the final hundred yards. How did he get to us so fast? I shouldn't have taken my eyes off him.

"Did you angel's fall from heaven to grace this Yuletide?" He sips his beer with a leering gaze over his rim.

"Morris." I sigh. "Annalee said you've been demanding she, well, do things that are illegal considering her age." I decide to clean it up in case anyone is hitting the eavesdropping potions a little hard tonight. "This is going to stop. I'm never going to date you. None of my sisters is going to date you."

He makes a face. "I was joking. Yesh, Lipski, lighten up."

"We can't be partners anymore—"

He grabs the front of my shirt, jerking me from my sister's arms, but we're all connected. A strong, unified front, so they pull forward with me. Annalee falls, going down hard on her knee.

"You asshole." I shove him back hard.

Piper bends to pick up our sister. We're still out of view from most of the crowd.

Realizing this, I tell her, "Go get Dad."

She nods and makes like she's going to run, but Morris holds out a hex bag. "I wouldn't do that."

Piper snorts. "We're gremlin-trolls. Magic is useless against us."

"Not this magic," Morris assures her. "I searched high and low to find a hex that would penetrate through that magic resistance your family likes to lord over everyone else." Morris is gremlin too, but it's really the gremlin-troll combo that makes us unique.

"We don't lord it. It's in our DNA," Annalee says and dusts herself off. She limps to Piper.

Morris ignores them. "It's Bogwood and cinnamon of all things. Plus a few chants that have proven successful. A little surprise in the Book of the Dead."

I shiver at the mention of the book Ali had spent a considerable amount of time destroying a while back. It took us a long time to figure out the secret, but copies of some spells had slipped through while she'd been tracking down the mystery.

"All right. What does it do?"

"It will help you loosen up, for one."

Okay, so, a date rape drug. Great.

"So, none of you are going anywhere until you hear me out. I'm really a nice guy, so I don't like it that you've made me go to extremes. You'll listen to my side."

A flicker in the shadows of the alley catches my attention. I glance back at Morris before he notices my attention has wavered. I gesture, "Go ahead," and move as if I'm attempting to join my sisters against the wall. Not a great fighting stance to be backed into a corner, but it will do for now.

A Jackal takes shape from the darkness.

Morris straightens as if preparing a speech he's memorized. "You come from a long line of cops, and even though your talents are mediocre, that status gives you a lot of respect."

Piper groans. "Seriously? You open with an insult?"

"I said she was respected. I'm from a long line of cops too, but I worked hard." He shrugs as if he's thought of something, a little consolation to give me. "Men are naturally stronger. I know I have to pull more of the weight and I accept that." He squeezes the hex bag. "And I have the hex. You don't argue with the person who has the strongest magic. Lesson one, if you decide to follow your dad and sister into this business."

I narrow my eyes at Morris. "That's not lesson one."

Eze's form becomes clearer as he approaches.

"Whatever," Morris says and crosses his arms. "I forgot the order, but strongest magic is in there."

"Lesson one is pretty important." I inch forward, keeping Morris's attention on me. Eze closes in on him from behind. "Lesson one. Always watch your back?"

"Ha! This is what I mean by you being mediocre. It's you always watch your *partner's* back."

"Oh, right," I concede and lunge forward, knocking my forehead into Morris, stunning him.

Eze bites his arm, causing him to drop the hex. Piper scampers to pick it up, using her scarf to preserve the prints.

A knee to the back: me to Morris. A slap in the face: Morris getting a move on me. A hair pull: Annalee on Morris from behind. Eze wraps a plastic tie around Morris's wrists, and it puts an immediate end to the struggle.

"Next time you preplan an ambush of the Lipski clan, never forget that their father has them all set up on alerts," Eze says, growing into Morris's ear. "I was kinda boggled how come, even after

the riot was prevented, you, Morris, were *still* on the injury list."

I'm breathing heavily as I push myself up from the ground and check on my sisters.

Eze takes a huge sniff of Morris. "And now that I'm finally up close enough, I can see why you bother me so much."

"Because I got Grayson after you discarded her?" Morris spits as he speaks.

Eze presses Morris's face into the pavement. "No, asshole, because it's your scent I smelled when I went to her apartment after her surgery. Were you planning a little delusional romantic breaking and entering?"

"You can't hold forecasts that never materialize against a criminal," Morris says, which isn't exactly a denial. It wouldn't be enough for a conviction, but I shake my head at how easily that will be used as enough information to shove him so hard off the force for reasons of instability, his body will flatten from the impact.

Dad rounds the corner at a full run, taking in the scene. Mom gathers Annalee and Piper into a hug and would sweep me up too except Eze is already there, holding me and checking me for scrapes.

"Gods, I thought it would be too late. When I checked the reports, I kicked myself for leaving you alone."

"But we'd prevented the riot. How were we to know my name and then Annalee's name appearing on the list were completely separate events from that bigger one?"

"A better actuary would have thought through all the scenarios." Eze's hold on me eases.

I don't let him pull away. "Don't say that. It was an honest mistake, and you *did* get here in time."

"And thank the gods for that." My dad slaps Eze on the back. "I knew you'd be the best investigator to break any case that involved Grayson." His eyes twinkle, and he looks back to me. "And I approve of this match," he says as if that's the one thing holding us back.

He gives us both one last back pound and then heads to my other sisters.

"There you go." I squeeze Eze close. "You know, Becker told me that there is a lot of strategic effort done by the criminal if they can force a prediction, a harmful one, to come to be. The prediction should mean we have the upper hand to prevent it. But, sometimes the same events keep replaying, and they prevent them over and over, and it's only once they can catch the culprits *in the act*, that's when they can finally bring them in, and they can serve time for their crimes. If you'd come in any sooner, Morris would still be my partner, and I'd be fighting him until he did something much worse and with more forethought the next time. Your timing was perfect."

Eze nods, seeming to see my point, his natural jackel protectiveness making it impossible for him to *like* the necessity of Morris attacking me, my family, before they could apprehend him.

I kiss his cheek. "And you know? Morris's idiocy aside, I couldn't think of a better way to spend my Yule."

Eze arches an eyebrow. "Because you got free reign on an important case?"

I pull him closer and drop to a tone only he can hear. I rub my nose against his in a gesture I've seen his sisters do with their Jackal husbands and Eze once told me was a sign of affection between mates. "No, the case was amazing, don't get me wrong. It was the best Yuletide and First Fruit ceremony because I got to spend them with you." Eze glances around to be sure my Mom and Dad are now away from the scene, tending to their other daughters, giving us some privacy. They approve of our mating, but I agree we don't want to share too much of our relationship too soon. Then he kisses me. No mistletoe needed.

USA Today *bestselling author and two-time RITA nominee Anthea's books have received starred reviews in* Library Journal *and* Publisher's Weekly, *and she has been named "one of new stars of historical romance" by* Booklist. *Make sure to pick up her full-length spicy historical romances, available online at all digital retailers. Anthea lives with her husband and daughter in sunny Southern California. In addition to writing historical romance, she plays the Irish fiddle and pens award-winning YA Urban Fantasy as Anthea Sharp.*

A COUNTESS FOR CHRISTMAS

by Anthea Lawson

November 6, 1814
Tarrick Hall, Suffolk

Dear Miss Cecilia Fairfax,

Do not be unduly alarmed, but I am writing on behalf of your brother, Marcus. He is well, but suffered a hunting accident that has left his eyesight temporarily damaged, and I have agreed to help him navigate his correspondence.

His first wish was to write to you, and assure you he is (mostly) unharmed. Although he believes your first impulse will be to rush to his side, he would urge most strongly that you remain at home, tending to your father. In addition, Marcus asks that you make no mention of his current infirmity, so as not to lay an additional burden upon the viscount so soon after the loss of your mother.

As the accident occurred here at my estate, I am taking every measure to provide for your brother and ensure he is receiving the best of medical care. The doctor is confident Marcus will regain his eyesight within the month.

Marcus would like to assure you he plans to return as usual to Wiltshire for the Christmas season. He sends his love and reminds you that you are "a willow in the wind."

Yours, etc.
Liam Cahill Barrett, 5th Earl of Tarrick

Cecilia Fairfax sank back into the tapestry-upholstered chair, the letter trembling slightly in her hand. A hunting accident? Oh, Marcus!

The fire burning in the parlor grate did little to ward off the chill creeping through her. She supposed she should be grateful her twin brother hadn't blown his foot off, or shot the Earl of Tarrick in the shoulder, but still—the timing was wretched.

Forcing her breathing to calm, Cecilia sat forward and re-read the letter, searching for clues to Marcus's true condition. The "mostly" was clearly the earl's addition, as her brother was known to always put things in the rosiest light possible.

"Mostly" unharmed. It was small comfort.

She had known, the previous week, that something had happened to Marcus, through that curious bond they shared as twins. On Tuesday afternoon, while sitting with Father, her eyes had suddenly stung and burned, and her heart thumped like an enormous drum, tuned so tightly the next beat might make it burst. She had gasped aloud, and Father had asked what was the matter.

She'd made a vague reply, and the episode passed, but anxiety for Marcus had lodged like an iron splinter in her chest.

And now she knew.

The splinter still ached and pricked, however. She *did* want to rush to his side—but he was right. Father was fragile, and there was no reasonable excuse she could make for leaving Wiltshire.

You are a willow in the wind. How she wished it were so, but ever since Mother's death—a slow, consuming illness that had claimed her life in early January—Cecilia had felt brittle. A sharp wind could snap her in half.

If she let it.

Cecilia refolded the letter into crisp lines. She was strong enough to carry on, despite her idiotic twin rendering himself blind. Despite Father's recurring cough that left him weak and irritable. Despite the approaching holiday season—drat Marcus for reminding her.

Last Christmas, Mother had been ill, and the holiday had passed with none of the spirit and gaiety that usually filled Wilton House. This year, she fully expected Christmas to be excruciating, especially as Father had decreed it was time to put off their mourning.

"Your mother would not have wanted to see us so dreary, all in black." He had patted her cheek. "The color makes you look terribly pale, my dear. No, we shall make an end of mourning and celebrate Christmas in her honor—with life and light and color, as befits her favorite season."

How could Cecilia deny him? For well over a year the house had been swathed in sadness. And so, she was determined to make the holidays everything her father wanted—despite the absence of the viscountess, who had filled their lives with warmth.

Ignoring the chasm of grief inside her, as she ignored it every day, Cecilia went to her writing desk to compose a reply.

November 12
Wilton House, Wiltshire

Dear Lord Tarrick,

Thank you for your letter. I am not pleased with my brother for his continual exploits, but most relieved to hear the injury is not permanent. In our family, tales of his near-fatalities are notorious. Please keep him away from any sharp corners and stairs—secure him to the bed if necessary, or perhaps a leash might be in order.

As soon as he is recovered enough to travel, inform him his presence at home is greatly desired. Do keep me informed as to his wellbeing.

And thank you, sir, for tending to him. I commend your willingness to host what must be a demanding houseguest. Remind him that he is a stone in the sea.

We are in your debt.

Very sincerely yours,
Cecilia Fairfax

"A stone in the sea?" Liam Barrett glanced over the top of the page to where his reluctant guest, Marcus, lay on the bed, a bandage over his eyes.

The guest suite where Marcus was installed was dim, on the doctor's orders. Floor-to-ceiling green drapes were drawn across the tall windows, and coals glowed redly on the hearth, lending heat but no light to the room. Liam had drawn a chair up directly beside the bed and lit the lamp on the bedside table. The warm yellow glow fell over the page, illuminating the firm curves of Cecilia Fairfax's writing.

Marcus smiled, though the expression was closer to a grimace. "No matter what trouble I'm in, I'll get washed back to shore eventually."

Liam scanned the letter again. There was a sharp humor to Cecilia Fairfax's words. He wasn't entirely certain if he liked the woman for it.

"Your sister is all kindness. A leash?"

"No doubt Cecy pictures me leaping about blindly without a care in the world." Marcus let out a low breath. "Despite what she says, I am not constantly risking my life."

"Only occasionally?" Liam lifted a brow. "Although we were but acquaintances at Oxford, I heard stories of your escapades."

Marcus flushed, his fair coloring showing his reaction clearly. No doubt he was glad of the linen laid across his face, so he would not to have to meet Liam's eyes.

"I was young then, as you know," Marcus said. "My mother insisted I enter school early, though perhaps I should have waited."

He was still young, to Liam's mind. Although Liam was two years his elder, it felt as though a decade gaped between them. Perhaps that was due to the burdens of the Earldom falling early on Liam's shoulders, while Marcus was a carefree younger son. Or perhaps because of the cheerful way the young man strode into whatever life offered, while Liam knew himself to be far more dour in nature.

"You may regale me with stories of your exploits later," Liam said, curiously interested to hear them; perhaps because he himself had led a rather staid life as a student. "Doctor Smith will be here shortly, and after his visit you may dictate more assurances to your sister."

❖

November 18
Tarrick Hall, Suffolk

Dear Miss Fairfax,

I am writing again at your brother's direction, to say that a leash will not be necessary. I have personally provided a cane for his perambulations about the house, and the stairs are well-guarded by attack lions. Rest assured no more accidents will befall Marcus while he is under my roof.

His recovery is proceeding apace, and the doctor is encouraged that he will be able to travel in two weeks' time.

Yours, etc.
Liam Barrett, Earl of Tarrick

Cecilia couldn't help smiling at the earl's letter, despite her ongoing concern for Marcus. Attack lions, indeed. The Earl of Tarrick was reputed to be a rather grim fellow, but his letter somewhat belied that reputation.

She absently stared at the mottled November sky through the parlor windows, trying to recall what she knew of the earl. There was some history of family tragedy, and the unfortunate fact of his Irish blood. Not only had his mother been Irish, but, horrifyingly, Catholic as well, according to the gossips. He did not spend much time about in Society.

The winter light shone weakly into the parlor, making the wallpaper seem more gray than peach. She held the letter up to the mullioned windows and studied the vigorous, looping handwriting. It was impossible to tell anything about the writer, other than he crossed his T's with a line a trifle too broad.

"Mistress?" Martha, one of the maids, stepped into the parlor. "Begging your pardon, but Mrs. Bess would like to speak with you concerning the draperies."

"Of course." Cecilia swallowed a sigh. "I must reply to a letter, but inform her I will be down shortly."

"Yes, mistress." Martha bobbed a quick curtsey and was gone as quickly as she had come.

She was one of the village girls, hired less than a year ago, and so full of darting energy that she made Cecilia feel a bit tattered around the edges.

Fingers chilled, she rose and pulled her shawl more tightly about her shoulders. The dark brown wool was unbecoming, but it was the warmest she had. This time of year, she was always cold—but a cup of tea would revive her, certainly. Enough to meet with Bess.

Dear Bess. She had been the housekeeper for as long as Cecilia could recall, and even then she had been old.

Mother's illness had taxed all of them. Father most of all, but Bess had suffered as well. Recently, she had taken to wandering in her attention, sometimes leaving crucial things undone. It was past time to provide her a proper retirement, but somehow Cecilia had been unable to bring herself to break the news to Bess that she was relieved of her longtime position as housekeeper to the Fairfaxes.

Soon, though. Once the household was out of mourning, and the holidays endured—*celebrated*, she amended—there would be time enough to restructure the running of Wilton House.

"Another letter from Wiltshire, my lord." The butler bowed before Liam's desk, then handed him the correspondence. The envelope, addressed in Cecilia Farfax's neatly swirling script, was smooth beneath Liam's fingers.

"Thank you, Hobbs. Please alert the cook to send luncheon up to Mr. Fairfax's room." Liam rose, glad enough to leave the estate business untended for a short while.

It was foolish, how such a small thing as a letter could become the brightest thing in his day. A letter that was not even written to him.

He did not like to think how empty his house would feel, once Marcus departed. It was not that Liam was lonely, exactly. But solitude was a heavy weight, and he had become accustomed, over the last handful of weeks, to having that weight lightened.

Marcus Fairfax was an unfailingly cheerful fellow, with an amazing number of stories. He had a witty way of spinning them out, the fire crackling cheerfully in his room, the warmth of brandy settling in Liam's stomach while the warmth of words settled in his mind. Marcus's tales of his times at Oxford were amusing, yet Liam found himself enjoying the stories of Marcus's childhood even more.

Perhaps it was because his own youth had been empty of siblings, and a mother, and the type of family home that Wilton House sounded to be. It was like peeping into a baker's shop and seeing the warm loaves, golden on the racks, when all one had ever eaten was stale, hard bread. Even though Liam had never tasted that life, he liked to hear that it existed outside the pages of treacley books written for children.

Though Marcus's claims that Wilton was haunted did strain credulity a bit—especially the stories where he and his sister had played hide-and-seek with the ghost of a young girl.

"She almost always won," Marcus told him. "The ghost, I mean."

"One would think."

"You don't believe me, but she exists. Or existed. She died from influenza in 1783, at the age of nine—it's in the family bible. Elizabeth Fairfax. Would have been my and Cecy's great-great aunt."

"How do you know it's her?" Despite his skepticism, Liam found himself interested.

"The clothing, mostly. She's not dressed as a serving girl—her skirts are wide and very old-fashioned. Besides, the Fairfaxes have lived at Wilton House for over two-hundred years. So even if she's not Lizzy, she's an ancestor."

Liam shook his head and, letter in hand, ascended the broad staircase. What a fanciful fellow his guest was.

He paused a moment to set his palm atop one of the carved marble lions standing guard at the top of the stairs. The stone was cool against his hand. So far, the statues had done their job, and Marcus had not tumbled down the stairs. Of course, the maids were happy to assist and accompany the cheerful young gentleman about the house whenever he tired of the confines of his rooms.

"Another letter," Liam said, striding into the suite where Marcus was currently housed.

The rooms were done up in deep green—a soothing color, if only Marcus had been able to see it.

"Cecilia is nothing if not punctual," Marcus said, glancing up from his seat by the fire. The linen bandage across his eyes gave him the look of a jaunty oracle. "Come, read it to me."

Liam joined him, settling into the second armchair pulled before the hearth. When he opened the letter, he smelled the distant memory of flowers.

November 24
Wilton House, Wiltshire

Dear Lord Tarrick,

I am relieved to hear of the lions guarding your stairs. Perhaps you could send one home with Marcus, as he could use such a pet to keep him out of harm's way—although I hesitate to think what such a beast would do for his reception in Society, once he returns to London.

Now, Marcus, I must tell you it has not yet snowed here, so you may give up any thoughts of pelting me with snowballs the moment you walk in the door, as is your wont. Besides, with your recent injury, I would be forced to aim for your chest and not your head, so it is just as well the season remains cold and clear.

In all seriousness, will you need any extra provision made for your care when you arrive? I am not entirely certain I trust the reports that your eyesight will be completely cured—and if such is the case, I implore you to strain Lord Tarrick's hospitality a bit longer, and do not undertake to travel until you are truly ready to do so.

Your loving sister,
Cecilia

Marcus leaned back, his face turned toward the fire.

"Will I be fit for travel, do you think?" For a moment his smile slipped, revealing the worry beneath.

"Doctor Smith is planning to remove the bandages tomorrow, is he not?" Liam asked.

"Well." Marcus leaned his chin on his fist. "I confess, I've peeked a time or two. I'm afraid my sight will not be miraculously restored overnight."

"Can you see anything at all?"

Guilt rose up like briars in Liam's throat. If he had blinded Marcus Fairfax, he owed the man a debt he could never repay.

As if sensing the direction of his thoughts, Marcus shook his head. "See here, Tarrick, guns misfire. It was my great misfortune to be behind the barrel of one at the time—but that is a risk a gentleman takes when shooting."

"It was my gun," Liam said. "I bear the responsibility."

"To answer your question—I can make out shapes. I can see the brightness of the fire, and lighter patches in the room that might be the windows. It is an improvement, certainly."

Liam crossed his arms. An improvement—but not a recovery.

"Your family has suffered some hardships recently, correct?" he asked.

"I do not remain here simply for your scintillating company," Marcus said. "My mother has been dead

nearly a year, and I am not certain Father is finding it worthwhile enough to stay on this mortal plane without her."

"He must have loved her very much." Liam couldn't imagine.

Marcus let out a sigh edged with sorrow. "She was the sun the entire household revolved around. They are struggling enough, without me casting another dark cloud upon their existence."

"Your sister seems well enough." Liam waved the letter, again catching the faint scent of flowers.

"Cecy puts on an admirable front." Marcus frowned. "A pity about the snow. She needs something to make her smile, especially now."

"Now?" Liam leaned forward.

"She is caring for Father, readying the house for the holidays, and carrying the secret of my injury. Too many burdens."

"You called her a willow in the wind." Liam could imagine her—a slender, pale thing like her brother, bowed down by the weight of her obligations.

Marcus nodded slowly. "I only hope she doesn't break."

❖

December 1
Tarrick Hall, Suffolk

Dear Cecy,

You will notice that Lord Tarrick is still serving as my secretary. I believe he missed his true calling in life—it's a pity he was born into the gentry. (Miss Fairfax, I cannot let such a slight upon the characters of secretaries pass. I assure you that, even were I not the Earl of Tarrick, I would make a poor secretary. Indeed, if you can decipher my writing, I commend you.)

Do not be alarmed, but the doctor has ordered me to wait another week until I travel. He fears the jouncing of a coach may disrupt the progress of my returning sight. And it is returning, have no fears on that account.

You have not written much of Father. Is everything well? Will our esteemed elder brother be joining us for the holidays, or will we be lucky enough to avoid his family this go-round?

Expect me to arrive by 20 December. The earl has kindly offered his coach to transport me to Wiltshire, so you see I'll be traveling in great comfort.

Until then I remain,

Your loving brother,
Marcus

(P.S. I must add that your brother's eyesight is slow to return. He is reluctant to speak of it and add to your burdens, but I do believe you'd be happier forewarned. T)

Cecilia smiled as she read the angular, dark writing. The earl's letters were not difficult to decipher—although she noticed his penmanship had declined slightly from the first, more formal missive he'd sent on her brother's behalf.

She tapped the letter thoughtfully against her lips. Was the Earl of Tarrick as dark and angular as his handwriting?

Oh, foolishness. She needed to be readying rooms for Marcus, and discussing meals with the cook, and making sure Mrs. Bess had not ordered the servants to hang all the washing outside to freeze, forgetting it was winter.

There was, too, the work to be done in preparation for her brother's visit. Edward and his fretful wife, Honoria, and their clamorous set of boys would be descending imminently—like a flock of harpies, Marcus was fond of saying. Cecilia did not, quite, agree. Honoria was not as strident as a harpy, though she did find fault with almost everything around her. And everyone. Poor Edward.

Still, receiving the earl's—or rather, Marcus's—letters, provided a welcome respite. A few stolen minutes where she could retire to the parlor, sink into the overstuffed wingback, and be *elsewhere* for a brief time.

Always too brief, however. Letting out a low breath, Cecilia went to her desk to compose a reply to the earl. She certainly had no time to spin fancies about a man she was likely never to meet.

A pang went through her as she pulled out a fresh sheet of paper. She would not receive another letter from Tarrick Hall, as Marcus would be departing there within the week. She was glad the earl had warned her that her brother's recovery was not as complete as he would have her believe. He seemed quite the gentleman, the Earl of Tarrick. Swallowing back something that tasted suspiciously of disappointment, Cecilia dipped her pen and began to write.

December 8
Wilton House

Dear Lord Tarrick,

I am not certain this letter will reach you before my brother's departure, so I shall not include exhortations for safe travel (which no doubt he will ignore in any case).

Again, thank you for caring for him whilst he recovered from his injuries, and for your frequent letters. And the guard lions, of course. Please give them a pat of gratitude from me—provided they do not bite your fingers off.

~~Perhaps some day we will have the good fortune to meet in London.~~

My brother and I are deeply in your debt.

Most gratefully,
Cecilia Fairfax

"There you are," Liam said, slipping the letter back into its envelope and nodding to Marcus, seated across from him. The cozy fire burning on the hearth belied the chill in Liam's bones. "Homeward bound at last. No doubt you'll be happy to shake the dust of Tarrick Hall from your feet."

How long would it be until another guest graced the set of rooms? Years? Liam crossed his arms, banishing the thought.

"You've been an excellent host." Marcus squinted happily at him. "In fact, I have a splendid idea."

"If it involves remaining here another few weeks, I can't say I agree. Your vision is improving daily, and you are wanted home for Christmas. Is your sister-in-law truly that dreadful, that you'd wish to remain here?" Liam glanced at the half-packed trunks lined up by the door of Marcus's room.

Marcus waved his hand in dismissal. "Cecy and I manage to prop one another up during Horrible Honoria's visits. No, I think you ought to come with me to Wiltshire for Christmas!" He grinned. "I'll be able to repay your hospitality, and you'll have a marvelous time."

"You expect me to believe that, after regaling me with tales of your sour relatives?" Liam tamped down the sudden surge of interest that ran warmly through his veins. "I am quite content here at Tarrick Hall, though I thank you for your offer."

He tried not to think of the empty hallways, the lack of greenery and holiday cheer. Did he not, every Christmas Eve, sit beside the fire and drink a fine glass of port? Did he not go for a long ramble about his estate, savoring his property, despite the winter's cold?

"Quite content?" Marcus let out a snort. "Let me guess. You give the servants a Christmas holiday and send them off, then sit alone beside the hearth in your study, eating cold ham. Perhaps indulging in a brandy or two."

"It is not a bad life." Liam lifted one shoulder in what was meant to be a shrug. "I'm happy enough."

He did not examine too closely the itch that had lodged beneath his ribs at the thought of going to Wiltshire with Marcus Fairfax. And meeting Miss Cecilia Fairfax.

"If you're happy here, then you're easily pleased, and my sister-in-law will prove no obstacle to your greater joy." Marcus reached forward and took him by the shoulder. "Do come, Tarrick. Or are you afraid of the ghost?"

"I take no alarm at the figments of a boy's overactive imagination."

"Lizzy's real," Marcus said, letting go of Liam's shoulder. "It would serve you right to meet her in the upper hallway. You must come to Wilton House, just for that comeuppance. Besides, I know Cecilia would like to meet you."

Liam had not read him that crossed-out line in Miss Fairfax's letter—the one about possibly meeting some day, that had made him stumble briefly in his narrative—but clearly her brother knew her well.

"I hardly think your sister would welcome the unexpected burden of my arrival."

"How often has she said we are in your debt?" Marcus raised a blond eyebrow. "She will be glad to repay it, I assure you. Besides, I am still not recovered enough to read, or count out my bills correctly.

What if the coachman takes a wrong turn? What if the innkeeper decides to take advantage of my infirmity? I need you, sir, to see me safely home."

"That's a patent lie."

"I wager it won't take you long to pack." Marcus leaned back, smiling. "You'll be ready to leave before I am."

"I'm not coming with you, Mr. Fairfax."

Cecilia sat at her desk, resolutely keeping herself from rereading the earl's—Marcus's—letters. Instead, she busied herself with making lists of all the tasks still looming, before the holidays at last came to a close. The maid, Martha, hurried into her sitting room—a welcome distraction.

"Mistress," Martha said, "the Earl of Tarrick's coach is coming up the drive."

"Indeed?" Cecilia rose from her desk and went to the window.

As the maid had said, a large black coach was approaching, the side emblazoned with the earl's coat of arms. Thank goodness. Having Marcus home would lift some of the weight pressing down upon her. And he had arrived just in time—Christmas was only a handful of days away.

Giving her hair a quick smooth, Cecilia hurried down the stairs. No need to change from her worn gray muslin. It was just Marcus, after all.

She arrived in the entryway as the butler opened the door.

Marcus strode in. "Cecy?" he called.

"Here," she said.

As soon as she spoke, he turned toward her, a wide smile on his face, and opened his arms.

She embraced him, then drew back, grasping his shoulders.

"You still can't see," she said.

"Why of course I—"

"Don't deny it." She gave him a little shake. Drat her brother, pretending he was well.

His smile faded. "I can see—but details are blurry. You blended with the shadows."

At least the earl had forewarned her. She sent a prayer of thanks to the man, wherever he might be.

"There's one more thing," her brother said. "I brought a guest for Christmas."

"What?" Sudden apprehension jolted through her, and her fingers tightened on his shoulders. "Who is with you?"

She knew the answer, however. Who else could it be?

"The Earl of Tarrick," her brother said. "You don't mind, do you?"

"I…"

"He's just outside. I'll go fetch him."

Her throat was dry, her nerves suddenly fluttering. A pox on her impulsive, generous brother. As if the holidays were not complicated enough.

Whirling, she rang for the maid, counting the seconds until the girl hurried up.

"Martha, we need another set of rooms made up immediately. Marcus has brought the Earl of Tarrick to stay for the holidays."

The maid's eyes went wide. "Of course, Mistress. The gold rooms?"

"Those will do very well. Make haste."

Martha bobbed a curtsy and hurried off.

Moments later, Marcus reappeared in the doorway, followed by his guest. The Earl of Tarrick was tall and solidly built. As she had imagined, he was dark and angular, with steely gray eyes set in a forbiddingly remote face. Judging from his expression, he rarely smiled.

He removed his hat, revealing hair as black as a raven's wing.

Marcus stepped forward. "Tarrick, allow me to present my sister, Miss Cecilia Fairfax. Cecy, this is Liam Barrett, the Earl of Tarrick."

"Miss Fairfax, the pleasure is mine." The earl made her a stiffly correct bow.

Judging by his appearance, she would have expected his voice to be rough and growly, but the earl's tone was surprisingly smooth—like a cup of warm chocolate.

Cecilia dipped a curtsey, wishing she were not wearing her drabbest gown. Would the earl mistake her for a shadow, as her brother had? No. Indeed, his gaze rested on her a trifle too long, and she felt heat rush into her cheeks. What dreadful stories had Marcus told about her?

"Lord Tarrick," she said. "Please, come into the parlor. Your rooms will be ready as soon as possible, given that I had no notice of your arrival."

She shot her brother a narrow-eyed glare. Surely Marcus could not see her expression, but he grinned back at her anyhow.

"My apologies for the unexpected visit," the earl said. "Your brother insisted."

Cecilia ushered them into the parlor, where a fire was burning merrily, thank heavens.

"Marcus is too persuasive for his own good," she said, wishing the earl had resisted. Well, half-wishing. "Make yourselves comfortable. I must see to the maids."

"Cecy, sit with us." Marcus made a grab for her hand, and missed. "Let Mrs. Bess arrange things."

"I cannot. Please excuse me." She nodded at the earl. "Marcus, offer our guest some brandy. It's on the sideboard."

"I'll pour," the earl said, an unexpected dry humor in his tone.

Cecilia shot him a glance, but his eyes were as cool as ever. Heart pounding in her chest, she hurried out of the room. Heavens, she had so much to arrange.

Liam watched Miss Fairfax leave the parlor, her step firm, her chin high. She was, as he'd suspected, as fair as her brother, with the same long, slim nose and smoky blue eyes. There, the similarities ended. Her brother was more sturdily built, while she was— yes, willowy was the word. Where Marcus was full of open humor about the world, his sister seemed much more contained, her expression guarded.

He glanced about the room, which seemed cheery and warm. No black draperies hung at the windows to signal the family's ongoing grief, yet Miss Fairfax had been wearing a markedly dreary gown.

"Is your family still in mourning?" Liam asked.

"No," Marcus said. "Father has declared we'll celebrate the holidays without that pall. Mother loved this season. I forgot to warn you—there will be singing. And a yule log, and greenery, and the best pudding you've ever tasted."

"It sounds splendid." And like no Christmas he'd ever known.

"Brandy?" Marcus gestured in the general direction of the sideboard. "When Cecy commands, we must obey."

Liam found the crystal decanter and poured them two glasses. He made a point of handing Marcus his brandy, not releasing it until he was certain his host had a firm grip.

"How will you keep your father from noticing your blindness?" Liam asked. He took a swallow of brandy, a bright fire warming the inside of his mouth.

"Father is…" Marcus threw back a swig of his own drink. "The last time I visited home, he was so overtaken by his own infirmity he would not notice anyone else's."

"What's the nature of his illness?"

"A broken heart, mostly, with gout and rheumatism complicating matters." A rare, pensive look crossed Marcus's face. "He's old, you know. Cecy and I were rather a surprise, coming a good fifteen years after Edward was born."

At least they had been loved—that much was clear. Liam drank his brandy and stared out the window. Bare branches etched a sky pearling into evening.

"Your brother and his family arrive soon?"

"Tomorrow or the next day. At which point, you and I shall go riding, and make many expeditions to gather boughs in the forest."

"Are evergreens that difficult to find in this part of Wiltshire?"

Marcus made a face. "No. The difficulty lies within the walls. Come, I'll introduce you to Father, and we'll see about settling you into your rooms."

Liam set his half-empty glass of brandy aside, and followed Marcus. Not for the first time, he wondered if coming here had been a mistake. Well, and he could always leave again. He'd delivered Marcus safely home, and met the pale, lovely Cecilia Fairfax. His escape was parked in the stables, should family interactions prove too difficult for his taste.

And what of Miss Fairfax? an errant voice inside him whispered. Has she any refuge at all? A coach to bear her away? The excuse of rambling about in the woods?

The uncomfortable answer was, no. There had been a shadow behind her eyes, a trapped look like that of a hare pursued by the shivering howls of wolves.

He suspected Cecilia Fairfax was running nearly as fast as she could, inside, where no one would ever see.

❖

"Begging your pardon, Mistress, but Martha said as how there was nest in the chimney of the gold bedroom. Well, there was, and now the carpets are sooty. And there's, er, a pair of swallows loose in the room."

"The laundry soap is wet through, completely ruined—how shall we wash all the linens in time for your elder brother's arrival tomorrow?"

"Mistress, cook says the partridges are all burnt on one side. So sorry—would half a bird each do for dinner?"

"Mrs. Bess has set herself to polishing the silver, and there's no forks fit to dine with. Please come!"

"Milady, the best bottle of claret has gone missing. Perhaps you might check your father's study?"

Cecilia paused inside the study, her fingers tight around the neck of the half-full claret bottle. Instead of opening the door and returning to the hallway, she leaned against it, resting her forehead against the slab of oak. If only she could keep all her troubles from reaching her, held at bay by the solid wooden door.

Dinner was going to be dreadful; all the mishaps of the afternoon compounded by the presence of the Earl of Tarrick. If it were only family, they could smile through their difficulties, but having a stranger in their midst made everything more difficult.

She could hear Martha calling for her. Taking a deep breath, Cecilia opened the door and stepped into the hallway. They would have to make the best of it, as ever.

As she had feared, dinner was a strained affair. The earl, seated on Father's right, watched everything with his cool gray eyes and said very little. Father had nipped too much of the claret and alternately pontificated at length about the joys of family and lapsed into long silences.

Marcus was his usual cheerful self, though he was using his utensils in an odd manner. Both knife and fork were engaged in poking and chasing bits of food around the china, and each successful mouthful was lifted carefully to his lips, with a few near-misses. Luckily, Father was too far gone to notice when a stray piece of turnip tumbled off Marcus's fork to lie forlornly on the white tablecloth.

"You have a charming home, sir," the earl said to Cecilia's father.

" 'Twas all my wife's doing. She had the touch, you know. Domesticity. Children about the knee." He peered from beneath his bushy white brows and scanned the table. "I say, where is Edward and his brood?"

"They arrive tomorrow," Cecilia said, doing her utmost to keep her voice even, though her heart pounded at the thought.

There was so very much to do.

Liam slept well enough, though it had been years since he'd slumbered on a mattress other than his own. The maid had come in that morning to rake up the coals, and a fresh fire burned merrily on the hearth. Before leaving the room, she informed him that breakfast would be laid out shortly in the morning room.

He rose to dress, for the first time regretting the lack of a valet. Not that he was incapable of donning his own clothing, but he was well aware he did not possess any elegant flair. He did not know the most fashionable ways of tying his cravat, he did not have anyone to pull his coat just so across his shoulders or keep his boots polished to a high shine.

Vanity. Liam shook his head, but still spent an extra moment in front of the mirror, tidying his sleep-rumpled hair. He leaned forward, trying to see his face as a stranger might.

His eyes were unremarkable. His jaw too wide, his cheeks too hollowed. His hair might hold a certain appeal—years ago a young lady had told him it was like black silk—but other than that, he had very little to recommend him.

With a sigh, he straightened and tugged his cravat back into place. Truly, he would be better off finding some excuse to leave. This moping about in front of mirrors was inexcusable.

The Fairfaxes kept country hours, for which he was thankful, being an early riser. The smell of eggs and bacon wafted down the hall, and he increased his strides. A true English breakfast would be a pleasurable change from his usual bowl of oatmeal. Of course, his servants would cook him bacon and eggs if he asked, but it was simpler to have a bowl of porridge each morning. Less trouble for everyone.

A strange noise reached his ears, and he paused. He did not think the household boasted any pets, yet a quiet mewling issued from a nearby passageway.

For a scant second, his skin prickled. Was it the fabled ghost of Wilton House?

Certainly not. It was the sound of a living creature in distress. Liam turned the corner and paused outside a small paneled door—a closet of some kind. By the sound of it, the creature had been prisoned within.

He turned the knob and gently opened the door a few inches. Light slanted into the small room, revealing shelves stacked high with linens.

"Here, now," he said softly. "Come out, kitten."

No sign of the creature. Liam pulled the door wide, then jumped back in surprise as the *ghost*—no, no, it was only Miss Fairfax—whirled to face him. He caught a glimpse of tear-wet cheeks and disheveled blonde hair before she turned her face from the light.

"Go away." Her voice wavered unsteadily.

"I beg your pardon," he said.

Gentlemanly courtesy demanded he shut the door and depart, never to mention the fact that he had found Cecilia Fairfax weeping inconsolably in the upstairs linen closet.

She sniffed, her hands balled in a pillowcase that had no doubt been muffling her sobs, and something within Liam gave way.

Instead of withdrawing, he stepped into the closet and shut the door behind him. The air smelled of lavender, and he heard Cecilia's skirts rustle in the dimness.

"Whatever are you—"

"Come here." He opened his arms.

She could not see him, he was certain of it, yet she stepped forward, just enough that he could touch her shoulders. She let out a shivering sob, and he folded her against him, murmuring hushing syllables from some long-forgotten time.

Her hands fastened on his coat and she clung there, crying, while he held her. In the close darkness they were not mere acquaintances, not earl and miss. No, they were elements of the world, meeting as inexorably as shadow and light. Greif and comfort. Loss, and love.

A strange, perfect contentment settled over Liam. He would stand there for centuries letting Cecilia

Fairfax drench his shoulder with her tears, if that was what she required of him.

At last, the storm of weeping abated. Cecilia's sobs turned to sniffles.

"Oh dear," she said, stepping back. "I must beg your pardon, Lord Tarrick. This is most—irregular."

Liam reluctantly let her go, the cloth of her sleeve wisping against his fingers. He supposed she was correct. Proper young ladies did not inhabit linen closets, weeping into the arms of unexpected guests. Still, he could not be sorry for the circumstance.

"Are you sufficiently recovered, Miss Fairfax?"

She drew in a breath, yet did not speak. Liam felt the gossamer touch of her fingertips across his cheek, so light he might have imagined it. But he had not. He held very still, the scent of linens and lavender suffusing his senses.

"Yes," she finally said. "Thank you."

He wished there was light enough for him to see her, so that he might take her hand and press a warm kiss across the back of it.

There was no good way to bid her farewell. He reached behind him, the knob cool beneath his fingers, and opened the door just wide enough to slip out into the hallway. She did not follow, and Liam gently closed the door behind him, wishing for something he could not name.

Cecilia scrubbed her face with the pillowcase, then inhaled, trying to catch a last hint of the earl's spicy scent. She'd been beyond shocked when he'd come into her hiding place, and for a panicked moment had thought he was going to press his advances upon her.

But no—he had offered his warm, broad shoulder for her to weep upon, without hesitation. Without questions.

And then he had left, and a treacherously large part of her wished he had not.

She cracked open the closet door. The hallway was empty—everyone no doubt gone down to breakfast. She could not face the earl across the table. Nor her brother, who though he might not see her red-rimmed eyes and tearstained face, would be able to hear the remnants of weeping in her voice.

Besides, there was too much to do, and her stomach tangled in knots again just thinking of it.

Clutching the crumpled pillowcase, Cecilia stole back to her room and the towering list of tasks awaiting her. She would have Martha bring her up some tea and toast, and spend the morning planning Christmas dinner, including provisions for the staff. And then Boxing Day, with father's usual gifts to the servants…

Three hours later, the butler interrupted her.

"Miss Fairfax, the Widow Pomfrey has come to call," he said.

Cecilia loosened her grip on her teacup. For a stark moment she thought Edward and his family had arrived, too early. But she welcomed the stout widow's company, enough to take a respite from her work.

"My dear girl," Widow Pomfrey said when Cecilia entered the parlor. "You look a bit pale. Come, tell me—how fares your family?"

She held out her hands. Cecilia took them and let the widow draw her over by the fire. Widow Pomfrey was the physical opposite of the late Lady Fairfax—small and plump, with merry dark eyes and a hardy constitution. Yet the two women had shared a warmth of spirit that had made them fast friends.

"Marcus is home now for Christmas," Cecilia said. "He is…well. Edward is expected later today."

"And your father?"

The widow's tone revealed nothing but kind interest, but Cecilia suspected the woman nurtured a fondness for Lord Fairfax. After Mother's death, Widow Pomfrey had been a frequent visitor, providing help and advice to Cecilia, and bringing the family her famous pies. Indeed, the widow's pies were one of the few things that could tempt Father into eating, those first dreadful months.

"Father is regaining his strength, and his cheer." It was only a small lie.

"I am most pleased to hear it." The widow smiled, her eyes crinkling almost closed in the roundness of her face.

On impulse, Cecilia squeezed her hands. "Come spend Christmas Eve with us."

"Oh, well, I…"

Was that a blush on Widow Pomfrey's cheeks? She had no children to spend the holiday with, no family nearby. Indeed, the more Cecilia contemplated the idea, the more it satisfied her. Marcus was not the only one who could invite guests, after all.

"Please, do come," Cecilia said. "It will save me from having to explain to Father why we must have inferior pies. We need you."

"In that case, I shall come. And bring mince, and apple. It will be lovely to see your entire family again."

"We also have another guest." Cecilia withdrew her hands from the widow's soft grasp. "The Earl of Tarrick is visiting. He's a friend of Marcus."

"Do tell." The widow's eyebrows rose, nearly to the edge of her lace cap. "Is he handsome?"

Now Cecilia feared it was her turn to blush—though perhaps the widow would attribute the flush on her cheeks to the warmth of the fire, instead of the thought of the earl's arms around her.

"I suppose he is," Cecilia said. "Though I haven't given the matter much thought."

My, she was becoming an accomplished liar. The instant Liam Barrett had stepped into the front entry, she had been struck by his appearance. And a bit intimidated—though his gray eyes and lack of smiles seemed less remote to her, now that she had sobbed upon his shoulder.

Perhaps he was not aloof, so much as shy? She blinked at the thought. Not everyone was as outgoing as Marcus. The earl's reserve was understandable. And beneath that cool exterior was a surprisingly kindhearted man.

"Have you any brighter gowns?" Widow Pomfrey asked, glancing at the dark blue wool Cecilia wore. It was clear the widow had inclinations toward matchmaking.

"I've only just met the earl," Cecilia said.

It was true—although it was *also* true she'd been corresponding with him for well over a month. Not that the widow needed more fuel for her fire.

"Something to bring out the color in your cheeks." Widow Pomfrey tilted her head.

Cecilia had a red gown—a beautiful satin one, edged in white. It had been made up, along with dozens of others, for the Season she was supposed to have had in London. Before Mother fell ill, and their plans for Cecilia's grand coming-out fell into ruin.

Swallowing past the sudden tears crowding her throat, she nodded. "I do have a red gown."

"Then you must wear it. You are a lovely young lady, Cecilia, and if the earl does not see as much, he must be a blind man."

Not as blind as Marcus, she hoped. Was her brother's eyesight ever going to fully recover? What would Father do, once he knew?

The widow must have seen the worry in her eyes, for she gave Cecilia another smile, and rose to her feet.

"I've kept you long enough, my dear. Do tender my regards to your father. And your brothers, of course."

Cecilia showed her to the door, then stood on the step as the Widow Pomfrey departed. The winter chill seeped into her bones. The sky was low, clouds promising snow. She only hoped it would bide another few days—until Edward and his family arrived, until the greenery had been collected from the woods. Tomorrow she must send Marcus out to gather boughs and holly.

As the afternoon wore on, Cecilia found it difficult to concentrate. Every noise had her jumping up to scan the drive for Edward's coach. She had checked and double-checked that his rooms were ready, that the fires were lit, the water for washing brought up—although none of it would be to Honoria's satisfaction.

Evening descended early, and still they had not arrived.

At dinner—another quiet affair—the butler approached the head of the table.

"I beg your pardon, my lord," he said to Cecilia's father, "but this message was just delivered by one of the village boys."

Fear darted through Cecilia. She had not wanted Edward to come, but she hoped no ill had befallen him or his family. Across the table, Marcus tensed. He set his fork down, the tines clinking against his plate.

"Read it, Father," he urged.

Their father unfolded the paper and read the note aloud.

Dearest Father,

I regret to inform you that my family will be unable to spend Christmas at Wilton House. The boys have fallen ill—nothing too dire, the doctor assures us, just an upset of the digestion that seems to be striking many in the neighborhood. Still we thought it best we not travel during this time.

"Thank goodness," Marcus said under his breath. "Can you imagine having the urchins here, spewing their dinner about?"

"Marcus!" Cecilia sent him a quelling glance.

In addition, we wanted to share the joyous news that Honoria is in a delicate condition—which, however, adds to the inadvisability of travel.

Our thoughts are with you and my siblings, and know that my family will be celebrating Christmas with you in spirit, if not in person.

Your respectful son,
Edward

Cecilia swayed back against her chair, relief deflating the tension that had filled her almost to bursting all day.

Edward and his family were not coming! She would not have to bear Honoria's sharp words when nothing met her impossibly high expectations, or run about after two wild and rambunctious boys, since Honoria refused to bring the nanny along yet pled a headache whenever her offspring needed tending. Best of all, Cecilia would not have to watch Edward silently endure his wife's scathing remarks, a trapped look tightening his features that she could do nothing to ease.

She closed her eyes in a silent prayer of thanks.

When she opened them again, she found the earl watching her from across the table. There was a sympathetic spark in his gray eyes, as if he could read her thoughts. She smiled at him, and for a moment thought he would smile in return.

Then Marcus knocked over his wineglass while groping for it, and the moment was broken, lost amidst the commotion of tidying up.

❖

Liam laid an armful of holly into the back of the wagon, ignoring the sharp pricks of the leaves. Despite his hat, his ears were tingling with cold. The sun remained hidden behind swirls of cloud, only occasionally peeping out to send a shaft of light through the bare winter woods.

"Well done," Marcus said, unloading his own burden of boughs. "That's more than enough to decorate all of Wiltshire in greenery. And look what I found."

He pointed to a balled mass of foliage growing on one of the branches.

"Your eyesight must be improving, to discover such a treasure," Liam said. "Er, what is it?"

Marcus clapped him on the back. "It's mistletoe, my good man! Full of berries to steal a kiss with."

"Ah." Liam knew of the tradition, of course, but to his recollection had never seen the plant, let alone put it to use.

"Is that your only response?" Marcus grinned. "My vision is clear enough to see how you and my sister nearly smile at one another, before you both recall yourselves."

Liam coughed—not an entirely feigned response. "I do beg your pardon."

"I won't forgive you."

"You won't?" Liam looked closely at Marcus. "Please understand, I have no designs upon your sister."

It was a small lie, but really, he couldn't confess to the man the growing warmth of feeling he had for Cecilia. No, it was not the done thing for a houseguest to suddenly fall in love with his host's sister.

His fingers closed hard around a sprig of holly, the thorned bite of it recalling him to his senses. In love? What an impossible notion.

Marcus had stopped smiling. "I see. That's a pity. Come, then—one more pile of boughs and we can return to the house."

They completed their task in silence, Liam turning over their conversation in his head like a handful of polished stones. Had Marcus been encouraging him, or simply trying to determine the lay of Liam's affections? Or had Marcus been warning him off in some oblique manner that he was too thick-skulled to fathom? How *did* the gentry go about these things?

Lord, he was thrice a fool. If he had any sense at all, he'd order his coach made ready and ride back to Tarrick Hall that very evening.

But somehow he could not bear the notion of jostling away in his empty, cold vehicle; away from the warmth of Wilton House, away from the holiday he had, curiously, come to anticipate. Away from a particular set of stormy blue eyes that hid a vulnerability he understood all too well.

Their return to the house was greeted with merry cries and the bustle of the servants bearing the greenery away. They would deck the hall later with swags of sweet-smelling boughs, and no doubt hang the kissing-ball of mistletoe someplace amusingly prominent. Perhaps at the center of the wide opening leading to the parlor.

"Come in," Cecilia said, her smile seeming to warm further as she turned it on him. "There's mulled cider. You must be chilled."

He was, but it was nothing a simple cup of cider could cure. No, it was the bleakness of the rest of his life, a windswept plain spread out before him, that chilled him to the bone. He should never have come to Wiltshire. A man dying of frostbite does not want any excruciating thawing. Far better to freeze solid without interruptions along the way.

Still, he let her lead him to the cozy parlor, took the cider and lifted it to his lips. Cecilia Fairfax should not suffer for this grim mood that had fallen upon him.

As soon as he had drained his cup, he made her a stiff bow. "I must attend to some estate business in my rooms. I beg that you will excuse me until dinner."

"Oh." The sparkle in her eyes dimmed, and he was sorry to be the cause. "Don't let us keep you."

Marcus made a disagreeable noise from his slouched position on the settee, but said nothing. Feeling unaccountably weary, Liam headed for the shelter of a door he could close behind him.

Four hours later, he emerged, a bit warmer in body, if not spirit, to find the hallway sifted in gray evening shadows. The maids had not yet lit the sconces on the wall.

As he closed his door, movement caught the corner of his eye. A slight figure in skirts stood at the end of the hall. He turned, prepared to give the errant maid a congenial nod, but no one was there.

Odd.

Liam blinked. He might have mistaken a hanging drapery for a maid, in the dim light—except that there were no draperies in the vicinity. Ignoring the chill at the back of his neck, he strode down the hall.

At the head of the stairs, he met a flushed maid carrying a candle. She bobbed him a quick curtsey and proceeded past him to light the sconces.

"Lord Tarrick?" It was Cecilia's voice. "Is that you? I was just coming to fetch you for supper."

"It is," Liam said, descending to where his hostess waited at the foot of the stairs, her slender hand resting on the carved newel-post. "My apologies for keeping you waiting."

He offered his arm, as a gentleman should. At least he knew *some* of the proper protocols.

"Not at all." She slipped her hand through his elbow, and together they proceeded toward the dining room.

As they passed the parlor, Cecilia let out a sharp cry and stumbled against him.

"Miss Fairfax!" He immediately caught her by the shoulders. "Are you well?"

She shook her head and glanced about, a suspicious tilt to her brows. Clearly not finding what she was looking for in the warmly-lit hall, she gave him a half-distracted smile.

"My apologies, my lord. I thought…well. No matter. Clearly I am clumsier than I'd imagined."

"I don't find you clumsy in the least." He ought to release her, now that she had regained her balance, but his hands seemed incapable of lifting from her shoulders.

A faint flush colored her cheeks as she lifted her head and met his gaze. Then her eyes slid to a point somewhat above his head, and her flush deepened.

What was…. Ah yes. If he was not mistaken, they stood directly below the ball of mistletoe.

He gave her a heartbeat's chance to pull away. Instead Cecilia swayed imperceptibly closer to him. Her lips, when they were not pressed into an anxious line, were full. And eminently kissable.

Locking away all rational thought, Liam leaned forward. Their gazes met, with a shiver that sped down his spine. Then, deliberately, she closed her eyes and tipped her face up to his.

Heart jolting like a runaway coach, he lowered his head and brushed his mouth over hers. Soft, warm—and then warmth sparked to vivid flame. He pressed his lips more firmly to hers, and she sighed, her mouth opening slightly beneath his. His tongue, most traitorous and ungentlemanly, took advantage, dipping in to taste her sweetness. Fire spiraled through him, and a curious sensation of rightness. Cecilia Fairfax belonged in his arms, her slender fingers curling through his hair, her body pressed close, her mouth pliable and delicious beneath his.

But they stood in the center of Wilton House, and a kiss that he'd meant to be a gentle caress had blazed all out of proportion. Liam forced his head to lift, away from the warmth of her lips; forced himself to step back and release her, though his blood clamored for more. *Sweep her into your arms, carry her up the stairs*, a wild, reckless part of him demanded.

She stared at him, her eyes bright, her cheeks becomingly rosy. Then, slowly, she smiled.

"Happy Christmas, Lord Tarrick," she said, no trace of disdain in her voice.

"Likewise, Cecy—Miss Fairfax. Though we are a bit early, are we not? Christmas is two days hence."

She glanced up. "There is no rule about when the mistletoe may be used. Though now you must pick a berry and give it to me."

He reached up and plucked one of the small white berries. It was hard and smooth, like wax. She held out her cupped hand and he dropped it in.

"What will you do with it?" he asked.

Her smile took on a mischievous edge as she slipped the berry in her pocket. "Come along, sir. Supper awaits."

He finished escorting her to the dining room, and they spoke no more of the kiss—the splendid, secret kiss now indelibly engraved in his memory. He would sleep, and wake, and sleep again with the remembered feeling of his lips on hers. For years, no doubt. Years upon years. He could not decide if that was a wonderful thing, or a terrible one.

Either way, he would never regret that kiss.

Christmas Eve came inexorably—and it *was* evening, despite Cecilia's best efforts to hold the day at bay. She had spent the hours in a whirlwind, making sure all was in readiness for the holiday. Cakes were baked, the Yule log ready to light in the parlor's hearth, and all her gifts wrapped.

The Widow Pomfrey had arrived, pies in hand, as promised. She was keeping Father company before dinner, while Cecilia dressed.

Cecilia sat before the glass in her room, brushing her hair. Martha had helped her don the red satin gown, and the fabric glowed richly in the light. Too richly, perhaps. Her skin looked pale in contrast, her eyes wide and weary. She was not certain she was worthy of such a pretty gown.

Although the earl had kissed her, pretty or not.

Ah, that kiss. She had lain awake far too long the previous night, rekindling the moment behind her closed eyes. The serious look he had given her, the warmth of his lips upon hers, the solid strength as his arms had closed about her, the stunning softness of his raven-black hair between her fingers.

She had not meant to end up beneath the mistletoe with the earl. Perhaps she had dreamed of it, but she never would have maneuvered him so blatantly. No—that had been the ghost's doing. Sneaky little thing, to push Cecilia so violently at just the opportune moment. It was unlike Lizzy, to make such an overt showing.

Not that the ghost of the girl had been visible, but still. Cecilia could hardly explain such a thing to their guest, and so had passed it off as clumsiness.

"Mistress?" Martha said, interrupting her thoughts. "Cook says all is in readiness. Shall I call the family to dinner?"

"Yes—in ten minutes."

Cecilia caught her hair up and coiled it into a bun. Watching her, Martha *tsked.*

"Now, mistress, let me fix your hair. It won't take but a moment."

Without waiting for assent, the maid set the curling iron in the fire, then pulled a few strands of pale hair free from Cecilia's bun. Deftly, she curled them, the soft ringlets falling about Cecilia's face.

"That's better," Martha said. "Though you need something more. Those ruby-studded combs."

"I couldn't." Cecilia's response was automatic.

The combs had belonged to Mother, and though Cecilia had inherited all her jewelry, she had not touched it since her mother's death.

"Now, mistress, your dear mother would have wanted you to look well. Especially tonight."

Martha winked at her, and Cecilia flushed. Did all the servants know of her growing affection for Lord Tarrick?

"Oh, very well. But be quick about it."

She waved at the jewelry box on the dressing table, where the mistletoe berry was concealed like a small, precious pearl. Smiling, Martha plucked the combs out and deftly inserted them into Cecilia's coiffure. The gems winked and shone, set off by her pale hair.

"Lovely," the maid said. "I'll go fetch the family now."

After she left, Cecilia spent a moment admiring her reflection. She did look well—in a waifish sort of way. Enough to please the earl, or so she hoped.

She rose and collected the last gift to bring down to the parlor—a book wrapped in brown paper and sealed with red wax, for Lord Tarrick. After hours of consideration, she had settled on her beloved copy of *Lyrical Ballads* by Wordsworth and Coleridge. The poems had often comforted her, and she wanted to give him something of personal value, that showed the esteem in which she held him.

Something that would thank him for that most splendid kiss.

Dinner was a jolly affair—in no small part because Cecilia could not help the little bubbles of joy that cascaded through her whenever she met the earl's gaze. Oh, it was foolish of her, but she could not help but indulge in her feelings.

He would leave soon enough, she knew it. But he was here now, and it was Christmas time, and so she let her smiles come freely. The Widow Pomfrey added to the air of merriment as well, with her unfailing good humor and witty stories of life in the village. And, of course, her delicious pies.

After dinner they repaired to the parlor, where the Yule log crackled merrily. Cecilia was careful to give the mistletoe a wide berth, though she could feel the earl's gaze upon her as she entered the room.

She went to the pianoforte and began to play the family's favorite carol; *God Rest Ye Merry Gentlemen*. Marcus took up the melody first, his baritone clear and strong. The widow joined him in a wobbly alto, quickly shored up by Father's tenor.

Cecilia sang softly, but it was difficult for her to keep her place in the music and sing out at the same time.

A shadow fell over the page, and she glanced up to see Lord Tarrick standing at her shoulder. Quietly, he began to sing as well, reading the words off the sheet music. His voice was low and deep, a bit husky as if from disuse, but tuneful enough.

When the carol ended, she turned and smiled at him.

"I didn't know you sang."

"I don't." His gray eyes were serious. "Until now."

Their gazes held, until Marcus cleared his throat.

"Here we Come a Wassailing!" he cried.

Despite the merry noise of caroling issuing from the parlor, no actual wassailers arrived at Wilton House. No doubt they thought the estate still in mourning. After the family and their guests had drunk their fill of the spiced wine, Cecilia directed the rest to be shared out among the servants.

At last, late into the evening, the small party wound to a close.

"My heavens," Widow Pomfrey exclaimed, glancing at the pocket watch pinned to her gown, "Look at the hour! I must be returning home."

"Oh, do stay," Cecilia said. "I had an extra room made ready, just in case."

It took very little coaxing to persuade the widow to stay, and soon enough they were all making for their beds. Cecilia lingered a moment in the parlor, to make sure the Yule log was well banked.

Satisfied, she stepped into the hall, only to catch light and movement near the kitchen. Likely it was only a servant nipping the last of the wine, but Cecilia turned her steps in that direction. The kitchen was empty, the door gaping wide, admitting the frigid night air.

She paused at the threshold, rubbing the gooseflesh from her arms.

"Hello?" she called. "Is anyone outside?"

At the corner of the house she caught sight of a white-capped figure carrying a lantern. Heedless of the cold, Cecilia hurried out.

"Mrs. Bess!" she cried, when she was near enough to recognize the figure. "Whatever are you doing?"

The old woman had descended the steps leading to the cellar and was fumbling with her keys. At Cecilia's voice, she looked up.

"We must have plum cordial for tomorrow."

"Certainly," Cecilia said, "but we can fetch it in the morning."

"No, no." Mrs. Bess's voice was anxious and thin. "It's a Wilton House tradition. Plum cordial for Christmas."

Clearly the old housekeeper's mind would not rest until she was holding a bottle of cordial. Cecilia descended the steps as Mrs. Bess unlocked the cellar door. She took the lantern from the housekeeper's chilled fingers.

"Stay here," Cecilia said. "I'll find the cordial."

She hurried into the musty confines of the cellar, once again wishing they had an interior access. But Wilton House was oddly built, and no-one had seen fit to make the cellar convenient to reach.

In the lamplight, the rows of glass jars and bottles glinted like foreign treasure; amber and verdigris and old rubies. Cecilia located the plum cordial at the far end of the cellar. The glass was cool beneath her fingers as she carried it to where Mrs. Bess waited by the door.

"Here we are." Cecilia handed the old housekeeper the cordial. "Now, back to our warm beds." Her words left a white plume in the air.

"Oh." Mrs. Bess squinted at the bottle. "Plum cordial. But oughtn't we to have two? For the guests?"

Reining in her impatience, Cecilia turned and proceeded back to the shelf. She set down the lantern and was just reaching for another bottle of cordial when the cellar door slammed shut.

"Mrs. Bess?" She whirled and hurried to the now-closed door. "Hello?"

She tried the latch. It was locked, and dismay crept through her, even colder than the chill night air. Had Mrs. Bess forgotten that she was in the cellar? It was entirely too plausible.

"Mrs. Bess? Let me out!" she called, pounding on the door. The wood absorbed her fistfalls, turning them to soft thumps.

Cecilia pivoted and grabbed a jar of pickles, beating it against the door until she feared the glass would shatter. There was no reply. Mrs. Bess did not return.

Still, Cecilia called and pounded until her throat was sore and her hands ached. Swallowing back her fear, she slumped against the cold stone wall. There was nothing for it—she would have to wait until morning, and hope that someone would venture out to the cellar. Although the kitchen was completely well-stocked with everything they would possibly need on the morrow. Her chances of being discovered were not good—unless Mrs. Bess recalled their night-time trip.

Shivering, Cecilia glanced about the cellar. Potatoes were lumped in one corner in their rough burlap sacks. Uncaring of the mess, she dumped them out and wrapped the coarse material around her. She was still cold beyond belief, but she would survive the night. She would—and in the morrow she would win free of the cellar. Somehow.

Clinging to that thought, Cecilia closed her eyes and sank into frost-laden, fitful sleep.

Liam woke, cold beneath his blankets despite the coals still glowing on the hearth. He pulled the covers up about his chin, but sleep was gone. After a solid half-hour of chasing after it, he gave up and rose, donning his clothing. A quick glance between the curtains showed the edge of dawn shading the horizon. Christmas Day was here—and he had nothing to give Cecilia.

Or perhaps he had everything to give. But would she accept?

He sat on the edge of the unmade bed, turning his signet ring back and forth between his fingers. The gold was warm, the sapphire bezel gleaming in the dim light. Hope and fear alternated, strobing across his soul until he was dizzy.

What was he even contemplating?

He could not ask Cecilia Fairfax to marry him. They scarcely knew one another. No, he would depart on the morrow. If they continued to correspond, or if Marcus invited him for another visit, *then* he might muster up the courage. But he could not do it now. It was the outside of foolishness, especially since she had no reason to tell him yes. Why would she?

Far better to wait.

Mind made up, the clamor of emotions beneath his skin stilled. Liam slid the signet ring back on his finger.

A quiet knock sounded at his door, and the dark-haired maid slipped into the room. She drew up short at the sight of him. Her eyes darted to the rumpled covers, then back to him, and she bobbed a quick curtsey.

"Good morning, milord." She hesitated a moment, then went to the hearth and began building up the fire.

Prompted by some impulse, Liam asked, "Is everything well?"

"Oh!" The maid glanced up at him. "Truthfully, milord? Miss Cecilia has disappeared."

"What?" He rose abruptly. "Disappeared, how?"

"No one knows. Her bed wasn't slept in, and she's nowhere to be found."

Ah, that explained the furtive glance at his bed—as if the servants had thought their errant mistress would perhaps be found there. He cleared his throat. "Is the family awake?"

"Yes, they're in the parlor. They're organizing search parties, if you want to ride out."

Cecilia Fairfax missing. An impossible hole opened in the fabric of his world. How could he come back to court her if she was *gone*?

Leaving the maid, he strode into the hallway. He could not believe Cecilia had simply disappeared. Not here, in the serene heart of Wiltshire, surrounded by family and friends.

A flicker of movement at the head of the stairs made him glance up, and Liam stumbled to a halt. A girl stood there, garbed in an odd, old-fashioned dress.

But that was not what sent a shiver prickling over his skin. It was that he could see right through her to the paneled walls, her figure transparent as mist.

"Lizzy?" he whispered, his mouth dry as paper.

She nodded and beckoned urgently, then glided down the staircase. Liam stood frozen for a heartbeat, then sprang forward. He did not think the ghost meant him harm. Did she know what had befallen Cecilia?

At the foot of the stairs, he glanced wildly about, then spotted Lizzy's pale form hovering near the front door.

"Outside?" he asked.

In answer, the ghost passed through the solid mahogany door and was gone. Liam hurried to follow.

He undid the lock and threw open the door, just as Marcus emerged from the parlor.

"Tarrick," Marcus said, "what the devil are you doing?"

"Lizzy went outside," Liam replied, a bit incoherently.

There wasn't time to explain. He bolted down the front steps, Marcus close behind. A tattered bit of mist rounded the corner of the house, and Liam pursued. He halted outside the mounded rows of the kitchen garden. There was no sign of the ghost.

"Where are you?" he cried, his voice cracking on the last syllable. Cecilia could not be lost to him. He would not allow it.

"Are you out of your head?" Marcus asked, drawing up beside him.

"Hush." Liam slashed his hand downward.

A muffled thumping issued from the far corner of the house. Liam hastened toward the sound, pausing at the head of a rough stone staircase running down the outside wall.

"The cellar!" Marcus said.

The two of them sprinted down the stairs to the door at the bottom. Liam grasped the handle, but the door was locked. At the sound of the rattling latch, the thumping ceased.

"Help!" It was Cecilia's voice, issuing from behind the cellar door.

"Cecy?" her brother called. "Can you hear me?"

"Marcus—I'm here." Her reply was faint, but present.

"Thank God."

Liam agreed—but Cecilia was still locked in the cellar. "Who has the keys?" he demanded.

Marcus frowned. "Mrs. Bess. I'll go find her." He ran up the steps, pausing at the top. "You stay here."

As if Liam would budge from the spot.

"Miss Fairfax," he called through the door, "Cecilia. Are you unharmed?"

"Mostly, though I'm a bit chilled." Her voice was weaker than he liked.

"Your brother has gone to find the keys. We'll have you out of there in a thrice."

"Liam?" There was a desperate ring to her words. "Please keep talking to me."

"What should I say?"

"Anything. I just—I need to hear the sound of someone's voice. Your voice."

He drew in a deep breath and then, before he could persuade himself otherwise, said the words.

"Miss Fairfax, will you marry me?"

Silence, underscored by the heavy beating of his heart.

"Excuse me? Are you jesting?"

"Never. I know the situation is hardly…" Damnation. What was he thinking, asking Cecilia to marry him through the thick expanse of a wooden door. He was a coward of the first order. "That is to say— here comes your brother."

Liam stepped back as Marcus bounded down the stairs, a ring of keys in his hand. Behind him came Lord Fairfax, the Widow Pomfrey, and a cluster of servants, white-haired Mrs. Bess among them.

"Which key is it, Cecy?" Marcus rattled the ring in frustration.

"The smaller iron one," she called back.

Marcus fitted it into the lock and, after another excruciating second, it turned. He threw open the door to reveal the wan and trembling form of his sister, coarse burlap sacks wrapped around her shoulders and upper body.

Without a word, Liam stepped into the dank interior and swept Cecilia up into his arms. She made no protest, only blinked and turned her face to his chest when they emerged into the light.

"Brandy," he said, ascending the stairs with her. "And blankets—in the parlor. Is there a closer entrance into the house?"

"Here," her father said, holding open a door that led into the kitchen.

Liam bore his precious burden to the parlor and sank down before the fire, still holding Cecilia. Shivers ran through her, and bedamned if he was going to let her go.

Unless, of course, she wanted him to. Terrible though the prospect might be.

"Here," Marcus said, holding out a glass of brandy.

Cecilia lifted her head, her eyes the color of a bruise, and took a tiny sip.

"More," Liam said. "You must get warm."

She took a larger drink, then coughed and shuddered as the brandy went down.

"Blankets, milord." The dark-haired maid hastened to the hearth, her arms full of woven wool.

As if the sight of the maid was a catalyst, Cecilia sat up and gently slid from Liam's arms. She pulled off the burlap sacking, leaving streaks of grime on her red dress and a smudge on her cheek. Before she could start shivering again, the maid draped a blanket about her shoulders, and another across her lap.

"Thank you," Cecilia said, glancing about the room. "Thank you all. I'm so glad you found me."

"How the devil did you get locked in the cellar?" Marcus said.

"Poor Mrs. Bess is wandering in her wits. She didn't mean to lock me in, but I fear she forgot my presence." Cecilia shook her head. "I didn't want to relieve her of her duties."

"And look at the cost to you, poor dear," the Widow Pomfrey said.

"She must be retired," Cecilia's father said, in a tone that brooked no argument. "Immediately."

Cecilia bit her lip. "Yes, but I have no one to take her place."

"As to that…" The widow glanced at Lord Fairfax, a faint blush suffusing her round cheeks. "Please let me assist you. I know a woman from the village who might suit admirably."

"Excellent," Cecilia said, meeting the widow's gaze.

Liam had the impression some small, secret communication known only to women passed between them, for the widow smiled and Cecilia nodded again.

"Lord Tarrick," Cecilia said, turning to him. "I believe you asked me a question."

He stiffened, the blood catching in his veins.

"I did."

"Would you do me the favor of asking it again?"

"Here?" He glanced about the parlor, from Marcus sitting on the carpet beside his sister, to Lord Fairfax and Widow Pomfrey, to the dark-haired maid.

"Yes." Cecilia's voice was clear and firm.

Very well. His chest tightened, but he was hers to command. Liam shifted onto his knees and faced her. Taking her hands in his—her fingers still too cold for his liking—he swallowed once, for courage.

"Miss Cecilia Fairfax. Would you do me the very great honor of becoming my wife?"

The room stilled. Even the flames in the hearth seemed to pause. Liam could scarcely breathe.

Cecilia tipped her head.

Liam wanted to close his eyes, wanted to leap to his feet and rush back to the isolated safety of Tarrick Hall, never to come out again. Instead he forced himself to wait, the signet ring heavy on his finger.

At last, Cecilia smiled, and it was like the sun coming out from behind the clouds after years of darkness. His heart gave a tremendous thump, then settled into a new, stronger rhythm, borne by a sense of hope beyond anything he had ever felt.

"Yes, Liam. I will marry you." She leaned forward and kissed him, gently, on the lips.

The world spun from that point of contact, the moon revolved, the planets danced, all because Cecilia Fairfax had consented to be his bride. Something inside Liam mended—something he had not even known was broken, until recently.

Marcus let out a whoop and clapped him on the back, the maid cheered, and Lord Fairfax smiled broadly.

"I beg your forgiveness, sir," Liam said, glancing up to her father. "I ought to have asked you first, but—"

"I understand," Cecilia's father said. "Sometimes the heart precedes the head in such matters. You have my blessing."

Liam slipped the gold signet of the Earls of Tarrick from his finger and handed it to Cecilia. The sapphire shone in her cupped hand.

"This is all I have to give you," he said. "My name, my title. My heart. Everything I am and everything I have is yours, Cecilia Fairfax."

"It is more than enough, Liam." Tears shone in her eyes, brighter than the sapphire in his ring. "More than I had ever hoped for."

"Happy Christmas, my countess," he said.

Something half-seen at the edge of his vision made him glance to the doorway. The transparent figure of Lizzy stood there, smiling. As he watched, she faded away, leaving only mortal joy to fill the parlor.

Which was, indeed, enough.

Our columnist, Julie Pitzel, has been a receptionist, radio DJ, bill collector, telemarketer, administrative assistant, community college instructor, and an expediter (aka professional nag). She's been involved in the Houston writing community for many years including two years as President of a local Romance Writers of America Chapter. She writes paranormal fiction from a geodesic dome south of Houston, where she lives with her husband and a pair of cats. Most recently, her story "The Dance" was published in The Death of All Things *anthology.*

YOU READ THAT?: HOLIDAY TROPES AND TRADITIONS
by Julie Pitzel

Pumpkin spice is in the air, Christmas songs are playing in the background, and Halloween is just around the corner. It's September as I write this, but it's never too early to start celebrating—right? Welcome to HallowThanksgiveMas, the time of year when the two most advertised holidays squeeze Thanksgiving off of the calendar.

As frustrated as I get about the mad dash for Christmas, I still enjoy reading holiday romances and the tropes that combine to make me want to read them while curled up with a mug of hot chocolate, a warm sweater, and fuzzy slippers. Note: I'm in Houston, so I will also need a fan blowing full blast to prevent melting.

All romance fiction contains certain tropes. They are the recognizable story elements that draw in readers. When we look at our lists of favorite stories, we'll see the same type of tale over and over: friends to lovers, enemies to lovers, secret babies, and second chances are a few examples. Some romance critics will point at tropes as an excuse to pan the genre—"See? They're all the same story," *said with a slightly nasal, pompous tone*—refusing to recognize that *all* genre fiction contains tropes. Mysteries with an amateur sleuth or thrillers with a race to save the world are as much tropes as a romance with a marriage of convenience. The tropes that make up a story are a framework for the plot. And holiday stories, especially holiday romances, have their own collection of elements.

While I'm aware that Christmas is not the only holiday happening at this time of year, it is the holiday I grew up with, the one that I'm most familiar. I don't know enough of the traditional stories of other beliefs to comfortably reference them. But whether you light a yule log, a menorah, or a Kinara, this is the season for family gatherings, gift giving, introspection, and food.

Some of the traditional holiday tropes include take-offs on *The Gift of the Magi*, *A Christmas Carol*, or *It's A Wonderful Life*. Other themes would be nostalgic accounts of older, simpler times, tales of forgiveness, and stories dealing with crazy families. There are stories of Santa or elves or angels fitting into the real world, usually to save a certain person. Holiday stories are filled with snow, ice-skating, tree trimming, and food—so much food. And most holiday stories end with a happily ever after. It's easy to see how those storylines could be intertwined with romances.

Second chances set in the holiday season are probably the most common mashup. They are usually romances are about couples with a failed relationship in their past. During the course of the story they will admit that they still love each other. Each character will—eventually—acknowledge their own complicity in the breakup, and together they figure out not only how to repair the relationship but how to make it stronger and avoid repeating their earlier mistakes. This type of story easily combines with holiday tropes of forgiveness, nostalgic romps, and crazy families. Second chances usually happen due to forced togetherness and the holiday season is rife with forced togetherness. A blizzard or avalanche traps everyone at the ancestral home or ski lodge where there are limited bedrooms. Frequently the couple is manipulated by a well-meaning relative or friend, both invited for the holiday and not informed the other will be there. But oops, you can't leave now, might as well make the best of it—wink, wink.

Friends to lovers is another frame that works with holiday stories. We're all familiar with this trope, two people who've been "buddies" forever finally figuring out that they want to be so much more. Usually one of them has been in love with the other but couldn't reveal their feelings because the other was in a relationship or there are age differences or they work together. Even when the barrier was removed, they fear ruining the friendship. The holidays are a good time for these characters to finally come together. There's often high family tension and loneliness issues that force them to communicate their feelings. Sometimes one or the other character will have returned to the hometown only to discover that their childhood friend has changed in the intervening years. Or they agree to spend time together so they won't be alone for the holidays. These are usually fun romps, wrapped around cold winter nights, roaring fireplaces, and the discovery that good friends can make great lovers.

Enemies to lovers at Christmas should be required to have a scene with mistletoe. These are the business rivals, the rancher versus the farmer, or the cop versus the thief. Two characters who don't trust each other and don't like each other but end up working together, discover that their differences are only superficial, and fall in love. When we bring in the holiday element, often one of the characters will be the embodiment of Ebenezer Scrooge or the Grinch. They don't like Christmas, they don't like charity, and they hate kids and puppies—at least, that's what they want everyone to believe. Then they're forced or tricked into running a holiday fundraiser, saving an orphanage, or taking care of a baby. Maybe one of them drank too much at the company holiday party and shenanigans ensued (or didn't but they think they did). And during the course of the story, trust and forgiveness happens. Enemies to lovers stories are a lot of fun when wrapped up in holiday ribbon.

One of my favorites is the fake relationship/marriage of convenience trope. One of the characters needs a spouse to qualify for an inheritance, or a fiancé to forestall getting matched with someone horrible, or because they claimed they were engaged and have to produce the fiancé at a family gathering. Then while the two characters spend days pretending, they actually fall in love. The conflict in these stories often revolves around the characters' fear of revealing their true feelings for each other. It's a storyline that fits well within a home-for-the-holidays tale. There will likely be an embarrassing gift exchange, with one or both not having anything to give. There's usually mistletoe, a crazy family, and maybe a snowball fight. And our gift is watching this couple discover they aren't pretending after all.

The holidays are stressful and busy. By the time this article prints, Black Friday will be a memory, parents are panicking over budgeting and finding this year's must-have toy, and if we hear *Little Drummer Boy* one more time we'll scream. We need to take the time to relax with fun and positive stories. I hope my descriptions brought to mind some of your favorite books and movies, and you'll have a chance to enjoy them with some mulled wine and your own special someone.

Now I have to get busy. We exchange gifts with the in-laws at Thanksgiving, so I need to get our gift buying done before we pack the car and drive five hours. I expect to once again earn the title of Little-Miss-Thanksgiving-Overachiever. A title I earned for baking two pies—pumpkin and pecan—with homemade crusts, a loaf of multigrain bread, and another of banana bread*. Of course, I also brought the expected and batch of fudge, and requested cranberry sauce made from whole cranberries with fresh-squeezed orange and lime juice. This year I'm thinking of adding some cookies to the list.

Copyright © 2018 by Julie Pitzel.

---

* Editor's Note: *salivating* Mmmm—yum! How do we get an invite to a Thanksgiving like that?

C.S. DeAvilla writes award-winning science fiction, fantasy, and romance under another pen name. She has been a romance fan since she sneaked a peek at her mother's massive historical romance bookcase and fell in love with all the characters. She reads every romance genre—as long as two people are falling in love, she'll give it a read. Her favorite authors are Jennifer Crusie, J.R. Ward, Darynda Jones, Suzanne Brockmann, Sarah MacLean, and Kristan Higgins. But she always has room for one more.

RECOMMENDED BOOKS

by C.S. DeAvilla

Title: ***By the Book***
Author: Julia Sonneborn
Publisher: Gallery Books (Simon and Schuster)
ASIN: B074ZPWLHH
Release Date: February 6th, 2018

The return of autumn always puts me in the mood for a school-themed romance, and *By the Book* delivered one in the form of professor Anne Corey. Anne needs desperately to snag a tenure position in the English department, but every obstacle blocks her goal. For one, she needs to get a book deal (good luck with that in today's market), and second, avoid her ex-fiancé (Adam Martinez) who has recently been hired as the new president of the university. Afraid the ladder will prevent her from obtaining a permanent position, Anna reads negatively into every interaction with Adam. And realizes she still may harbor feelings for him. After all, the breakup is completely her fault. Good thing a rock-star faculty member has taken an interest in her and she can use that new relationship as a distraction. See? She doesn't need Adam in her life! But when Adam attempts to explain he knows a little more about this rock-star faculty member and he's not a good person, Anna takes that as a threat to her personal life and to her career. *By the Book* serves as a great second chance romance and readers will find themselves cheering for Anna. Anyone who has had a partner or colleague sabotage their chances at success will relive that frustration by reading Anna stubble through who she can and can't trust. This is cute, sweet romance at its best.

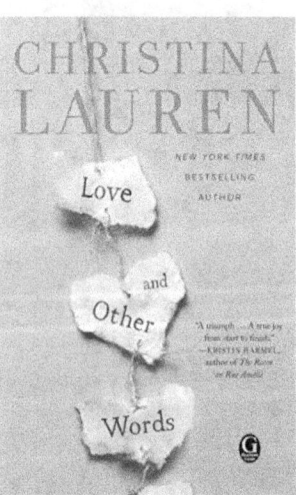

Title: ***Love and Other Words***
Author: Christina Lauren
Publisher: Galley Books (Simon and Schuster)
ASIN: B075CRQLKG
Release Date: April 10th, 2018

Christina Lauren is among my favorite writers of all time. A pseudonym for two friends writing together, Christina Lauren pens some of the best in contemporary romantic comedy available in bookstores. *Love and Other Words* is their first foray into women's fiction, but this book still stays true to the authors' romance roots. At its core, this book promises a deeply emotional journey between the two characters. It's difficult to understand how Macy Sorensen and Elliot Petropoulos could have ever stopped communicating; their friendship is portrayed as deep as one can be. Sharing a love for books, Macy and Elliot become fast friends when Macy's father buys a weekend house next door to Elliot's family, a few years after Macy's mother passes away. Elliot and his family provide a stable, sturdy environment for a grieving Macy and her father. Elliot continues to ask Macy her favorite word throughout the narrative which becomes part of their "thing" and is an excellent callback to the book's title. As expected from the electric chemistry these two characters share, they soon fall in love and become each other's firsts for everything. However, readers are aware that something major will happen to split these two and it will rock both of them in a way that effects both their futures. Elliot and Macy are in other, newer relationships at the start of the novel, but we get a sense that neither is truly as happy as they once were. Throughout the novel it's a gripping push and pull as to whether or not these two will find their way back to each other, or if there has been too much pain to allow that to happen. This book hit every one of my reader cookies: fantastic characters, tons of chemistry, lots of intimate moments, enticing dialog—the authors penning Christina Lauren are masters at their craft.

a push-pull love situation—for readers who like to have their love story teased over several books in a more true-to-life set up, they will be pleased with *Black Pearl Dreaming*.

Title: ***Black Pearl Dreaming*** (book two in the Portland Hafu series)
Author: K. Bird Lincoln
Publisher: World Weaver Press
ASIN: B07FPZ9KBW
Release Date: October 16th, 2018

Koi Pierce is Hafu, half-baku, a dream-eater. In this Urban Fantasy adventure, I knew I was starting the second book without having read the first and I worried it would be difficult to follow. It wasn't. Lincoln begins the novel where I'm assuming the first left off, but does an excellent job of catching the reader up. Koi is accompanying her father, also a baku, to Japan where they hope to find answers, but instead are thrust into a completely different set of issues with the Black Pearl—an imprisoned dragon. First of all, the man she's falling for might not be as trustworthy as she assumed. Though he helped them defeat a dragon back in Portland, he's got a lot of secrets of his own, and his family loyalty may stand in the way of their relationship. Ken is Kitsune: a fox shifter, and promptly seems to betray her once they land in Japan. However, not everything is as it seems in this installment. I really enjoyed Lincoln's writing style which was fast-paced, but still managed to lace in some great prose, humor, and character building. For readers who love to get immersed in a new world, this is definitely a book to pick up and get lost in. I really loved Ken and Koi's interactions which were

Title: ***The Light Over London***
Author: Julia Kelly
Publisher: Galley Books (Simon and Schuster)
ASIN: B075RLVVY7
Release Date: January 8th, 2019

I received an advanced reader's copy of *The Light Over London* while attending the Pocket/Galley spotlight at the *Romantic Times* convention. Julia Kelly's book was laying on my seat as if fate had demanded my reader-attention to this upcoming novel that tells the story of two women. Cara's story, set in modern day, begins when she's tasked with finding the best historical pieces at an estate sale. Cataloging the important items, she comes across a diary and immediately becomes curious over whose it is. There is no name, not a lot of clues, but it details the life of a woman who served in the Royal Army during WWII as a "gunner girl"—women who scored high on military exams in math and engineering, putting them in charge of anti-aircraft guns, shooting down enemy planes before they could bomb the city of London. The novel delves deeper into the story of Louise, the mysterious woman and the author of the diary, following her whirlwind and complicated romance with pilot Paul Bolton. Paul is charming and their romance unfolds as a quick, love-at-first-sight meeting. Except there are clues along the way that Paul isn't quite as he seems. Cara, reading as the story unfolds in modern day, sympathizes with this young woman, having recently been through a divorce with a man who shares a few similarities with Paul. Learning to trust and open up her heart again is difficult for Cara, especially with her adorable neighbor Liam willing to help her solve the puzzle of the diary. Will Louise find happily ever after, too? This book is compelling, and the two women's storylines are fast-paced as well as emotionally meaty. Though Louise starts out seemingly shy and meek, she proves herself to be forged of steel and a true warrior when it counts. Meanwhile, Cara's story centers on pulling herself out of a hermit-like status. I loved how the two storylines and romances mirrored each other symbiotically. If you're a fan of a little touch of historical transportation and a book you can sink your teeth into, then this is going to be a winner in the new year. Guaranteed great read.

Title: ***Undecided***
Author: Julianna Keyes
Publisher: Self-published
ASIN: B01BXZMCEW
Release Date: April 4th, 2016

I'm in love with the New Adult genre, ever since it exploded onto the romance scene a few years ago. Some of my favorite authors are writing New Adult, and often I crave a new tale, but with so many choices it can be hard to find one I know I'll like. *Undecided* was recommended by another New Adult author I follow, so I decided to take a chance—it ended up being a great find. Nora Kincaid is a reformed party girl. Once a star student in high school, Nora went a little crazy her freshmen year and needs to keep it tame this year to make up for all her mistakes the year before: two failed classes and criminal charges. Yikes! But the perfect roommate situation turns out to be another reformed partier, a track star she hooked up with in a closet at a wild party. Not recognizing her, he begs her to be his roommate, hoping that their dedication to keeping the apartment a party-free zone will keep him on the straight and narrow as well. Then there's Crosbie Lucas, her new roommate's best friend and party king extraordinaire. Crosbie's sweet gestures of friendship slowly win Nora over, but her wild past soon catches up to her and she must come clean or lose the deepest love she's ever had. *Undecided* is filled with high drama and conflict at every turn, characteristics that have become cornerstones to the New Adult genre. Keyes keeps the stakes high and raises them just when it seems the characters might be getting comfortable. This is a good one if you're itching for a good tension-filled read that is still fun and humorous at the same time.

Copyright © 2018 by C.S. DeAvilla.

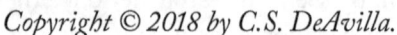

Andrea attended The Culinary Institute of America in Hyde Park, New York to+ study Culinary Arts in 1998. Upon graduation, she continued on at Johnson & Wales University in Providence, RI to study Food Service Management. After a few years of getting hands-on experience, Andrea was drawn to Chicago to the famed Charlie Trotters Restaurant. There, Andrea was exposed to one-of-a-kind wine cellar in which she received one of the best wine educations in the world, tasting & serving some to the most rare and most special wines ever produced. She worked with some of the world's top ingredients, Chef's, Farmers, food lover's and wine aficionados, but homesick, Andrea returned to Santa Fe, NM, where she was Partner & Head Chef at Rasa Juice Bar & Ayurveda. Andrea received many rave reviews and won the Local Hero Award 2 years in a row for her organic, plant-based café. Her attention to detail to her beautifully plated and delicious food is enhanced with the love and care she infuses into every bite! She is currently the Owner and Chef of The Temptress Private Chef & Catering, *operated out of her home town of Santa Fe, NM.*

THE TEMPTRESS PRESENTS:
CHOCOLATE GANACHE CAKE

Raw, Vegan & Gluten Free

by Andrea Abedi

The Temptress Private Chef would love to wish everyone a warm and wintery holiday season. What a better way to get into the holiday spirit than with chocolate! Raw Cacao has so many magical healing benefits for the body and mind. Cacao is a natural mood elevator and antidepressant, has more calcium than cow's milk, and has forty times the antioxidants than blueberries! The benefits are endless and chocolate tastes oh so good! I have created a raw chocolate recipe that will warm you up during the holiday season! Enjoy lovers!

CRUST INGREDIENTS

1 ½ cups pecans
¼ cup sprouted buckwheat
½ cup cacao powder
1 cup medjool dates, pitted and roughly chopped
1 teaspoon vanilla extract
Pinch salt

1. Pulse in food processor until all ingredients stick together, almost like rough sand texture. You want to be sure that the mixture will slightly stick together. If too dry add about 1 Tbsp of water.

2. Press into a round 9" spring form pan to form a crust along the bottom of the pan. Place in freezer for an hour or more.

CREAM INGREDIENTS

4 cups raw unsalted cashews, soaked for 2-3 hours
½ cup water
1 cup maple syrup
1 cup cacao powder
Pinch of salt
2 teaspoons vanilla extract
1 cup coconut oil, slightly heated into liquid, do not let boil.

1. Blend all ingredients in a Vitamix blender, except coconut oil, until a mousse like consistency.

2. On slow speed, drizzle in coconut oil. Make sure oil is fully blended with the mousse. Stir in by hand if needed.

3. Pour over the crust and freeze for 2 hours.

CHOCOLATE ICING

2/3 cups coconut oil, not heated

2 teaspoons vanilla extract

6 tablespoons agave

4 tablespoons cacao powder

1. Take the cake out of the freezer. Let it stand for at least 5 minutes at room temperature.

2. Combine all ingredients in the Vitamix blender until the icing is thick and fully blended.

3. Pour the icing over the cake. Tip the cake side to side to evenly distribute the icing.

4. Place in freezer to firm up icing for about 2 hours. Loosen the edges of the cake with a warm knife, then pop out of the spring form pan.

5. Place cake on a flat plate or cake stand. Dust 1 cup of cacao dust through a sieve on the top of the cake.

6. Add any edible flowers you have on hand, fresh berries, dehydrated fruit and you are ready for a romantic night together!

Copyright © 2018 by Andrea Abedi.

Christine Feehan (https://www.christinefeehan.com) is a #1 New York Times *bestselling author, with seventy-five published works in seven different series: Dark Series, GhostWalker Series, Leopard Series, Drake Sisters Series, Sea Haven Series, Shadow Series, and Torpedo Ink Series. All seven of her series have hit the #1 spot on the New York Times bestseller list.* Judgment Road, *the first book in her newest series,* Torpedo Ink, *debuted at #1 on the* New York Times *bestseller list.*

A CHANGE IN THE CARPATHIAN SERIES

by Christine Feehan

Dark Sentinel is the thirty-second book in my Carpathian series and this story is important to the evolution of this series. It's not new that vampires are the enemy of the Carpathians. They're cunning, not only because they're evil, but because they were once Carpathian. They know the history, strengths, weaknesses, culture, spells, secrets, and safeguards. When a Carpathian warrior chooses to cross the line and become a vampire, that knowledge remains. They retain information, strength, power, abilities and are freed from any morals, ethics or honor that might keep them from doing heinous things.

In the beginning, starting from *Dark Prince*, many vampires were also clearly insane. They had little restraint or patience. They acted on impulse, without much strategy because their insanity propelled them beyond the ability to utilize all the knowledge they had. They were killing machines.

Over time, however, it became clear that not all vampires were the same. While the Carpathians spent their time addressing their inability to have children and the near extinction of their race, a few vampires looked for ways to become more strategic. They turned to technology, which the Carpathians paid no attention to.

With the Carpathian people working to survive, they left themselves vulnerable. Now that the story has come back to the United States you find there's a concerted effort by a large group of vampires who have learned how to focus, work together and use technology. And, they have a plan.

Bringing the story back to the US, which started with *Dark Crime*, we're introduced to a new group. In *Dark Carousel* we get Tariq Asenguard's story and find out that he has been chosen by Mikhail, the Prince of the Carpathian people, to represent the Prince with Carpathians in the United States. Mikhail has come to realize that the vampires are out-maneuvering them using modern technology and a better understanding of the modern world. He needs someone who has been paying attention to both and Tariq is that someone.

The new and the ancient collide as some of the oldest and most powerful Carpathians leave a monastery that's hidden away in the Carpathian Mountains in order to assist Tariq, but also because they've discovered that human women can be lifemates to them, which gives them hope. So, now Tariq has help from these powerful ancients. He's set up a stronghold in an area where the vampires have congregated and he's been sent a powerful healer as his second. The fight is on.

Dark Sentinel furthers this new story arc and adds to it. Just as we learned of vampires in the earlier books, we also learned of a secret society of humans who hunt "vampires" which, to them, include Carpathians. That society has been fairly docile for several books, but comes back in full force in *Dark Sentinel*. The cards continue to be stacked against our Carpathian heroes throughout this new installment.

Without giving too much away, I can say that this book shows the vampires are continuing with whatever plan they have, continuing to work together and using new strategies to further their ultimate goal. I can also say that the vampires are after something the Carpathians have, but the Carpathians aren't clear on what that is. Of course, *I* know, but I'm not telling. LOL.

CLOSING EDITORIAL

by Tina Smith

Well, dear reader, I'm finally writing a closing editorial where my seasons aren't too extreme. There's a blustery breeze outside and a biting chill in the air that brings with it the threat of winter. Winter has long signified an end to the cycle of the seasons, a death of sorts—but it promises new life and changes as well. In other parts of the world, they are experiencing seasons much differently or in another order, as Lezli reminds me often, being a native Aussie.

Since the start of the magazine we've been planning this holiday issue and what exactly we wanted to include in it—which was a mix of different kinds of traditions and cultures represented and what the winter holidays mean to many outside of the typical western understanding because love takes on many forms just as traditions do.

Lezli and I have wrapped up one full year—a milestone we are ecstatic about—and we have been looking back at some of our best stories (all of them, in their own way, of course!), but also looking forward to what we plan for *Heart's Kiss* in 2019.

Spoilers! It's going to be amazing. We have a been in talks with several known and up-and-coming writers who have promised to bring you the very best in cutting-edge romance entertainment. Brenda Jackson, for example, will be starring in our Valentine's issue along with many other fan favorites and *Heart's Kiss* regular contributors, such as L. Penelope. So, subscribe for a year, and get under the sheets with us in time for the holiday of love.

www.HeartsKiss.com